Playing for Keeps

Also by Deborah Fletcher Mello

The Sweetest Thing

Craving Temptation

Don't miss Deborah Fletcher Mello in:

A Christmas Kiss

All I Want Is You

Playing For Keeps

Deborah
Fletcher
Mello

Kensington Publishing Corp.
http://www.kensingtonbooks.com

To the extent that the image or images on the cover of this book depict a person or persons, such person or persons are merely models, and are not intended to portray any character or characters featured in this book.

DAFINA BOOKS are published by

Kensington Publishing Corp.
119 West 40th Street
New York, NY 10018

All Kensington Titles, Imprints, and Distributed Lines are available at special quantity discounts for bulk purchases for sales promotions, premiums, fund-raising, and educational or institutional use. Special book excerpts or customized printings can also be created to fit specific needs. For details, write or phone the office of the Kensington special sales manager: Kensington Publishing Corp., 119 West 40th Street, New York, NY 10018, attn: Special Sales Department, Phone: 1-800-221-2647.

ISBN-13: 978-1-61773-778-7
ISBN-10: 1-61773-778-X
First Kensington Mass Market Edition: November 2015

eISBN-13: 978-1-61773-779-4
eISBN-10: 1-61773-779-8
First Kensington Electronic Edition: November 2015

10 9 8 7 6 5 4 3 2 1

Printed in the United States of America

Playing for Keeps

Chapter One

The employees at the Glenwood Avenue Starbucks greeted Malcolm Cobb by name. It was just past six-thirty in the morning and their cheery demeanors always amazed the man. He had finished his morning run ahead of schedule and was one of the first in line to get his coffee to kick off his day.

"Will you be having your usual today?" a young woman named Allison questioned.

Malcolm nodded. "I will, Allie."

The girl gave him a bright smile. "One venti caramel macchiato, skim milk and extra caramel coming right up!"

Malcolm nodded. "Thank you."

"We had a great time at your nightclub this past Saturday," another Starbucks employee chimed as he blended coffee and cream into an oversize container. "I took my girl and her sister. They're still talking about it!"

"I appreciate that," Malcolm said as he moved from the order lane to the pickup counter. While he waited he made conversation with the staff and the man in line behind him. The morning chatter was casual and easy as they caught up on their weekend escapades and mused over the news headlines.

Malcolm looked across the room as the bell chimed over the entrance door, announcing a customer's arrival. His eyes widened as he caught sight of the woman coming through the door. He knew beyond any doubt that the stunning beauty was a woman who garnered a lot of attention when she came into a room because she definitely had his.

She had an air of sophistication and glamour that few other women he knew possessed. She was dressed in a form-fitting pencil skirt and top that showcased her curves and four-inch pumps, and she carried a high-end leather bag across her arm. Her hair was thick and healthy, a precision cut bob stopping just at her shoulders. Her makeup was meticulous and flattering to her walnut brown complexion. She actually took his breath away, and it was only when the Starbucks employee called for his attention that he realized he was staring.

"Mr. Cobb, is there anything else we can get for you?"

Malcolm's head snapped as he pulled his attention back to the young employee looking at him, a bright smile across her face. He nodded. "Yes, there is something you can do," he said as he leaned over the counter, his voice dropping to a whisper. "Charge my credit card for that woman's order. Whatever she wants."

Allison looked toward the end of the line. "The woman in the blue print dress?" she asked.

Malcolm nodded. "Yes."

The girl smiled. "Not a problem, sir."

Moving out of the line Malcolm took his macchiato and a cinnamon Danish to a corner table. Settling down in his seat he watched as the woman placed her order. As she reached into her handbag for her wallet, Allison pointed in his direction. He smiled and waved a slight hand.

Cilla Jameson had noticed him when she'd entered, the handsome stranger catching the eye of a few women in the room. She'd barely given him a second glance though as her mind had been elsewhere, too many thoughts racing through her head. Foremost was whether or not she had paid her credit card bill and if her card would be accepted when they swiped it to pay for her morning coffee. She was desperate for a good cup of coffee. His generosity was a welcome blessing.

She studied him curiously. She recognized him from somewhere but was having a hard time remembering where. It wasn't often that she couldn't remember a handsome face when she saw one and the man was definitely handsome. He was tall and dark, his beautiful complexion smooth and clear like chocolate ice. He had a slim build but he was fit and from his running shoes, shorts, and sweat-stained shirt she reasoned he'd either just left the gym or had finished a long run. His hair was jet-black and cropped low and close to his head, the cut and meticulously lined edges flattering to his face. There was an abundance of attitude shimmering in his dark eyes and a bad-boy aura that surrounded him. If a stranger picked up the tab for her morning meal she was thankful he was a good-looking stranger.

Picking up her order, she crossed over to where he sat, a bright smile across her face. "Thank you. That was very kind of you," she said, nodding her head in appreciation.

Malcolm smiled back as he gestured to the empty seat on the other side of the table. "Do you have a minute to join me?"

Cilla hesitated for a brief second before she said, "I think I do have a minute." She placed her beverage against the tabletop. She was only slightly surprised when he stood up and moved behind her, pulling out her chair. She tossed him a quick look over her shoulder. "Thank you."

He nodded as he sat back down. "My name's Malcolm. Malcolm Cobb."

"It's a pleasure to meet you, Malcolm. I'm Priscilla Jameson but everyone calls me Cilla."

"Cilla . . . that's a beautiful name. So, do you have a husband or a maybe a boyfriend I need to be concerned about, Cilla Jameson?"

She laughed. "Aren't you a little presumptuous?"

"Why would you say that?"

"We're just meeting. Why would you need to be concerned about any personal relationship of mine?"

His eyes danced over her face, amusement shimmering in his eyes. He shifted forward in his seat. "Because if you do have a husband, then I would have to recuse myself from pursuing you any further. If you just have a boyfriend . . . well . . . all would be fair in love and war."

She laughed heartily, her head bobbing slightly. "Interesting." There was a momentary pause as they eyed each other intently. She shook her head. "No. I'm not married and I don't have a boyfriend. You?"

Malcolm grinned broadly. "I'm very single."

She smiled. "I keep thinking that I know you from someplace but I can't figure out from where."

"Did you go to school here in Raleigh?"

She shook her head. "I was born and raised in Charlotte. But I graduated from UNC-Chapel Hill."

"I went to school here. I did my undergrad at Shaw University and my graduate work at NC State. I studied industrial design and engineering."

"I majored in prelaw but I'm working in pharmaceuticals at the moment."

Malcolm smiled. "I'm not sure how to take that," he said, the hint of laughter in his tone.

"I don't deal drugs if that's what you're implying," Cilla said with a slight roll of her eyes. "I'm a healthcare administrator for a biotech company in Research Park."

"Well, I own a nightclub downtown."

Cilla snapped her fingers. "That's where I know you from. You and your business partner were featured in the *News and Observer.*"

Malcolm smiled. Since its grand opening, the nightclub had been featured in the local newspaper a number of times. Most recently, word of their success had reached a national level, The Playground being named a must-stop on things to do in Raleigh, North Carolina.

Co-owned with Romeo Marshall, his best friend and fraternity brother, their nightspot was now the place to be, and both of them, the men to know. The success of The Playground had propelled them right into the spotlight. "It wasn't a good picture," he said. "They didn't get my best side."

Cilla laughed. "So which is your best side?"

"The one they didn't show."

There was a moment of pause as the two sat grinning foolishly at each other.

"So, your club is a jazz and blues bar, right?" Cilla questioned.

"It is, with a hint of R&B and soul." He reached into his pocket for his wallet and pulled a business card from inside. "If you have some time maybe you can stop by," he said as he passed it to her.

She studied it momentarily. "The Playground . . . sounds like it would be a good time."

"It will be," he said, his tone smug. "I'll be there."

She smiled. "You don't know when I'm coming."

He shrugged. "I'm always there so you can't miss me."

Cilla took a quick glance down to her wristwatch. She took one last sip of her morning brew. "Thank you again for the coffee. I really appreciate it."

He stood up with her. "I'm here every morning, same time," he said. "In case you're interested in another cup. And I really do hope you'll be interested in having another cup of coffee with me."

Cilla laughed, the soft lilt of it stirring a wave of heat through Malcolm's spirit. "Always here, always at the club, doesn't sound like you have any time for much else," she said.

Malcolm's mouth pulled into a seductive grin. "I would make time for you, Cilla Jameson."

* * *

"I said now!" Claudette Cobb shouted, her deep alto voice vibrating through the home. "And I mean it!" the matriarch concluded.

Malcolm Cobb laughed as he moved from his downstairs office into the home's foyer. He leaned to kiss his mother's cheek.

"Where have you been?" she exclaimed, pressing a hand to her chest. "You scared me!"

"Sorry about that but I snuck in through the back door. I went for a run and then grabbed a cup of coffee from Starbucks. I thought I'd get some paperwork done before I lie down for a nap."

"I don't know why you waste good money when we have that coffeepot sitting right there in that kitchen."

"I like Starbucks. It helps to clear my head after a long night."

"Humph!" his mother grunted, her expression strained.

"But good morning to you!" Malcolm exclaimed, changing the subject.

"It was a good morning until them girls decided to work my one good nerve," she said, her smile brightening her face.

Malcolm chucked warmly. "Math test today. Neither one wants to go to school."

Claudette shook her head. "I don't know why. They both always do well. They whine that they're going to fail and then they always pass with flying colors."

Her son shrugged his broad shoulders. "I don't know what to tell you." He leaned against the banister and called upward. "Cleo! Claudia! If you're late for school, you will both be grounded for the weekend and I mean what I say. Get a move on it."

Seconds later his thirteen-year-old twin daughters both shuffled across the hardwood floors and down the stairs. Malcolm eyed one and then the other. Identical, the two girls were making it their mission to express their individuality in their attire. Claudia, the eldest, was going for a *Little House on the Prairie* look with a ruffled maxi skirt, a blouse buttoned up to her neck, and low-heeled boots. Cleo, the younger of the twins by minutes, was hoping for more of a video vixen look.

He shook his head and pointed skyward.

"Change, Cleo. Now!" he snapped, his brusque tone voicing his displeasure.

"What's wrong with what I'm wearing?" the girl snapped back, defiance billowing across her face.

"You don't have on any clothes," her grandmother quipped.

Malcolm moved quickly in the child's direction, her eyes widening as her father took the first four steps in one swift leap. He stood eye to eye with her, everything about his expression declaring there would be no discussion.

"I'm changing!" the girl muttered as she turned abruptly and raced back to her room.

Her sister stood laughing. Malcolm shifted his gaze, eyeing her with a narrowed stare. "Your lunch is on the counter. Grab a Pop-Tart or a banana for breakfast and get your tail to the bus stop."

"Yes, sir," Claudia responded, moving quickly toward the kitchen.

Minutes later Cleo returned, her skirt more modest and her blouse appropriate. She eased her way cautiously past her father, not bothering to comment as he repeated the same instructions to her. As the two girls headed out the front door he kissed both their cheeks and slipped a five-dollar bill into each child's pocket.

"Bye, Daddy," Claudia said as she kissed him back.

"Love you, Daddy," Cleo whispered.

He nodded. "I love you, too, baby girl. And you and I will talk when you get home this afternoon."

"We're going to Mommy's this afternoon," the girl responded, reminding him of their weekday visitation with his ex-wife.

"Then we'll talk when you get back," he said.

"Do we have to go with Mommy?" Cleo questioned. She met the look her father was giving her.

Interrupting, their grandmother pushed her way between them. "You're going to be late and if you miss the bus I'm going to have to take you to school. Let's go and I'll pick you up when school gets out so we can meet your mother on time. You know how she gets if you're late."

Malcolm watched as the girls hurried to the corner, their grandmother standing at the end of the driveway to see them get on the bus. Both had thrown him one last look and he wished he could have told them no, that they didn't have to visit with their mother if they didn't want to. But that wasn't an option for either of them, his divorce ruling dictating their mother's visitation rights. One weekend per month, one month each summer, and every other Monday the girls had to spend time with their other parent whether any of them liked it or not. And none of them liked it.

Malcolm blew a deep sigh. He knew he would

eventually have to take it back to court and allow the girls to express their own wishes but he wasn't ready for the turmoil that would ensue. Dealing with his ex-wife had always come with much drama. So much so that he'd purposely avoided pursuing a serious relationship since they'd split. He'd been burned, badly, and hadn't been willing to put his heart on the line since.

He suddenly thought about the beautiful woman who'd taken his business card. Cilla Jameson had him intrigued and although she'd captured his attention he didn't know if he could see it going but so far. As he reflected on their morning exchange he couldn't help but wonder exactly how far that might be.

Minutes later, with a deep sigh, Malcolm headed back to his office. There were a dozen calls he needed to make before heading back to the nightclub and he hoped against all odds to get at least a thirty-minute nap before that had to happen.

Cilla was reading the last FDA report on a new line of organic narcotics when her best friend, Bianca Torres, rushed into her office, hurriedly closing the door behind her. Bianca moved to the glass wall that bordered the reception and secretarial areas and closed the blinds. The gesture was conspiratorial, like something between them needed to be kept secret.

"What's up?" Cilla questioned, lifting her eyes from the mountain of paperwork that rested on her desk. She peered past Bianca's shoulder, catching her own secretary's eye briefly before the curtains were drawn closed between them. "Why are you acting all squirrelly?"

"Did you know Donna got engaged?" Bianca whispered loudly as she dropped into the cushioned seat in front of Cilla's desk. With a flip of her head she tossed her waist-length, jet-black hair over her shoulder.

"I didn't know she was dating anyone."

"She got engaged this weekend!"

"I guess that's exciting and I'm happy for her but why does that have you acting so weird?"

"Her fiancé's down the hall. She wanted everyone to meet him."

"I'm still not understanding," Cilla said as she reclined back in her seat, crossing her hands together in her lap.

"We know her fiancé already," Bianca continued.

Cilla eyed her with a raised brow, still questioning where the story was going.

Bianca tossed up her hands. "It's Wes. She's engaged to Wesley Brooks."

Cilla's eyes widened at the name of their old friend and Bianca's ex-lover. Neither had spoken to Wes since he'd been caught red-handed, his infidelity caught on camera and posted on the internet for all to see. Before then they'd all been friends. He and Cilla had been sales partners and Bianca had been convinced he was the one. Wes's getting caught making out with a blond bombshell had been the beginning of the end.

Cilla rolled her eyes toward the ceiling. She rose from her seat and reopened her office blinds. "Really, Bianca? I thought you were over him?"

"I am. I am happily committed to my favorite guy.

That snake doesn't come close to the man Ethan is," she said, referring to the boyfriend she'd met before the New Year. "I just enjoyed giving Wes a hard time. He deserved it."

Her friend laughed. "I met a man this morning," she said, changing the subject.

Bianca shifted in her seat. "Where'd you meet a man?"

"Starbucks."

"What's wrong with him?"

"There's nothing wrong with him."

"There is always something wrong with them. Every man I've ever met hanging out in a coffee shop has had some issues."

"Well, this man doesn't. He really seemed to have his 'ish' together." Cilla passed Malcolm's business card to her friend. "He owns a nightclub downtown."

Bianca's eyes widened with excitement. "I know this place! This is the joint I was telling you about. This club is off the chain!"

"So, do you want to go with me? He invited me to stop by sometime. I'm thinking I might go tonight."

"You better take me with you but you can't go anytime soon. And definitely not tonight!"

Cilla rolled her eyes. "Why not?"

"Desperate much? Don't you know you need to keep a man guessing?"

"Like you did with Wes?" A wide smile pulled at Cilla's thin lips as she lifted her hand and waved.

"He's behind us, isn't he?"

Cilla nodded. "And about to come into the office," she mumbled between gritted teeth.

Bianca winced as she took a deep breath. She

twisted around in her seat just as the door opened and her ex-boyfriend, Wesley Brooks, stuck his head inside.

Wesley waved his hand nervously. Both women smiled, amusement dancing across their faces as their associate Donna chattered excitedly.

"Hey, y'all! I just wanted to introduce you to my fiancé!" the petite blond said excitedly. "This is Wesley. Wesley Brooks. We just got engaged!"

Bianca forced a wide grin to her face. "We're all old friends!" she said smugly. "How are you, Wes?"

Cilla nodded. "Wesley, hey! It's good to see you again."

The man smiled sheepishly. "Cilla, Bianca, how are you?" He and Bianca exchanged a look, her arms crossed tightly across her chest.

Cilla smiled. "We're good," she said quickly. "Congratulations! Engaged! That's so exciting."

Donna grinned. "It's going to be a short engagement. The wedding is in six weeks."

Bianca eyed the man with a raised brow. "Well, Wes does *short* well," she said as she held up her hand, her thumb and forefinger just millimeters apart. "How's Gwen?" she suddenly asked. "You two still making movies together?"

Cilla stifled a laugh as the man blushed profusely. The insult blew right over Donna's head. The rest of the conversation was swift and tense, polite small talk as both women wished the newly engaged couple well.

When the two lovebirds had moved off down the hallway, Bianca blew a deep sigh. "As I was saying, if you race on down there to see some guy you just met, you're going to seem desperate. It's not a pretty look."

"You mean like you just looked when you told Wes to call you sometime so you two could catch up?"

Bianca shrugged, a wry smile pulling at her mouth. "I was just making conversation."

"That wasn't all you were trying to make and he and Donna *both* knew it."

"You can't blame a girl for trying to start a mess when she can. Did you see him start to sweat?"

"Okay," Cilla said, laughing heartily. The jovial moment passed as she moved back to her seat.

"So what do you plan to do about this Malcolm guy?" Bianca questioned as she twisted his business card between her fingers.

"That reminds me," Cilla quipped as she opened her laptop and typed in her password. "I need to make sure I paid all of my bills this month. Lately I've had so much on my mind that I think I could forget my head if it weren't screwed onto my neck."

Confusion washed over Bianca's expression.

Cilla chuckled. "He bought my coffee this morning," she said as though it all should have made sense to her friend. When it didn't she explained about her credit card situation and Malcolm's timely gesture.

Bianca shook her head as she moved back onto her feet. "Just tell me what you decide to do about tonight so I know if I need to go home and change." She moved to the door, turning as Cilla called after her.

"Why do you need to change?"

"Because everyone who's anyone is showing up at The Playground. You don't know who I might meet!"

Cilla shook her head. "Did you forget about Ethan? You do have a boyfriend, remember?

Bianca laughed. "Girl, I will never forget about Ethan! Don't you know I *love* that man!"

Chapter Two

The Playground Jazz and Blues Club sat off Glenwood Avenue in downtown Raleigh, the old brick building neighbored by Lem Young's Chinese Cleaners and Harper's Florist. A line of college students, young adults, and old souls was already forming, a growing crowd trying their best to get inside.

Malcolm walked a dimly lit corridor, past a mirrored wall into the nightclub's interior. He had barely made it down the length of the hallway when a random female suddenly pressed her body to his and trapped his mouth beneath her own. The kiss tasted of stale tobacco and bourbon. As he pushed her from him, both his hands holding tight to her shoulders, she gave him a toothy grin and laughed. The wispy giggle filled her face and she looked no older than his daughters. He felt himself tense, gesturing for one of the members of their security team.

"Hahaha, you ain't my boyfriend," the girl said with a waiflike cackle.

"No, I'm not," Malcolm said as he guided her to

an empty chair and pushed her into it. "Did you come with your boyfriend?" he questioned as he stole a quick glance around the room.

A look of confusion shimmered in her dark eyes as she stared at him.

"What's your name, sweetheart?"

Before she could answer another young woman rushed between them. "I'm sorry, Mr. Cobb. This is my friend Tina and she's had way too much to drink!"

He looked toward the young woman who'd called him by his name, not recognizing her face. She sensed his perplexity and smiled brightly. "I'm Nikki Procter. My mom is Bernadette Procter. She goes to your church and is on the usher board with Miss Claudette."

Malcolm nodded as he made the connection. "Nikki, how old are you? And how old is your friend Tina?"

The girl laughed. "We're both twenty-one. Today's her birthday and we all came out to celebrate." She pointed to a crowded table of young women who sat behind them. "The man at the door and the man at the bar both checked our IDs twice. We're legal."

"Well, I think Tina's had too much celebration. It's time to say good night." He pointed to the security guard. "Ryan here will help you get her to the car," he said, his statement a direct order.

The girl named Nikki nodded. "I'm the designated driver tonight so I'll make sure she gets home safe."

Malcolm's head waved up and down against his broad shoulders. He blew a low sigh. He understood the rite of passage. Had himself overindulged when he'd been able to drink legally. But overindulging had become a bad habit that had almost destroyed his life. It made him ultrasensitive to the behavior of the younger crowd that seemed to enjoy the club's happenings to excess.

He blew another deep sigh as he eased through the crowd to the bar. Lawrence "Romeo" Marshall, his best friend and the co-owner, stood behind the wooden structure pouring vodka into a glass.

The two men had been friends since pledging Alpha Phi Alpha. They'd been line brothers, their bond irrefutable. After college both had gone in different directions. Returning home to North Carolina had reestablished their connection. They'd been working the bar together almost since Romeo had gotten the bright idea and Malcolm had agreed to be his cohort in crime. Going against the grain of everything else they both knew, neither could fathom any reason why running a juke joint together wouldn't work for them. And since it had, the association afforded them both something they'd been missing.

Malcolm lifted an easy hand in greeting. "Hey there, Romeo."

"Hey, Malcolm," his friend answered. "What's got you here? I thought you were going to take the night off?"

He shrugged, his broad shoulders pushing toward the ceiling as he settled himself against a barstool. "A woman."

Romeo laughed heartily, noting the wistful expression that crossed his friend's face. "As good a reason as any!"

Malcolm laughed with him. "Actually, the girls are with their mother. I couldn't sleep so I figured I might as well get some work done. I need to reorganize that storage room. We keep having to increase the inventory and we're running out of space." He tossed another quick look around the room. "Besides, you look like you could use an extra hand," he concluded.

The room was filled to capacity. Both men were amazed at the number of bodies who'd shown up on a Monday night. All the media attention was serving them well. They'd had record sales for weeks and it didn't look like it was going to slow down anytime soon.

Romeo nodded. "It's been crazy like this all night!"

"I guess when you consider the alternative we really can't complain!" Malcolm said, a low chuckle blowing past his lips.

Romeo filled three more drink orders then leaned across the bar, sipping on a cup of hot coffee. He pushed another in his friend's direction. "So tell me about this woman," he said as he took a slow sip.

Malcolm laughed again. "There's nothing to tell. *Yet.* Give me a few days and I'll let you know."

Lifting his cup in salute, Romeo nodded and smiled, then both men shifted into work mode.

The crowd at The Playground was just shy of being rowdy. The music was loud and the throng of partygoers was animated. The staff was working diligently to keep the masses satisfied. Onstage, the new piano player, Walter "Lightning" Lewis was playing a slow seductive number that had couples clinging hungrily to one another. He was a tall, thin young man with skin like melted caramel. Reddish brown hair curled smoothly atop his head complementing his dark eyes and chiseled jawline. The women loved him and they owed the insurgence of youth in the room to his presence.

The band behind him was a motley crew of musicians who'd come for the music; friends and acquaintances who appreciated every opportunity they could find to jam together. Some were transient, faces they might not see again for months, if at all. And then the regulars, who showed up at the first tinkling of the piano keys. Payment was the money Romeo and Malcolm slipped into their pockets at the end of each set and the one or two shots of liquid fuel permitted at the end of the evening. Life was simple and easy and the appreciation danced around the room enough to make it all worth doing again and again.

Odetta Brown, the head waitress, slapped a silver tray against the bar top. She was a gregarious, big-boned, voluptuous woman with a chocolate-kissed complexion. Short, jet-black hair framed a full face resplendent with large, nut-brown eyes, and a full pout. Brusque in her manners, she was loudly expressive and the customers loved her, something about her unencumbered style and curt mannerisms was refreshing. Malcolm grinned as she bumped her shoulder against his.

"They are working my nerves tonight!" Odetta exclaimed. Her eyebrows were raised sky high and her eyes were open wide, exasperation painting her expression.

Malcolm laughed. "You say that every night!"

Odetta snapped her requisite piece of chewing gum, blowing a large bubble and popping it a second time. "Well, they're really doing it tonight! I swear, some of these kids act like they ain't had no home training!"

Malcolm tossed Romeo a quick look. "I'm starting to think we should raise the minimum age limit to twenty-five. These young kids don't know how to have a good time without getting unruly."

"That's exactly what I'm saying," Odetta chimed.

Romeo nodded. "Let's talk about it at the next staff meeting."

With a roll of her eyes and one last snap of her gum, Odetta blew a loud sigh. Both men shook their heads.

Across the way the sweetest voice brought the room to a sudden standstill. Onstage, their resident songbird, Sharon Wallace, had drawn everyone's attention in her direction, eyes widened and mouths agape. She was a tiny young woman standing just over five feet tall. Seeming almost fragile, there was an air of innocence about her. A mass of copper-colored curls set off her peach-toned skin and dark freckles danced lightly across her pug nose. She wore a casual, off-the-shoulder top and form-fitting pants that complemented her petite figure. Standing against the backdrop of that black piano, she looked like a superstar on the rise.

Malcolm, Romeo, and Odetta all grinned, tossing each other a quick look. Sharon had initially been hired as a waitress but it hadn't taken long to discover her talent lay in the booming voice that billowed out of her small body. Malcolm lay claim to discovering her after finding her singing in a small storefront Baptist church one crisp Sunday afternoon. To hear him tell it she'd been heaven sent. He had sat in the rear pew of that old church every Sunday for over a month. It had taken two weeks before he'd discovered her name. By the third week, he knew that the closest thing to home for her had been the West Creedmoor Women's Shelter and that she had no family and no job to speak of. At the end of the month, he'd taken her under his wing and into his heart and had been hell-bent on delivering her from her miseries. The rest was history in the making.

Even the new hires, the waitresses, Michelle Clifton and Leslie Trammel, and the bartender, Frank Pierce, had come to a halt, all lost in the moment. The two women looked toward their employers for approval and when Malcolm and Romeo both smiled and nodded, each relaxed and enjoyed the entertainment. Everyone in the room was mesmerized as Sharon sang like her life depended on it. It was just another night at The Playground, leaving those lucky to be there with much to remember.

The house was quiet when Malcolm eased his way inside. His mother had left one light on in the family room and when he tiptoed in that direction to turn it off he found her curled beneath a blanket in the window seat, an opened book in her hand.

"Hey there, beautiful, you're still up," Malcolm said, his voice a loud whisper.

Miss Claudette smiled as she pulled a pair of wire-rimmed reading glasses from her face. "The house is too quiet when the girls are gone. I couldn't fall asleep so I thought I'd finish my book," she said, gesturing with the novel in her hand.

Malcolm caught a quick glimpse of the cover, the image of a little girl shimmering beneath a watery surface. The title was *Rested Waters* and he noted the worn pages and the binding creased from wear. "Is it good?" he questioned. He moved to his favorite seat and sat down, the leather recliner seeming to wrap him in a warm embrace.

Miss Claudette nodded, her gray hair waving against her narrow shoulders. "It's very good. It's our book club selection this month," she said as she rested the paperback against her lap. "I can't wait for the discussion next week. This is my third time reading it."

Malcolm smiled, his head bobbing slightly. "Maybe I'll read it when you're done," he said softly.

"So, how did it go tonight?" his mother questioned.

Malcolm flipped his hand upward. "Crazy busy. I hadn't planned on working so hard but the crowd was outrageous."

"That's good," his mother responded. "That means business is booming."

Malcolm nodded, drifting off into thought. A blanket of silence eased between them and minutes passed before he spoke again.

"I met someone today. My God, was she beautiful!" he exclaimed, the comment slipping out of his mouth before he could catch it. His eyes widened as he realized the words he'd just spoken. He shot his mother a quick look.

Miss Claudette lifted her gaze to meet her son's. She didn't bother to respond sensing there was more that he wanted to share as he questioned whether he should say anything at all. When he finally did speak she listened intently.

"Her name's Cilla. She was grabbing coffee this morning at Starbucks and we talked for a few minutes. She was funny . . . and smart," he said with a brief pause. "I think I really liked her."

Miss Claudette nodded. "Maybe you'll get a chance to see her again," his mother said. Her tone was calm, and hopeful. A hint of concern echoed in her inflection. "If anything can come of it you know you need to take it slow, and be respectful. I raised you to be a gentleman and the girls need to see that from you. You need to be the example they look to when those little boys start sniffing around them," she said as if it were necessary to remind him.

Malcolm nodded then smiled. "I'm not sure why I told you that. I'll probably never see that woman again."

His mother shrugged. "It sounds like you want to see her again and that means something. That's why you told me."

He contemplated her comment for only a brief second before ending the conversation. "I think I'll go on up and get a shower," he said, rising from his seat. "Good night."

Miss Claudette smiled back. She lifted her face

upward as he leaned to give her cheek a kiss. "Sweet dreams, Son-shine. Mama loves you!"

"I love you, too, Mama."

Malcolm eased his way up the stairwell. Behind the closed door of his bedroom he fell back against the mattress, pulling his arm up over his head. He'd been thinking about Cilla Jameson since that morning. He had half-hoped that she might have shown up at the club but there'd been no sign of her. When he and Romeo had finally locked the doors, he'd actually been disappointed and the emotion surprised him. There had been no lack of beautiful women at the nightclub vying for his attention but he hadn't been interested because thoughts of Cilla had consumed him. He blew a deep sigh as he sat upright, unable to fathom what had gotten into him and wondering what it was going to take to shake the emotion from his spirit.

Since his divorce Malcolm had made dating something of a sport. He enjoyed it. He did it casually and it was only an investment of his time and energy when he wanted it to be. Over the years he'd met some incredible women and some who only thought they were. But what each of them had in common was a need or desire to make things between them permanent and Malcolm wholeheartedly had no interest in doing forever with any woman.

Commitment scared Malcolm, most especially since his first relationship had failed so miserably. He and his ex-wife, Shanell, had been college sweethearts. Back then he'd loved everything about Shanell, even the bad habits that had eventually torn them apart. With Shanell he'd been blinded by love, refusing to see the worst of their relationship even when he'd been slapped in the face with it time and time again.

The lies had been the start. Half-truths and blatant omissions. There wasn't anything Malcolm could ever ask of Shanell that didn't come with a wealth of excuses and a plethora of misunderstandings. The end had finally come after her arrest for prostitution. The first arrest of many more that had followed. The wealth of drama in between had only been the icing on some very bitter cake. Malcolm had missed all the signs of her addiction and mostly because he'd been lost knee-deep in his own. Now that he'd been sober far longer than not, Malcolm had no problems admitting that he was an alcoholic. He lived to tell his story in hopes that he could help just one soul take that first step toward recovery. His daughters had been one year old the last time he'd had a drink and even though the club put him directly in the line of fire more times than not, there was nothing and no one that could ever bring him back to the bottle and some of the darkest days of his life. The bar served as a daily reminder of what he could lose if he ever thought to drink again.

Shanell though still had not learned that lesson. Despite her constant assurances that she had changed and her life was different, Malcolm wasn't so sure. Trusting his daughters with their mother was the hardest thing for him to do, but she'd become adept at convincing the girl's court appointed attorney and the crew at child protective services that she only had their best interests at heart. But each and every court-mandated visit felt like punishment and he hated that his girls were both suffering for the mistakes he and Shanell had made.

Turning his life around for Cleo and Claudia had come without a second thought. There was nothing Malcolm would not do for his girls. Time and time again Shanell had pledged to do the same and with every broken promise Malcolm had found himself equally shattered. So much so that when he'd finally declared the marriage done and finished his heart had been a fragmented semblance of its original self.

For years after, he'd struggled with issues of intimacy and trust and his self-esteem had been crushed. The road back had taught him much about himself and his inner strength. Discovering the best and worst of himself had also taught him what he wanted, and needed, from the woman who might one day lay claim to his heart. More importantly, it taught him what he didn't need or want in return and what he absolutely refused to accept and tolerate.

Malcolm liked the man he now was. He was proud of his accomplishments. He was a great father and he knew that one day he'd be a dynamic partner for the right woman. But as far as Malcolm was concerned "one day" was a long way away and not something he saw himself giving any immediate thought to. Nor did he have any interest or desire in discovering who that right woman was, even if it was by happenstance. But in spite of that proclamation he still couldn't for the life of him get thoughts of Cilla Jameson out of his head.

Cilla peeked out of the window of her new condominium. The couple who lived two doors away were arguing in the parking lot, she not happy with something he had done. They had been screaming back and forth at each other for the last ten minutes. As they stood beneath the lights that illuminated the outdoor space it was easy to see the frustration that painted both of their expressions. When the man finally stormed off, leaving his female companion standing there in tears, Cilla felt for both of them. But watching them reminded her of why she didn't do relationships. Her own personal experiences had taught her that most never ended well.

She stole a quick glance to the grandfather clock that decorated her front entrance. It was late and she should have been in bed hours ago. It was going to make for a difficult time when her alarm clock would sound at five-thirty A.M. She blew a deep breath as she moved from the window into her kitchen to fill a glass with water.

Minutes later she eased her body back into bed, drawing the sheet and covers up to her shoulders. She suddenly thought about the evening she might have missed at that jazz club, having thought it better that she stay home and not take Malcolm Cobb up on his invitation. She clutched the sheets as she thought about the man. It had taken more than an ounce of fortitude not to give in to the curiosity that had kept him in her thoughts. But then she remembered the old adage about curiosity killing some cat and she knew that no good could have come from her going. At least that was what she'd been telling herself since she'd gotten home from work, determined to justify the regret she was suddenly feeling.

Her head waved from side to side. She should have gone. She had wanted to see Malcolm Cobb again. She wanted to talk to him, to laugh at his jokes and to see him on his own turf. If nothing else, she was intrigued by the flutter of desire she felt during their encounter, wondering if there was any sustenance to it or if it was just a fleeting feeling. She was suddenly kicking herself for not following her instincts. Second-guessing herself surely had not served her well because here she was, wide awake, alone, and thinking about a man who had managed to capture her attention. Wondering what might have been.

Second-guessing her instincts had never served Cilla well and she knew it. She had second-guessed her last relationship only to discover that every suspicion she had about John Parker had been even worse than she imagined. She'd suspected infidelity. She hadn't banked on a wife and three kids, the discovery a complete devastation. She had also second-guessed her relationship with that college frat boy, the blond, blue-eyed banker's son, an admitted pot-smoking horticulturalist. She thought he was a slacker while they were together, but after Colorado's legalization of the organic buzz, he'd become a multibillionaire overnight. Now he and her former college roommate were living the good life on three continents. Second-guessing herself had never boded well and Cilla was determined to stop. For once in her twenty-nine years she was determined to follow her intuition to see where that led her. The more she thought about Malcolm, the more she reasoned she didn't have anything at all to lose.

Chapter Three

Despite another restless night Malcolm was up and out early. His morning run was timed perfectly, early enough for him to avoid the rising heat and humidity the local weather forecasts were promising for the day. And like clockwork once he was done running he headed toward his local Starbucks, arriving at the door shortly after their opening.

Cilla had already made herself comfortable at the corner table when Malcolm eased his way inside. She smiled brightly when she caught his eye, lifting two beverage cups in the air. Malcolm's grin was miles wide as he made his way to her side. It had been two whole weeks since he'd last laid eyes on her. He'd actually given up hope that they might run into each other again so he couldn't help but wonder what had brought her there.

"Good morning!" she chimed sweetly. "They told me this was your favorite. I hope they got it right," she said as she shot a quick look toward the Starbucks employee who was beaming at them both.

"I'm sure it's perfect," Malcolm said as he took

the seat beside her. He was still grinning foolishly, the sight of her a welcome surprise.

"I thought I'd repay the favor," Cilla said, answering his unspoken question. "And I wanted to see you again."

Malcolm's eyes widened. He was taken aback by her comment. Any other woman and he might have questioned her motives. But there was something about the shimmer in Cilla's dark eyes that felt genuine. The words out of her mouth felt open and honest. He never gave a second thought to believing Cilla. It had been some time since he'd met a woman who felt so forthcoming when he knew so little about her.

He nodded. "I take that to mean I made a good first impression."

Cilla smiled. "You did all right," she said teasingly. Her laugh was magnetic and the more she smiled the more she made him want to smile.

"I didn't think I was going to ever see you again," Malcolm said matter-of-factly. "I kept looking for you at the club."

She nodded. "I've had a really hectic schedule. I still plan to come check you and your business out though."

"I hope you do. I think you'll have a good time. But I'm glad you're here now," Malcolm said, his voice sweet and rich like a thick blend of honey and molasses.

She laughed heartily, a blush of color washing over her expression. "So am I," she said as she leaned back in her seat.

She took a slow sip of her morning coffee, her

gaze locking with his. She was excited to find him staring so intently as if he were trying to memorize each line and dimple of her profile. Staring back, their gazes danced together and she realized it would take very little for her to lose herself in the depths of his stare.

She closed her eyes and inhaled deeply as she shook her head from side to side. When she reopened them he was still staring, his bright smile radiating over her. She took another deep breath. She suddenly needed conversation to stall the rising emotion flowing between them.

"So, if you're at the club nights what do you do during the day?" she asked as she rested her cup against the table. Malcolm shifted his own beverage cup next to hers. "Well, this morning I'm flying to Baltimore. I have an architectural business there and every few weeks I fly in to show my face and make sure things are on track."

"So you're running two businesses?"

He nodded. "I am. Two very successful businesses," he said, his broad chest seeming to push forward ever so slightly.

She found his bravado entertaining. "When do you come back?"

His eyes skated back and forth as if he were trying to remember his itinerary. "That depends. When are you going to have dinner with me?"

Cilla laughed. "When you get back from Baltimore," she said, her seductive tone matching his.

"Then I'll be back tonight." Malcolm grinned as he leaned forward in his seat. "What time should I pick you up?"

Cilla reached for the cell phone he'd rested on the tabletop. He never once flinched as he watched her. It was one of the newest Android smartphones and it wasn't password protected. She slid a manicured nail across the screen, moving through all his apps until she found his contact list. As she scrolled through the numbers she lifted her eyes to his for a brief second. Amusement painted his expression as he stared. Dropping her gaze back to the device she pushed the ADD button then entered her contact information. Once it was saved she passed the phone back to him.

"Call me when you land. We can figure out the rest then," she said.

Malcolm nodded. He picked up his phone, scrolled through his numbers, and pushed the DIAL button. Seconds later Cilla's own phone rang in her pocket.

She laughed. "You didn't trust me?"

He shook his head. "Nothing of the kind. I just wanted to make sure you recognized the number. And, now that you have my contact information, I hope you'll use it."

She rose from her seat. "Have a great day, Mr. Cobb!"

"I'm sure dinner and dessert will put the great in this day, Ms. Jameson."

With a low giggle Cilla crossed the room and headed for the exit. As she reached the door she tossed him a glance over her shoulder. Malcolm was staring after her, his eyes following the side-to-side sway of her hips as he bit down against his bottom lip. She shook her head, her eyes rolling as she met the look he was giving her.

She called to him from across the room. "Really?"

Malcolm laughed heartily, his shoulders pushed into a deep shrug, his palms opened toward the ceiling. With another wave of her head, Cilla turned and disappeared out the door. Malcolm grinned. Dinner couldn't happen fast enough.

Despite the tight schedule, Malcolm had showered, shaved, kissed his daughters off to school, and had made his charter flight from Raleigh-Durham International Airport to BWI Marshall with time to spare. By ten forty-five he was opening the door to his East Pratt Street design firm, the staff greeting him warmly.

His dream come true, the opening of 3C Innovative Designs was one of his most successful accomplishments. After graduating with an engineering degree he'd been committed to building an architectural firm that ran circles around its competitors. Sheer drive and love for his craft had pushed them to the forefront in the industry. They were now listed as one of the top five companies in the nation.

His leaving Baltimore and moving his family to Raleigh had come with some reservations and much risk but had been one of the best decisions he could have made. The business had survived, and excelled, in spite of him having to travel back and forth to do what he needed to do. He credited a talented staff and dedicated employees for helping him accomplish what many had said would be impossible.

Maxine Perry peeked her head into his office

and said hello. "Did you already have your morning coffee or can I get you a cup?"

He crossed the room to give the woman a hug. His administrative assistant for as long as he had the business, she was soft and sweet like warm cookie dough but polished like a vintage jewel. The business suit she wore was an Anne Klein classic design, one she had probably purchased years ago and had taken meticulous care of. "I'm good this morning, Miss Maxine. How've you been?"

He leaned back against the circular conference table that sat in the center of the room. Crossing his arms over his chest he focused his attention on his ex-wife's mother.

Miss Maxine nodded. "Every morning I get up is a good morning," she said with a soft cackle. "How's the nightclub business treating you?"

"It's kicking my butt. I'm really starting to feel like I'm too old for all this," he said with a deep chuckle.

Miss Maxine laughed with him. "You don't know old yet!"

Malcolm nodded as he moved to the back side of the desk and took a seat in the leather executive's chair. "Other than feeling twice my age sometimes, I really can't complain. The club is thriving and you're holding things together here. What more could a man ask for?"

She smiled. "So how are my grandbabies?"

"The girls are doing very well. Both of them made the honor roll and Claudia was chosen to do a solo at her dance recital next month. Shanell will have them with her this weekend."

Miss Maxine frowned. "Shanell was just here in

Baltimore. She came by the house the other night wanting to borrow some money. I got the impression she was planning to be here for a while. She didn't say anything about driving back to Raleigh to get the girls."

Malcolm blew a low sigh. "Well, I haven't heard that she doesn't plan to pick them up but if I do, I'll let you know."

"I miss my girls. I like that we can do that video chat during the week."

Malcolm laughed. "They get a kick out of it, too. But I have to keep my eye on Cleo. She'll chat all day and all night with anyone and everyone."

The matriarch chuckled warmly. "I'm glad she's got you to keep her in check. You're a good man, Malcolm Cobb. I wish my daughter could have seen that."

Malcolm didn't bother to reply and his former mother-in-law didn't expect him to. She continued, "You have a meeting with the design team in thirty minutes and with the rest of the staff at one o'clock. There's a stack of papers on your desk that need your signature and we have a new client coming in at three."

He nodded. "I was planning to fly back tomorrow but something's come up. I really need to fly back this evening. Can you please . . . ?"

Holding up her hand she stalled his comment. She gave him a smile and a wink of her eye. "I'll take care of it. What time do you need to be in Raleigh?"

"Before eight if we can swing it," he answered.

"Do you need reservations on that end?"

Malcolm hesitated, his eyes shifting as his mind suddenly raced. His gaze finally rested on the woman's face and he felt himself blush under the stare she was giving him. Despite his best efforts his intentions showed all over his face. He suddenly felt like he'd been caught red-handed, with his arm trapped deep in the cookie jar.

She laughed, the wealth of it feeling like a warm embrace. "I'll take care of everything," she said. She moved forward and hugged him one more time. "It's good to have you back, even if it is just for a hot minute," she said as she moved back out of the office.

Watching her shuffle back to her own desk, Malcolm blew a soft sigh. Maxine Perry was one of his favorite people in the whole world. The day he'd met Shanell he'd fallen head over heels in love with her mother. It had taken some time before he felt that way about Shanell. Few women had as kind a spirit as Maxine. She was always encouraging and confident and optimism prevailed despite the hardships handed to her. Born and raised in Maryland the woman had not had an easy life. She'd been a single mother who'd managed to put herself through college and had been determined to do the same for her children. Of her six kids she'd buried all of her sons, the five young men having succumbed to the streets of Baltimore. Shanell was all she had left and the matriarch had given up everything she had to keep her daughter on the straight and narrow, despite Shanell's insistence on walking a crooked line.

Malcolm would always be in Maxine Perry's debt because during his darkest days it had been Maxine who'd pushed him back to the light. She'd held his hands, his head, and had been at his back without him ever asking, her presence and love as steadfast as that of his own mother. As he stood thinking about her she moved back into the room, snapping her fingers for his attention. He jumped slightly as his gaze shifted to where she pointed. Her index finger waved from the clock to the conference room.

"You don't want to be late," she said as she dropped a hand onto her full hips.

He nodded. "No, ma'am. I certainly don't!"

At six-fifteen Malcolm was well past Baltimore's evening traffic, sitting on the tarmac. He had dinner reservations for eight-thirty and he knew the two dozen yellow roses resting on the seat beside him was Maxine's way of giving him her approval and support even though he hadn't told her anything at all about the woman she was making plans for. He hoped Cilla loved them as much as he loved the gesture.

Just minutes before the pilot announced that they were ready for takeoff he called home. His mother answered just as he was about to hang up.

"Is everything okay?" Malcolm questioned, concern ringing in his tone.

Miss Claudette nodded into the receiver. "We're fine. The girls and I were outside planting some rosebushes. I left the phone inside on the kitchen table and had to run for it."

"You should have made one of the girls run."

"They both had their hands dirty and I didn't

want them to stop doing what they were doing. So how's Baltimore?"

He shrugged. "No different since the last time you asked me."

Miss Claudette laughed. "Well then how is my friend Maxine?"

"She's holding it down."

"My girl always does. God bless her!"

"She said she's going to call you because she wants to arrange for you and the girls to drive up and meet her at Potomac Mills for a weekend shopping spree."

"That sounds like fun."

"I told her I'd treat."

"Then we will definitely take you up on that! If I don't hear from her in the next day or two I'll call her."

"Well, as long as you and the girls are doing okay, I'll let you go. I'll give the girls a call later, right before they go to bed."

"Do you need a ride from the airport tomorrow?"

There was a moment of pause as he debated whether or not to tell his mother he was on his way home. He took a deep breath. "No. I've got it covered."

Not missing a beat his mother chuckled softly, mother's intuition kicking in high gear. "I just bet you do," she said.

Malcolm laughed with her. "I'm actually coming home now but I have a dinner date. In case it runs late I didn't want you looking for me."

"Uh huh . . . in case . . ."

He laughed again. "Okay, Mama."

"I didn't say anything. Just keep in touch so I know you're safe, please."

"You know I will."

"Love you, Son-shine!"

"I love you, too, Mama!"

Takeoff was smooth and easy and when the pilot gave his okay, the private plane sailing midair, he dialed Cilla. She answered on the second ring.

"I was just about to give up on you," Cilla said in greeting, the caller ID giving him away.

"Oh, ye of little faith!"

She laughed. "Have you landed?"

"The pilot says we should be in Raleigh in less than an hour. Can you pick me up from the airport?"

Cilla laughed. "I guess I could do that."

"Do you know where the private terminals are?"

"I'm sure I can find my way."

"I'll be coming in at the TAC Air building."

"I'll find it. And then what? Where are we eating?"

"It's a surprise."

"At least tell a girl how to dress. I don't want to be in five-inch heels and a little black dress if we're just going to Snoopy's for a hotdog."

"Something tight and short always works."

"So, we are going to Snoopy's!" Cilla responded with a giggle.

"Tight and short works wherever."

"Uh no. Try again."

"You've already made a great first impression. I'm sure you'll be beautiful in whatever you wear."

"You're very good with the compliments, Mr. Cobb!"

Malcolm grinned into the receiver. "I aim to please!"

"Safe landing and I'll see you soon," Cilla said, her voice dropping an octave.

Just before he disconnected the call, Malcolm responded. "I can't wait to see you, too!"

An hour later Cilla saw him before he saw her. She was standing on the second floor of the General Aviation Terminal, staring out at the private planes that were coming and going with relative frequency. The luxury aircraft landed easily and her eyes followed as it moved down the taxiway to the hangar. The Cessna Citation Sovereign was lean and sleek, looking like a winged Maybach. It had to be one of the sexiest sights Cilla had ever seen.

Minutes later Malcolm exited the aircraft. His attire was business casual; silver-gray slacks, a white dress shirt, and a black silk blazer. He carried a black leather attaché in one hand and the most beautiful bouquet of flowers in the other. He was even sexier in his dress clothes. That flutter of attraction rippled with a vengeance through her abdomen and she smiled, her excitement reaching an all-time high.

Rushing down the expanse of stairway to the first floor, she followed the path to the building next door. By the time she reached the reception area Malcolm had made his way inside. He stood nervously, his gaze dancing around the space as he searched for her and when their eyes connected, both stood staring and grinning foolishly. Cilla moved quickly to his side. They stood face-to-face, their bodies mere inches from each other. Heat wafted between them, abundant and full, seeming to take on a life of its own.

Malcolm suddenly laughed and Cilla laughed with him. His deep chortle helped to ease the rise of tension that had swept over them both and they relaxed easily into the moment like their meeting was something they did every day.

"Hey, you!" he said as he extended the roses in her direction.

"Hey, yourself," she said as she paused to sniff the sweet aroma wafting off the long stems. She lifted her eyes to stare back into his. "How was your flight?"

He nodded. "Perfect now."

"Now?"

"It brought me back to you."

Cilla laughed again as she rolled her eyes upward. "That was so cheesy!"

"It was, wasn't it!" he said with a deep chuckle. He wrapped an arm around her shoulders and hugged her warmly. "Thanks for coming to pick me up."

Leaning into his side Cilla liked how it felt. He was the perfect height, standing just tall enough where even in heels she had to tilt her head to stare up at him, but not so tall that she couldn't rest her head easily against his shoulder if she were so inclined. She felt comfortable against him and her whole body eased into his as if it were the most natural thing for her to do.

"Thank you for the flowers," she said. "They're beautiful."

"You're beautiful," Malcolm said as he took a step back.

She was wearing tailored chocolate-brown palazzo shorts that stopped at her calves and a brown and cream, short, cropped, herringbone blazer. Beneath the jacket she wore a silk tank that was a brilliant shade of peach, the coloration a perfect complement to her light brown complexion. She was perfectly proportioned with a full bustline and wide hips and enough curve to her backside to make him wonder what she'd feel like cushioned close against him. The neckline of her top dipped just low enough to show off her cleavage, the round of her breasts teasing him. High-heeled pumps in a wonderful shade of emerald green, gold bangles around her wrists, and a thin beaded gold and diamond chain around her neck completed her ensemble. It wasn't enough to call her beautiful, he thought. Cilla Jameson was absolutely stunning.

A blush of color tinted Cilla's cheeks at his compliment. "Thank you." She took a deep breath. "So, where do we go next?" she asked, her curiosity consuming her.

Malcolm took his own deep breath as he gave her a wry smile. "Do you mind if I drive your car?" he asked, ignoring her question.

She shook her head. Reaching into her leather purse she pulled the keys from inside and handed them to him. Malcolm reached for her hand and entwined his fingers between hers as he pulled her along beside him. Outside, she pointed to the black Lexus IS 350 convertible parked off to the side.

"Nice ride," Malcolm said as he tossed her a quick look. He guided her to the passenger-side door then opened it to let her inside. "Very nice ride," he echoed as he made his way to the driver's side and took the seat beside her.

"It was my birthday present to myself."

His head bobbed. "I can't wait to see what you get me for my birthday," Malcolm said teasingly. He engaged the engine and pulled into airport traffic.

Cilla laughed. "When is your birthday?"

"November first. I'll be thirty-seven."

She smiled. "They'll be sending you your AARP card soon."

He cut an eye in her direction. "I said thirty-seven, not fifty-seven."

"I heard what you said." She laughed heartily. "A little sensitive about your age, aren't you?"

"Not at all. He gave her a wide-eyed look, a humorous smirk across his face. "How old are you?" he asked, flipping the conversation.

"Twenty-nine."

"So what do you plan to get yourself for your thirtieth birthday?"

"The question should be what do *you* plan to get me?"

He laughed. "Good question. I'm glad I have some time to think about it."

"'Cause it better be good!" Cilla countered with her own soft giggle.

Malcolm shook his head as he cut another eye at her, his smile miles wide.

It was a short ride from the airport parking lot to the Angus Barn, the city's premier steakhouse. Cilla's eyes widened as he turned her car into the restaurant's parking lot to an open space and brought it to a stop. Dining at the exclusive eatery had been on Cilla's bucket list of things to do. Wanting to share the experience with someone special, and having no one who fit the bill, had been the only thing to deter her from making this experience a reality. She gave Malcolm a look but said nothing as he exited the vehicle, circled around the car, and opened her door for her. He reached for her hand to help her out, his palm and fingers warm and teasing against her own.

"This is very nice," she said as they headed toward the entrance hand in hand.

"Walter Royal is an old friend of mine," he said as he referred to the restaurant's executive chef, a former *Iron Chef America* winner.

"You know Mr. Royal personally?" She eyed him with a hint of reservation in her gaze.

Malcolm nodded. "We go way back," he said.

Cilla's reservations were cast away once they were inside. At the door, the hostess greeted Malcolm by name. She was duly impressed when the owner made his way over to shake the man's hand, the two having a brief conversation about a potential joint fundraising venture between their two businesses. The man personally escorted them to the restaurant's kitchen and the infamous chef's table that was known to be a popular attraction.

Cilla felt like a deer caught in headlights as she tried to take it all in. With all the introductions, everyone's name and face had become a confusion of who was who. Despite her best efforts Cilla knew that she would never remember who everyone was regardless of the tidbits of personal information Malcolm offered after each introduction. Then there were the sights, the sounds, and the tantalizing smells coming from the bustling kitchen area as they were treated to an exclusive behind-the-scenes look at the Barn's operations. It was sensory overload and definitely more than she'd been prepared for.

There was a brief moment of quiet after the sommelier uncorked a bottle of wine and poured her a glass. Malcolm's glass was filled with a beverage of fresh pomegranate puree, lemon juice, and seltzer water.

"You don't drink?" Cilla questioned after he'd lifted his glass in toast, encouraging her to savor the delicate spirits.

He shook his head. "No. I've been sober for thirteen years. They blend this concoction especially for me."

"Sober?"

"I'm a recovering alcoholic," he said matter-of-factly.

"But you said it's been thirteen years. If you haven't had a drink in all that time wouldn't you consider yourself recovered?"

Malcolm shrugged. "I don't ever want to make the mistake of forgetting how bad things were in the midst of my addiction. There is a wise saying that says those who forget their mistakes are doomed to repeat them. I don't want to ever forget because I have no intentions of ever going back there."

"Was it that bad?"

He hesitated for a brief moment. "I'm not a very nice drunk," he said. "It got really ugly. I stopped drinking when I realized everyone in my life deserved better."

"So why would you own a bar?" she asked, suddenly curious to know more about the man. "Don't you ever get tempted?"

He shook his head. "No. I refuse to be tempted. But I love being in the bar business. I love the people and the atmosphere. And every day that I'm successful reminds me of just how strong I am and how strong I need to be for my daughters and my family."

Cilla suddenly sat upright, shifting in her seat. "Daughters?"

He smiled and nodded. "I have two daughters. Twin girls that I have custody of."

"So you have a wife?" There was suddenly an air of attitude in her tone.

He laughed as he shook his head. "I have an *ex-wife.* We've been divorced for over ten years."

"So you're raising your daughters alone?"

"My mother lives with me and helps me take care of the girls."

Cilla's expression made Malcolm laugh. "It's really not that bad," he said with a wry chuckle. "I come with luggage but I assure you it's all unpacked and put away."

Cilla laughed with him. "I'm just . . . well . . . wow!" she suddenly exclaimed. "I didn't know what to expect from you but I didn't expect all that."

He nodded. "Too much for you to handle?"

She met the look he was giving her, his stare intense. "No, it's not too much. I appreciate you being open and honest with me," she said.

He smiled sweetly. "You will always get that. I don't have anything to hide and I believe in being transparent. With me, you'll always know what you're going to get."

Before she could respond one of the many chefs stood tableside, serving up the first course of their sumptuous five-course meal. The crab cakes were a succulent blend of large lump crabmeat and the barest hint of bread crumbs and seasoning. It was sheer delight for a seafood lover. As the chef detailed the dish, Malcolm found himself drifting off into thought.

He'd opened up to Cilla right out of the gate. He had never before done that with any woman and definitely never on a first date. Malcolm had learned years ago that one or two dates would never make it to three or four so there had been no reason to make himself vulnerable by revealing too many details about his personal life. Only a woman he was interested in introducing to his mother needed to know about his children. And if the discussion of his drinking came up, it was only after he was certain she was someone he wanted to know better. As the chef stepped away his gaze moved over her face. Meeting her eyes he stared and she stared back, the intensity of it like nothing he'd ever experienced before. He suddenly realized that with Cilla, he couldn't see himself *not* telling her all there was to tell about himself. But he couldn't help but wonder what she thought about that, and him. Before he had an opportunity to ask, the second course arrived. It was a lobster bisque with a corn and red pepper relish. The flavor was light and delicate and absolutely mind-boggling.

"Why do you look so serious?" Cilla suddenly questioned, interrupting his thoughts.

He shrugged, a slight smile pulling at his mouth. He swallowed a spoonful of soup then swiped at his mouth with a cloth napkin. "I was actually thinking about you and wondering what you might be thinking."

"I'm having a wonderful time. The food is magnificent and I'm enjoying the company."

He nodded, his smile widening. "So tell me about yourself. Since I've shared my deep dark secrets it's only fair that you share yours." He leaned back in his seat, an arm thrown over the back of it as he waited for her to talk.

Cilla laughed and the warmth of it flooded his spirit. "My deep dark secrets," she said as her gaze floated around the room. "I'm not sure I have any."

"Oh, I'm sure you have a few."

She shrugged, her narrow shoulders pushing toward the ceiling. "Not really. I was a military brat. I grew up on the base in Adana, Turkey. My parents divorced when I was nine and my biological father didn't have anything to do with me after that. My mother moved here to North Carolina with her second husband who turned out to be a perfect father-figure. I was so desperate to have their approval that I was an absolute angel. I got good grades, never missed a curfew, dated all the right boys, and did everything I was supposed to do. Even during college and after I moved out on my own, I've always played by the rules. There's nothing deep or dark there."

"So, would dating me break that vicious cycle you seem to be caught in?"

Cilla grinned. "Probably not. I don't think my parents would see you as a bad boy. You've got too much going for you."

The conversation continued through the salad; a blend of baby arugula leaves, roasted sweet potatoes, bell peppers, red onion, Parmigiano cheese, and a honeyed balsamic vinaigrette. Laughter was abundant as they teased back and forth, sharing stories about their childhoods and their families.

"Being an only child I was spoiled rotten," Cilla said, her smile bright. "And I'm very much a girlie girl. I kept Barbie dolls, hair bows, and all things pink in my bag of tricks. My father hated it!"

"Couldn't make a tomboy out of you, huh?"

"Not even a little!"

"Did you play any sports?" Malcolm questioned as he took a bite of his salad.

"Cheerleading!"

"That's not a sport!" he said with a laugh.

"You wish! You try doing sequences of back handsprings and double twisting layouts over and over again during a football or basketball game. The tumbling required is very much a sport."

"Well, I was an athletic God! If it required a ball I had to play. But there was just one problem."

Her lips lifted in a slight smile. "And what was that?"

"I really wasn't any good!" Malcolm answered with a hearty laugh. "In fact, I was really bad! More missed passes than I care to count and I couldn't make a free throw to save my life!"

By the time their entrée arrived both had shared more about each other than either had ever shared with anyone else before. They were served their meal by Walter Royal himself, the master chef, who was excited to see his friend again. He shook Cilla's hand earnestly as Malcolm introduced them. The chateaubriand was exquisite, cut from the tenderloin and served with pan-roasted fingerling potatoes and sautéed vegetables with ramekins of béarnaise sauce and shitake mushroom au jus. Both the meal and the conversation were satisfying beyond measure.

"So, what's your secret passion?" Malcolm asked, his eyebrows lifting curiously.

She took a moment to reflect on his question. "I love to quilt."

"Quilt? Like in blankets?"

She shook her head. "No. I like creating artistic quilts. I'm sort of a closet textile artist. I make wall hangings out of fiber."

"Wow! I can't wait to see your work," he said.

"One day", she said as she took a sip of her beverage. She placed the glass back on the table. "Tell me more about your business."

"Well," he started, as he gave her some history about the company he'd built and told her about his plans for expansion. As he spoke she listened intently, her eyes never leaving his face as she found herself caught up in his excitement. Time seemed to stand still as the two talked on and on.

"Mmmm!" Cilla moaned when they brought the

dessert tray, the decadent treats making her mouth water.

It featured a variety of freshly baked cheesecakes, cobblers, pies, and multiple ice cream delicacies. Malcolm selected the blackberry cobbler; a fragrant dish of large, firm berries in a flaky, butter-laden crust served with a large scoop of vanilla ice cream. Cilla was unable to resist the Sawdust Pie, their award-winning, signature dessert topped with a dollop of sweetened whipped cream.

"This is my deep, dark secret," she said as she slowly licked her dessert fork. She pulled the metal tines past her lips. "I have a weakness for sweets. I cannot pass up dessert. Ever. It's my addiction."

Malcolm laughed. "Maybe I need to take you to one of my meetings. I go regularly. It's amazing what a twelve-step program will do for you."

Cilla suddenly laid her fork along the side of her plate. Contrition washed over her expression. "I'm sorry. That was really insensitive of me, wasn't it?" she said, her apology shining brightly in her dark eyes. Malcolm shook his head.

"Nothing for you to apologize for. Addiction is an awkward subject for some people to discuss. I make jokes to help folks feel more comfortable. I don't want you to think you have to censor yourself around me. Ever. If there's something you need to say, then I want you to say it."

Cilla took a deep breath. She nodded her head slightly. "I appreciate you being open with me. A lot of men wouldn't have done that. And if you're okay with it, as long as it doesn't impact our relationship from this point forward, we don't really need to talk about it again unless you just want to."

"So, we have a relationship now?"

Her grin widened. "You bought me dinner. And dessert. I might start stalking you."

He nodded. "If that's the case, and I'm laying all my cards on the table, I guess I should tell you that I did some time in prison, too."

Cilla's fork came to an abrupt stop in midair, waving just inches from her open mouth. She cut her eye at him meeting the look he was giving her. She held his gaze, studying the look in his eyes. Taking a deep breath she drew her tongue across her lips as she closed her mouth and rested the fork back onto her plate.

"Prison?"

"Well, not really prison. It was actually county jail."

"What was the charge?"

"Assault. It was some guy my ex-wife was sleeping with and I didn't take it well."

"And that's the only thing you've done time for?"

"It was only eight months and when I got out, I got myself together. I stopped drinking and I haven't had any charges or committed any crimes since, nor do I plan to."

Her expression suddenly went blank, her gaze shifting to some spot just past his shoulders. Malcolm could almost see her brain processing what she'd just learned. A wave of anxiety rushed the length of his spine, his stomach starting to tighten into a knot. He felt himself holding onto the air in his lungs as he waited for her to respond.

"So you're a convicted felon?"

He shook his head. "No. My crime was classified as a mid-level misdemeanor."

There was another lengthy pause but this time she stared directly at him, their gazes locked tightly together.

Cilla finally nodded. "Under any other circumstances, with any other man, this would probably be our one and only date," she said matter-of-factly. "I'd be too scared to take this any further. Wondering what other dark secrets you might decide to spring on me when I least expect it." She paused.

"But?"

"But, I'm just overwhelmingly impressed by your honesty. And you don't frighten me. I actually like you."

Malcom smiled, finally releasing that breath he'd been holding.

She picked up her fork and began eating again, her gaze still locked with his as she drew it to her mouth. She chewed slowly, then swallowed before speaking again. "I think the next time we go out we should go to Snoopy's for hotdogs. I'll even treat," she said with a slight smile.

"It's a date!" Malcolm answered.

"It will be so don't you forget it," Cilla replied.

Malcolm laughed. "I like you, too, Cilla Jameson. I really like you a lot."

Cilla gave him a wink of her eye as she reached her fork into his plate and took a bite of his blackberry cobbler. Drawing it to her mouth she closed her eyes and purred softly, savoring the delicate flavors. When she opened them again, Malcolm was eyeing her intently, biting down against his bottom lip. Without her saying a word, he knew without any doubts that liking each other was just the tip of the iceberg of what they were both beginning to feel for each other.

Despite the late night hour, the evening ended too quickly. When they finally finished their meal neither was ready to part ways. Malcolm drove slowly back to the airport, and his own car, which was still parked in the airport's daily parking lot. Pulling behind his vehicle he shifted her car into park and turned off the engine.

Exiting the driver's side he sauntered around to the passenger side door and opened it. Cilla eased herself up and out, standing tall as she met his intense gaze.

"Thank you," he said, his deep voice dropping to a loud whisper.

Cilla smiled. "I'm the one who needs to be thanking you. I had a really great time tonight."

He reached for her hand, entwining his fingers between hers. Her palm was soft and warm, the touch electric. He led her around the car to the driver's side.

He was still holding tightly to her. "Call me when you get home, please, so I know you got there safely."

"I will. Are you buying coffee in the morning?" she asked.

He grinned. "Are you meeting me?"

She nodded her head yes as she pressed her other hand to his chest, her finger tips burning hot through his dress shirt. She tilted her face upward, her eyes dancing in sync with his. Her mouth was opened slightly, anticipation blowing in the warm air that billowed past her moistened lips. She whispered. "Sweet dreams, Malcolm Cobb."

Malcolm smiled as he leaned forward, pressing his cheek against hers. His words were heated as they blew past her ear. "I'll be dreaming about you," he whispered.

He gave her hand one last squeeze as he kissed her cheek, his lips lingering briefly. Opening the car door he helped her inside. She gave him one last smile as she started the engine. With a slight wave of her hand she closed the door, shifted the car into gear and pulled off, Malcom staring after her until she disappeared out of sight.

Malcolm laughed heartily as he danced a two-step, his exuberance wafting through the air. He stole a quick glance to his wristwatch as he moved to his own vehicle. He was ready to get home to bed. Excited that morning coffee and seeing Cilla again was mere hours away.

Chapter Four

It was lunchtime and the summer sun was shining full and bright in the bluest of skies. The city sidewalk was bustling with people walking from point A to point B, everyone enjoying the warm temperatures as they took their lunch hour. Directly in front of the nightclub a line of traffic was at a standstill, waiting for the traffic light at the corner to shift from red to green.

Malcolm used his key to enter the brick building. Inside he stole a quick glance around the space, confirming that there was only one other person inside. Romeo stood behind the bar checking the inventory as he prepared them for the evening's festivities. His friend waved in his direction.

"Malcolm!"

"Hey, Rome!"

"How's it hangin'?"

"Straight as an arrow!"

"I hate to hear that. I had my fingers crossed that you might get you some last night. Get you out of that bad mood you've been in!"

Malcolm laughed. "You got jokes!"

Romeo held up both hands, the gesture as if he were surrendering. "What can I say?"

The two men laughed easily together.

Romeo gestured to a stack of manila folders that sat on the edge of the countertop. "That's the paperwork," he said, Malcolm understanding the reference.

Malcolm reached for the files and moved to one of the tables. He sat down as he flipped through the documents, pausing once and then a second time as he stopped to read the details. "What did the lawyer say?" he questioned, dropping the files back to the wood surface.

Romeo moved to where he sat and took the seat across from him. "He said it's a good deal. Both sides gave up some things and gained some things but bottom line, once we sign and write them a check, this building and the two next door will officially be ours. We'll collect rent instead of paying it and we get to fix all of the headaches by ourselves."

Malcolm nodded. "And you feel good about the deal?"

"Don't you?"

"I'm good if you're good."

"Then congratulations. Tomorrow, Marshall and Cobb Investments becomes a reality and we will officially own a piece of downtown real estate."

"We'll own three pieces of downtown real estate."

Romeo nodded. "Are you still thinking about expanding the architectural firm and opening up an office here?"

"I think so. If the flower shop doesn't renew their

lease and they leave I think I will be our first official *new* tenant. It just makes sense right now."

"Hey, I hear you and you know I'll support you however I can."

"How are Taryn and the baby doing?" Malcolm asked, changing the subject.

Romeo grinned. "Little man is *walking!* And I mean, high-stepping, kicking-butt walking!"

"Now the trouble starts! JB will be getting into everything now."

"Who are you telling? Taryn and I don't do anything but run behind him trying to keep up."

Malcolm's smile was wide. "God, I miss those days! They grow up too fast. Before you know it he'll be whining about getting his driver's license, talking back and working your last nerve! At least you won't have to worry about him wearing clothes that are too tight and too short like I have to with my girls!"

Romeo laughed. "That sounds like you're having some issues!"

Malcolm laughed with him. "Teenage daughters. I'm beginning to fully understand the rationale behind putting them in a chastity belt and locking them away."

"My goddaughters have always been perfect angels."

"Well, perfect and angelic have been long gone. They're trying me. Especially Cleo. It's become a daily battle with that one."

"Well, I'm sure your mother's keeping them in line."

"Mama's getting old. She can't beat them like she used to," Malcolm said teasingly.

Romeo chuckled. "Well, if you ever need a hand you can always borrow Taryn. My wife does not play!"

Malcolm shook his head. "Don't be surprised if I take you up on that offer."

Romeo nodded. "So, really, how was your date last night? I'm thinking she must be pretty special for you to cut your trip short just to take a woman to dinner."

"Her name's Cilla. Priscilla Jameson. And she is special. We had a great time last night! And we spent some time together this morning having coffee."

For a brief moment Malcolm drifted off into thought. He and Cilla had closed down the restaurant last night, exiting out the back with the chef and the owner. They had talked for hours. Malcolm had shared stories about his past, his daughters, and his businesses. Cilla had talked about her family, her job, her past relationships, and her hobbies. She knew everything about his relationship with his ex-wife and his stint in prison. He knew that her greatest fear was being a disappointment to her parents and that she one day hoped to own her own quilt business. She'd been excited to talk about her dreams for her future and he had shared his. The time had been illuminating for them both, discovering that they could be so open and feel so comfortable with each other. The memory of their time together brought a smile to Malcolm's face. His head bobbed up and down as he shook away the chill that had ripped up his spine.

Romeo had been watching him intently. He suddenly broke out in a deep guffaw and he howled for a good few minutes until tears ran from his eyes. He finally caught his breath as he swiped the back of his hand across his face. "Well, I'll be damned! That woman has you seriously twisted! Maybe we should get you to a doctor to get you checked."

Malcolm's head waved from side to side, his grin like a canyon across his face. "You don't know what you're talking about."

Romeo was still chuckling. "You've got it bad! I can see it all over you. That woman has you wide open!"

Malcolm rolled his eyes as the two men continued to banter and joke back and forth. As he pondered his best friend's comment, he couldn't help but think Romeo was right.

"So, let me get this right," Bianca said, amusement in her tone. "Now, you're dating an alcoholic convict?"

"He's a *recovered* alcoholic and a *former* convict," Cilla said, emphasizing the past tense.

"And you really believe there's a difference?"

"I believe he's a man who has changed his life around. He's a successful businessman running two high-profile companies, as well as starting a third. He's a pillar of the community, active in his church, is highly regarded by his friends, and anyone you talk to only has good things to say about him."

"Did you talk to his ex-wife?"

"I don't need to talk to his ex-wife."

"I'm just saying. She might not have good things to say about him and you may well want to hear what those things are. You don't know if he's told you about all his demons. There might be some dirt that you need to know about."

"I trust that Malcolm has told me everything I need to know."

Bianca shook her head. "And the brother has kids! Don't you know kids are the kiss of death for a new relationship? Especially girls. I made a point of not dating any man who had daughters that were walking and talking."

"He says his girls are very good."

"All men say their girls are good and that's because when they're with their daddies they're always on their best behavior trying to weasel cash out of his wallet. Ask me how I know. I was always good with my daddy. And if he and my mother hadn't been married since forever things would have been very different for any tramp he tried to date."

"You would have been difficult for no reason, Bianca. Besides, I am *not* a tramp."

"Trust me, you are to his daughters."

"I am not! Besides, they don't even know me yet."

Bianca chuckled. "I can't wait for us to revisit this conversation in six months!" she exclaimed. "Then tell me what wonderful girls they are."

Cilla rolled her eyes. "Are you ready yet?"

Bianca checked her makeup one last time, spinning in a circle in front of her full-length mirror. "I've been ready. Let's go check out your new badass boyfriend! See if he gets my seal of approval or not."

"If you embarrass me in front of Malcolm I will hurt you," Cilla said as she cut an eye toward her best friend.

Bianca laughed warmly. "Would I do something like that?"

A half hour later the two women entered The Playground. There was a nice crowd gathered and it was still early in the evening. As Cilla stepped into the club her eyes skated back and forth until they adjusted to the dim lights. She came to an abrupt stop when she spied Malcolm standing behind the bar.

As he spun bottles from one hand to the other he looked very much like a star mixologist. He was relaxed and comfortable, performing his own personal dance as he entertained his clients. Seeing him brought a full grin to Cilla's face.

Bianca gave her a not-so-gentle nudge, almost pushing her over as she shoved her in the shoulder. "Can you be more obvious," her friend said, giggling loudly. "You really aren't doing a good job of playing hard to get."

"Who says I want to play hard to get?" Cilla quipped.

Both women laughed heartily. They made their way to an empty table in a corner, Cilla continuing to steal glances at the man as she hoped to catch his eye. They'd only been sitting a few minutes when the waitress made her way over to take their drink orders.

"Hey, y'all. My name's Odetta," she chimed, one hand resting on her wide hip. "What can I do you for tonight?" She chewed a large wad of chewing gum, snapping it loudly between her lips.

"I'll have a white Russian," Bianca said. "And my friend here wants a Sex on the Beach from that guy," she said, pointing directly at Malcolm.

As the other two women both turned their heads

at the same time, staring in Malcolm's direction, he suddenly looked up from the drink he was pouring, meeting their stares. His wide grin pulled full as recognition registered on his dark face. He waved a slight hand toward them, suddenly looking like a ten-year-old with his first crush. Cilla's eyes widened as her own smile burst brightly.

Odetta looked from Malcolm to Cilla and back again, once and then a second time. "What am I missing?" Odetta questioned, her gaze skating back and forth between them. "Why is my boss looking at you like you're the last biscuit on the platter and he's got the only gravy in the room?"

Bianca laughed. "I'm Bianca and this is Cilla, your boss's new boo."

Cilla's mouth dropped open in surprise. "Bianca! I told you about embarrassing me tonight," she exclaimed, her eyes wide. She turned her gaze on Odetta. "I'm not his *boo.* Malcolm and I are just friends."

"Well, it looks like you're his something," Odetta said. "How long have you two known each other?" she questioned, her eyes narrowing in query.

Cilla felt her face flush red with color. "Not long. Not long at all. We're just friends!"

"Humph," Odetta grunted, flashing Malcolm another look. "Is that right?"

Across the way Malcolm was rushing to fill his drink orders. Odetta still standing at Cilla's table was beginning to make him nervous. The woman suddenly turned, moving in his direction. Before she reached the bar she stopped to whisper something to Romeo who was standing room center in conversation with another waitress and the club's featured performer. The trio turned to stare where Odetta had gestured, then back at Malcolm who suddenly looked nauseous. Cilla looked uneasy as well, her anxiety rising at the sudden attention. Bianca found it all too funny as she laughed hysterically.

Back at the bar Malcolm was shaking his head at Odetta. "Really, Odetta?"

"What?"

"You know what."

"Obviously I don't know anything. Like I didn't know you had a new girlfriend. So I don't know anything at all." She gave him the stink eye, her head lowered just so, her gaze nothing but thin slits and her mouth puckered in a full pout.

"We're just . . . we . . ." he stammered, then stopped, realizing there was no point in trying to explain himself so he didn't. He gave her a look and Odetta laughed.

"What are they drinking?" he asked instead.

Odetta recited the order verbatim. "But if you ask me," she added, "I think the sex on the beach she wants doesn't come in a glass, if you get my drift."

Malcolm blushed profusely. "I really don't need commentary from the peanut gallery," he said as he poured booze into two glasses.

He gestured toward Frank, the new bartender, to take the bar. "I'll deliver these," he said as he pointed Odetta toward the opposite direction.

"I just bet you will," she said with another deep chuckle.

As her laughter echoed behind him Malcolm

took a deep breath and then another. His smile returned to his face as he moved toward Cilla. He could feel his friends watching him intently, eyes following him across the room. He and Romeo shared a quick glance as his best friend gave him a thumbs-up. He suddenly felt nervous, perspiration breaking out across his brow.

"Hi," he said, his eyes meeting the stare Bianca was giving him.

He didn't wait for the woman to respond, his gaze shifting toward Cilla who was grinning at him. "Hey, you," he said, his voice dropping to a loud whisper.

Cilla nodded her head in greeting as she suddenly burst out laughing. Malcolm couldn't stop himself from laughing with her. The tension lifted instantly, feeling like a burst balloon deflating. He pressed a warm palm to her bare shoulder as he eased his body into the seat beside her and sat down. His touch was electric and it felt like a bolt of current was shooting through every one of her nerve endings. Cilla pressed her knees tight together to stall the quiver that suddenly pierced her. She shuddered ever so slightly as Malcolm gently kneaded the flesh beneath his hand.

"I'm glad you could make it," Malcolm said, his eyes still locked with hers.

Cilla's head bobbed a second time. "I told you I planned to check out your establishment."

He chuckled. "And I thought you were just here to see me."

Cilla tossed a quick glance over her shoulder. "Had I known I was going to cause all this commotion I might not have come all."

Malcolm leaned back in his seat. He looked toward the bar and around the room. Romeo, Odetta, Sharon, and Leslie were huddled together in front of the bar, each of them stealing glances in their direction. He blew a deep sigh, his brow furrowed. Before he could comment Bianca cleared her throat, pretending to cough to draw their attention.

Cilla shook her head as she gestured in the woman's direction. "Malcolm, this is my friend Bianca. Bianca, this is my friend Malcolm."

"It's very nice to meet you," Bianca said, extending her hand toward him. Her smile was bright and just shy of comedic.

He shook the appendage, noting her firm grip and soft hand. "It's very nice to meet you, too."

"I've heard a lot about you."

"Please, don't hold it against me. You can't believe everything you might have been told."

Bianca smiled. "I'll keep that in mind. So, my friend here was telling me that you . . ."

Cilla suddenly held up her hand to stall her friend's comment. "We are not going to do this. You are not going to interrogate Malcolm with your twenty questions."

Malcolm chuckled warmly.

"I was just trying to get to know your boyfriend," Bianca quipped.

Cilla shook her head. "You don't need to know him." She stood up abruptly and stretched her hand out to Malcolm. "I would really like to dance," she said, her eyes wide.

With a full smile Malcolm nodded and moved

onto his feet. Amusement flickered across his face as he tossed Bianca a look and shrugged his broad shoulders. He entwined his fingers between Cilla's and allowed her to guide him to the hardwood floors that surrounded the stage. Bianca made a face at them both as she gestured for their waitress and another drink.

Norah Jones was singing "Come Away with Me." The song was soft and seductive, the musical intonation absolutely irresistible. Only a handful of couples were on the floor, bodies pulled so tightly that in the dimly lit room it was almost difficult to see where one began and the other ended. Around the room others shuffled and shimmied in their seats.

They would have been better able to take the attention off them in a crowd than standing alone in the center of the floor with only three other couples, but neither seemed to notice. Cilla spun herself against Malcolm's body, looping her thin arms around his neck as she tucked her forehead beneath his chin. As she did he wrapped his arms around her torso and pulled her even closer. One large hand pressed hot against the curve of her lower back, his fingers grazing the round of her backside. The other hand snaked around her body to that spot between her shoulder blades. Everything about their connection was heated as they began to glide against each other.

Across the way Odetta dropped down into the seat Cilla had vacated. She and Bianca exchanged a look with each other. Odetta smiled.

"My boy Malcolm's a good guy. A *really* good guy. She *bet'* not break his heart."

Bianca nodded. "Cilla's my sister and she's probably *too* good for him. So if he hurts her, I will hurt him."

Odetta winked an eye at the woman. "Glad we could come to an understanding."

Bianca laughed. Her stare drifted back to the dance floor. "Looks like them two might work out all right."

"We might have to intervene every now and again but I think so. I think they look good together."

"Me, too," Bianca said in agreement. "Almost too good they're so cute."

Odetta chuckled. "Boss man said your drinks are on the house. Can I get you another?"

Bianca's eyes widened. "I usually stick to a two-drink maximum but since the boss is insisting, I don't want to be rude. I think one more wouldn't hurt. I don't think it'll hurt at all."

Odetta laughed again. "And by the way, the brother in the pinstriped suit at the bar has been eyeing you all night but between us, I hear he's lacking in the *meat* department, if you get my drift."

Bianca turned to give the man a stare. He lifted his head, nodding in her direction. "That's a damn shame," Bianca said, blowing a heavy gust of air past her lips. "'Cause he's not bad on the eyes. Not bad at all!"

Odetta nodded in agreement. "Yeah, girl! But you and I both know a few extra inches on the end of a shovel when you're digging for gold sure does help!"

Bianca laughed heartily. "Well, I'm really not looking. I'm off the market myself," she said, waving her ring finger in the air. "Got me a man already."

Odetta laughed. "Girl, just because you on a diet, don't mean you can't look at the menu!"

Bianca grinned. "I like that! I like that a lot."

Odetta winked her eye. "And a little taste every now and then won't hurt you either!"

When Michael Bublé began his rendition of Stevie Wonder's 1972 hit "You and I," Malcolm was still holding on to Cilla, unwilling to let her go. She felt good in his arms, like that was where she belonged. Every square inch of her body fit nicely against his. He had to admit that he liked having her there.

The music seemed to billow around them, pulling them to a place that was going to be difficult to come back from. Malcolm knew the playlist had undergone a change or two, someone spinning one love song after another but he didn't mind, knowing that eventually it would have to end way too soon. He blew a heavy sigh.

Cilla lifted her chin to stare up at him. Her smile was sugary sweet and sheer happiness gleamed from her dark eyes.

His mouth lifted, an even sweeter bend to his lips as he smiled back. "I apologize for my friends," he said softly.

She shook her head. "No apology necessary. They care about you. That's what family does."

He nodded. "They are my family. We look out for each other. I know that Romeo and the girls have my back if I ever need them."

"Trust me, Bianca's not much better! I'm going to hate it for you when she gets the opportunity to corner you alone!"

"Now I'm scared," Malcolm said, a deep laugh blowing past his full lips.

"I'm sure we're all going to get along just fine," Cilla said. She brushed the tips of her fingers against the back of his neck, teasing his hairline.

"I hope so. I'd hate for them not to like you. That would make it hard for me to be your boyfriend."

Cilla laughed, tossing her head back against her neck. "Who says you're my boyfriend?"

"You did."

"I did not!"

"Yes, you did. Your girl said she was trying to get to know your boyfriend and you said she didn't need to. You said it just before you pulled me onto the dance floor to seduce me."

"So now I'm seducing you, too?"

"Hell, yeah! Don't you know that at this very moment you could take full advantage of me and I'd be putty in your hands?"

Cilla giggled. "I think a lack of oxygen is beginning to go to your head."

He grinned. "Might be but that's what happens when you take a man's breath away!" He pressed a kiss to her forehead and hugged her warmly.

Closing her eyes Cilla savored the moment, enjoying the embrace. Leaning on him was easy and comfortable and she knew that it would take very little for her to get used to such a thing. She felt him press his cheek to hers, the warmth of his breath blowing gently against her earlobe and teasing her neck. She opened her eyes and met the look he was giving her. His stare was intoxicating, drawing her headfirst into the wealth of it.

"So, do you want to be my boyfriend?" she whispered, a wave of nervousness passing over her expression.

Malcolm smiled. "Woman, I thought you would never ask," he whispered back.

His large fingers cupped her chin, tilting her face to his. Cilla met his lips as he captured her mouth beneath his own. His kiss was eager and searching until his lips settled contentedly against hers. Both fell into the moment, the connection like nothing either had ever experienced before. Malcolm tightened the hold he had on her, his mouth like silk gliding against hers.

Cilla struggled to stay focused, to remember where she was and what she was doing. But her mind was mush, not one coherent thought to be found. She had no words for their first kiss. Nor could she explain the wealth of emotion that suddenly consumed her. She had wholeheartedly enjoyed their banter, being as quick with the quips and jokes as he had been. The laughter that always followed never felt forced or contrived, it being as natural as the two of them breathing.

But now, in Malcolm's arms, sharing such an intimate moment with a roomful of people watching, she was speechless, unable to articulate what she was feeling about his touch and the nearness of him. Because in that moment Malcolm Cobb felt too good to be true. Everything about the man seemed unreal, as if he were an apparition who might disappear if she ever woke from the dream she imagined she had fallen into. Her heart was suddenly racing and she felt her body trembling uncontrollably. Right then and there Cilla knew she never wanted to kiss anyone else again.

The moment was interrupted when Odessa abruptly bumped against Malcolm's back. "Excuse me," she said as the two parted, both eyeing each other anxiously. Malcolm took a deep breath and held it as Cilla panted softly.

"Y'all might want to get a room for all that," Odessa exclaimed as she brushed past them toward a back table.

Malcolm shook his head as Cilla's face flushed with color, her cheeks deepening to a deep red. "What were you saying about family?" he jibed.

Cilla grinned. She grabbed both his hands and reached up to press her lips to his one last time. "Why don't you introduce me to the rest of your friends," she said.

Chapter Five

"You're never home anymore!" Cleo exclaimed, her expression showing her displeasure with her father.

"I'm home all the time," Malcolm responded. "Just because I have a date tonight doesn't mean I'm never home."

"Who is she?" Claudia questioned.

Malcolm blew a low sigh. The twins sat in the center of his king-size bed, both eyeing him curiously. His personal life had suddenly become a point of discussion when he'd announced he had a date and wouldn't be able to join them at the community pool for an afternoon swim. The news had not gone over well and then the questions had come.

"I told you already. She's someone I met recently, that I'm getting to know. She invited me to join her at an art event this afternoon that one of her friends is hosting and I told her I would go."

"Is this the same woman you had dinner with two

nights ago and coffee with the other day?" Claudia asked.

He nodded, annoyance suddenly pulling at his expression. "She is. Is there something wrong with that?" He looked from one to the other.

"You two have been spending a lot of time together to only be friends," Cleo snapped.

Malcolm hesitated as he met the stare his daughter was giving him. He and Cilla had been spending a lot of time together. As much as both could manage without neglecting their many responsibilities. They'd been meeting for coffee on the regular, sneaking away for lunch a time or two, and had even managed a few late-night excursions at the club. Spending as much time with Cilla as he could had become one of his priorities behind his family and his businesses.

He took a deep breath. "First, you better watch your tone, young lady. Now, I said we were only friends and I meant that. How much time we spend together won't change that one way or the other."

"Can we meet her?" Claudia asked. She pulled her legs beneath her, sitting Indian-style as she eyed him curiously.

He blew another low sigh. Malcolm had never before introduced his daughters to anyone he'd ever dated. Knowing those relationships would never go but so far, he didn't think it right for him to shuffle women into and out of their lives. Lately though, with him and Cilla growing closer, he'd been giving some serious thought to her being the first to meet his girls. He looked from one to the other.

"You always insist on meeting all of our friends,"

Cleo retorted. "So I don't see why we can't meet yours."

He took another deep breath. "I'll make the decision when I think it's appropriate for you two to meet my friends, not you."

"You suck!" Cleo exclaimed as she jumped up abruptly, her eyes rolling toward the ceiling.

"Excuse me?" Malcolm snapped. "Watch your mouth, young lady!"

"You don't even follow your own rules," his daughter snapped back. "Why should we follow them?"

"You'll follow them because I said so," he said, his voice rising slightly. "I'm the parent and you're the child and you don't have to like my rules but as long as you're under my roof you're going to follow them. Now this conversation is done and finished. If you're going to the pool you need to go get ready before your grandmother changes her mind."

"You're such an asshole," Cleo muttered under her breath as she stomped out and down the hall, the door to her own bedroom slamming harshly.

For a brief moment Malcolm stood stunned, shocked by his daughter's mouth. He met Claudia's stare, the young woman watching him intently. Her eyes were wide, something like fear across her face as she paused, waiting to see if her father was going to follow behind her twin to discipline her for the profanity. When another few minutes passed without him moving from where he stood she lifted her slight frame from the mattress and moved to her father's side, throwing her arms around his waist.

"We just miss you, Daddy," she said as she hugged him. "Cleo didn't mean that."

Malcolm took a deep breath as he hugged her back. He leaned to kiss the top of her head. "Why don't you and your sister plan a daddy-daughter day for us this coming Sunday. Whatever you want to do. Within reason, of course. And I promise you'll both have me all to yourselves."

"The whole day?"

"From sunup to sundown."

"You promise?"

Malcolm nodded. "Cross my heart and swear."

Claudia smiled brightly. "I'll go tell Cleo. That will make her happy."

He pressed a hand to her cheek. "Thank you."

"Have fun on your date," Claudia said as she skipped toward the door, turning to give him one last wave of her hand.

As she disappeared from view, her footsteps echoing toward her own room, he blew out the breath he'd been holding, something telling him that Cleo's teenage angst was just the beginning to the tribulations his beloved daughters were going to put him through.

Cleo stood staring out her bedroom window as Malcolm left the house. When he pulled his SUV out of the driveway and into the cul de sac, Claudia entered her sister's room through their shared Jack and Jill bathroom. She moved to Cleo's side and stood with her as they watched their father until he was out of sight.

"You really need to stop being so mean toward

Daddy," Claudia said, cutting an eye in her twin's direction. "You just need to tell him what happened so he can fix it," she said.

"I'm not telling him," Cleo replied. "I can't."

"Then I will."

"No, you won't! You promised," Cleo said sharply, her head snapping as she turned to look at her sister. Saline suddenly burned hot behind her eyelids. "You swore, Claudia! Please, you can't tell anyone," she said as she struggled not to let the tears spill past her lashes.

Claudia shook her head. She wrapped her arms around her sister's neck and hugged her tightly. "But Daddy can make it right and you know he can. Then you two won't be fighting all the time, Cleo!"

Cleo shook her head. "He'll hate me if he ever finds out. Please, Claudia, you promised you wouldn't tell," she begged. "You promised me!"

Claudia hugged her sister tighter. "Okay," she finally whispered, "but only if you promise not to be so angry all the time. You're no fun anymore."

Cleo nodded her head. "I promise. I won't talk back or make Grandma or Daddy mad or anything. I swear, just please, please, please, don't tell," she pleaded.

"What are you two up to?" Miss Claudette suddenly questioned, throwing open the bedroom door. She looked from one girl to the other, not missing the tears that misted Cleo's large, round eyes. The matriarch moved into the room, her arms crossed in front of her robust chest. "Cleo, what's wrong? Why are you crying?"

Cleo shook her head, swiping at her eyes with the back of her hand. "Daddy yelled at me," she said.

She cut her eyes at her sister, the look she gave Claudia begging her to confirm the little white lie.

"She said some bad words," Claudia confirmed, her head bobbing against her thin shoulders.

Miss Claudette took a deep breath. She looked from one girl to the other, sensing that she was only being told half the truth. "Your daddy wouldn't have to yell if you would just do what you're told when he tells you without a whole lot of lip. It's not hard."

"Yes, ma'am," Cleo said.

Miss Claudette was still staring, her gaze sweeping over one and then the other and back again. She finally turned, heading back out the door. "If you still want to go to the pool then you better get ready. Maybe we'll go to Olive Garden for dinner afterward."

Both girls answered in unison. "Yes, ma'am!"

Claudia headed back to her own space, moving back through the shared bathroom.

Cleo called after her. "Thank you, sissy."

Claudia nodded, then disappeared through the door.

With no one eyeing her Cleo finally cried, her tears shadowing a wealth of hurt that she was holding too close to her heart. She would have given anything to go back to that time before the bad thing had happened and she suddenly had secrets from her father. When she could have told him anything, nothing and no one able to keep him from loving her. Now she didn't trust anything and was scared to death that if he ever discovered what she'd done, her daddy wouldn't love her anymore.

Cleo sobbed, her mournful weeping echoing

through the door. Hearing her sister cry, Claudia struggled not to let her own tears fall. Despite her promises, Claudia couldn't help but think her sister's secret wasn't going to be a good thing for any of them.

Cilla was laughing warmly. "They're teenagers!" she exclaimed. "Don't you remember what it was like when you were a teenager?"

"I never called my mother or my father an asshole," Malcolm said. "I liked having teeth and I wanted to live."

She and Malcolm were walking the exhibits at Gallery C, the art gallery housed in the historic Russ-Edwards House at the corner of Blount and Peace Streets. They stood in front of a lithograph by Romare Bearden, eyeing the image intently as they talked.

Cilla shook her head as she continued the conversation. "I'm sure you called them something at some time or another. You might not have done it to their face but you did it. It's part of growing up, thinking your parents don't know anything and hating the rules they set down for you. At that age you know everything, remember?"

"I'm sure there was a lot I didn't like but I wasn't crazy enough to disrespect either of them. My almost fourteen-year-old daughter told me I sucked and then she called me an asshole. It took everything I had not to seriously adjust her attitude."

He took a deep breath, still haunted by the exchange between him and Cleo. The girls had always been a challenge, but only because they were both so bright. Keeping them intellectually stimulated continued to keep him on his toes. Finding the school they currently attended had been a help, allowing them to progress with their education without compromising the innocence of their childhood.

Technically they were high school freshman but nothing and no one pushed them to be anything other than the sweet kids they were. He knew peer pressure would eventually become a problem but to the best of his knowledge, it wasn't an issue yet. But Malcolm knew that something wasn't right with his little girl and hadn't been for weeks. For the life of him though he didn't have a clue what was bothering her. He just knew enough to know that it wasn't typical teenage anguish.

"So what kind of things bothered you at thirteen?" he asked.

"Boys."

Malcolm's eyes spun toward the ceiling. He shook his head.

"I'm serious. Boys. It's just that age. They've got puberty going on, hormones are raging, cliques are forming, and being a girl is suddenly pure hell."

"It's not that bad."

"You were a boy. You wouldn't know."

"Boys have issues too."

"Y'all like to think you do," Cilla said teasingly. She gave him a look as she laughed.

Malcolm laughed with her. "Well, I need to figure out what's going on with her before I have to hurt her. She's getting out of control and I plan to nip that attitude in the butt before it gets any more out of hand."

"Don't you mean *the bud?*"

"Nope! I meant her *butt* because I will tear that ass up if she doesn't get herself straight. And I mean it."

"I can already see we're going to have a problem raising our sons together. I don't believe in beating children so there will be no spanking our boys."

Malcolm eyed her, amusement dancing in his eyes as he connected with the look she was giving him. "So, we're having sons together?"

"Did I say that?"

"You said that."

"I was talking hypothetically. *If* we were ever to have children together," Cilla said, her eyebrows lifting in jest.

Malcolm moved in front of her, nudging her back until she hit the wall, her body pressed tight against the cream-colored structure. They were surrounded by a collection of paintings by Haitian artists, the artwork color-filled and whimsical. Malcolm tossed an anxious glance over one shoulder and then the other. He stepped in closer to her as he leaned one hand against the wall and snaked the other hand across her abdomen and around her waist.

Leaning forward Malcolm coveted her mouth, holding her hostage to the desire that had risen with a vengeance between them. His kiss was possessive and urgent and Cilla could feel herself beginning to melt beneath his touch. When he finally broke the connection, both coming up for air, she pressed both of her palms against his chest to steady herself, her knees quivering like jelly.

"You keep doing that, Mr. Cobb, and our making

a baby might be more than hypothetical!" she gasped, fighting to catch her breath.

Malcolm chuckled softly. "Well, I'm sure we'd both enjoy the practice to make that baby," he said as he eyed her intently.

His stare was intoxicating. It took her breath away and Cilla suddenly realized that she'd been holding the oxygen in her lungs. She exhaled and then took another deep breath. She suddenly broke out into a sweat, perspiration beading across her brow as she imagined what that practice might entail. She shook her head, fighting back the emotion that was suddenly overwhelming her. She took a step to the side, easing herself from his grasp.

"I'm sure we would," she muttered as she spun herself in the other direction.

Behind her, Malcolm laughed, the wealth of it coming from deep in his midsection. Cilla tossed him a look over her shoulder, a faint smile pulling at her mouth. "You're not funny, Malcolm."

"I wasn't trying to be," he said as he moved behind her. "In fact, I was very serious." He grabbed her hand, entwining her fingers between his. They continued browsing through the collection of artwork, not saying another word and it was only when they were back in his car, their seatbelts tightened around their torsos, that Malcolm resumed the conversation.

"For the record," he said, as he twisted in his seat and turned to stare at her. "If we should ever have a son and he gets out of hand, I'll have no problem enforcing the appropriate punishment, even if it means taking a switch to his behind. We will raise a strong, decent man so I am not going to stand idly by while you over-pamper any boy child of mine like he's a baby."

"I beg your pardon!"

"I mean it. I've seen too many women babying grown-ass men who needed a size fourteen up their backsides and not a soft hand talking about 'my baby this' and 'my baby that.' That won't happen to any son of mine. Trust that."

Cilla laughed. "Have you ever given any consideration to having more children?" she asked.

Malcolm shook his head. "To be honest, I never thought I'd meet a woman I would want to have a child with." He paused and his gaze drifted for a brief second. "That is, not until you," he concluded, his eyes returning to her face.

Cilla smiled as they continued to stare at each other. "I always imagined that I would have at least two kids," she said. "Maybe even three."

Malcolm nodded. "Something for us both to consider, but understand, I don't do children out of wedlock. My mother is a card-carrying Baptist raised in the deep Deep South and she don't play, so if you want to have kids with me, Cilla Jameson, you'll have to marry me."

She laughed again. "So is that your way of asking me to marry you, Malcolm Cobb?"

He grinned. "That was full disclosure. You said you wanted to have my baby and I'm just making sure you know what that's going to entail."

Cilla shook her head. "How'd we get on this subject anyway?"

"You started it."

"Well, let's change it," she quipped.

Malcolm chuckled softly. "Whatever you want, beautiful, but I have to ask you one question first."

"Yes?"

"How do you feel about meeting my daughters? Because I really want you to get to know my girls."

Cilla couldn't stop grinning. Malcolm had left over an hour ago and thoughts of him still had her smiling like a Cheshire cat. After the exhibit they'd gone for hot dogs at Snoopy's, Cilla finally fulfilling her promise to treat him to the meal. They'd laughed, talked, teased, flirted, and had laughed some more. Before either realized it the time had flown by and Malcolm had needed to head to work. He had returned her to her home and had walked her to her front door, giving her a kiss that left her wanting so much more.

The kiss had been heated, his hands gliding the length of her body, as if on a mission of their own accord. His touch had been teasing, sending currents of electricity through every nerve ending. He'd grabbed her ass, kneading the soft tissue as he'd pulled her against the hardened member that had risen with a vengeance in his pants. His touch had taken her breath away and it would have taken very little for Cilla to open herself to him, excited to explore the sensual side of their relationship. Cilla had wanted him like she had never wanted any man before and she'd said so.

"Stay," she'd whispered, inviting him inside.

Malcolm had captured her mouth a second time,

his tongue searing her own. She'd gasped loudly as he'd trailed his fingers across the curve of one breast and then the other, her nipples hardening as they protruded against the fabric of her blouse.

When he'd pulled away he'd blown a soft sigh, dropping his forehead to hers. His fingers continued to play with the buttons on her top, teasing the lace that edged her bra.

"I can't," he'd finally whispered, sucking in the cool air that had finally drifted between them. "And God knows I want to, baby, but I have to go to work. You know that if I come inside that's not where I'm going to be headed."

Cilla had giggled softly, knowing that he was right. If he had come inside, Malcolm leaving would have been next to impossible. So he left, with the promise that he would call as soon as he was able.

She blew a soft, easy sigh, her smile filling her face one more time. She shook her head as she moved from the living room into the kitchen to fill a glass with ice and water, recalling everything they'd talked about during the time they'd spent together.

There had been an in-depth conversation about his children and his expectations regarding them and any woman he brought into their lives. Malcolm had admitted to having some anxieties and he'd been honest and open about his concerns. Cilla had been as forthcoming about her own apprehensions. She'd always known she wanted children but never before had she considered a ready-made family. In fact, she had always sworn off men with children. Until Malcolm. And now he was wanting her to meet his daughters, hopeful that they would actually like one another. The weight of that was heavy and Cilla didn't take what it would mean lightly.

Their conversation had run the gamut from thought-provoking to comical, one subject leading to another and then another. The two had discussed whatever had moved them at the moment and Cilla loved that she could talk to him so easily. Getting to know Malcolm was proving to be one pleasant surprise after another. She'd never known a man so transparent, his honesty and openness a refreshing change of pace from what she had known in the past. He was also a sweet romantic with a generous spirit. Her mother would have described him as a true Southern gentleman. Malcolm Cobb was proving himself to be one of the good guys and Cilla found that extremely attractive.

As she moved back into the living room and nestled herself comfortably against her upholstered recliner, she replayed their entire afternoon over again in her head. As the memories flooded back she shook her head. She thought back to how he'd touched her, his fingers hot against her skin and how delightfully sweet his kisses had been.

It was becoming increasingly difficult to temper her desire for him and the nearness of him had begun to feel like lighter fluid tossed on an already burning flame. Cilla had always maintained a ninety-day rule with men she dated, needing at least eighty-nine of them to figure out whether or not they were deserving of her sugar and sweets. But Malcolm already had her ready to toss aside her convictions and her panties, convinced that everything about the man warranted her giving up the goodies. His upstanding demeanor with his scorching touch made her hot as hell.

She took a sip of her water. Placing the glass back down on the table she reached for the paperback book she had rested there. It was a political-themed novel by Cheris Hodges, one of her favorite romance authors. As she flipped to where she'd marked the last page she'd read, she exhaled.

Being honest with herself Cilla knew she would have preferred to be strumming her fingertips across Malcolm's broad chest and back and not through the pages of a book. Since that first cup of coffee she'd been fantasizing about the man, imagining what it would be like to be in his arms as he made love to her. Envisioning each touch, the rich scent of his cologne teasing her nostrils, every hardened muscle connecting with her soft curves. And with each fantasy and every moment in his presence, Cilla wanted him like she had never wanted anything else before.

"Malcolm?" Miss Claudette called his name as he came through the garage door.

The house was still lit and music played softly through the speakers nestled in the walls.

Her voice echoed through the space a second time. "Malcolm, I need to speak with you."

He moved into the room where she sat upright in a wingback chair, her beloved Bible resting in her lap. "Hey, Mama," Malcolm whispered loudly. "I just knew you'd be asleep by now."

The matriarch shook her head. "Too much on my mind, son. How was work tonight?"

"Busy. Romeo took the night off to spend some time with Taryn and we were slammed."

"I ran into her and the baby at Harris Teeter the other day. He is just as precious as he can be and growing too, too fast."

"I miss those days," Malcolm said thoughtfully. "They fly by way too fast. The girls are growing up and I wish I could keep them from it."

His mother nodded. "That's what I want to talk to you about."

Malcolm reached for the ottoman and pulled it alongside his mother's chair. As he took a seat facing her he folded his hands in his lap. He gave her his full attention. "Is something wrong?"

"I'm worried about Cleo. Something's going on with her. She hasn't been herself since the last time they spent a week with their mother."

Malcolm's eyes shifted back and forth as he thought back to his daughter's last visit with her other parent. He'd been so focused on the nightclub, the property purchase, the business, and Cilla that he'd attributed Cleo's bad behavior to her being a teenager testing the boundaries. Despite his instincts screaming that she surely wasn't herself he'd never given any consideration to something having happened to her. His body suddenly tensed as he fathomed the possibilities. He inhaled swiftly.

Sensing his tension his mother pressed a hand to his knee, tapping it gently. "Now, don't you go getting crazy! I don't need you and Shanell at each other's throats before we figure out what's going on. You know how she gets and I don't want the girls to have to deal with her foolishness. Things are good right now and if there's no reason to upset the status quo then we're not going to do so."

Malcolm took another deep breath then swallowed hard. "Do you have any idea what it might be?"

Miss Claudette shook her head as she responded. "Not a clue. I point blank asked Claudia if she knew anything and she said that she didn't but I know she lied. Claudia always gets that twitch in her eye when she's telling a fib. She knows something and she's trying to protect her sister."

Malcolm nodded. "I'll talk to Cleo. She'll tell me if something's wrong."

His mother hesitated for a brief moment. "I hope that she does but I don't want you to be surprised if she shuts you out. It's the age but Cleo also has a lot of her mother's ways. She gets angry quick and she shuts down when she can't handle things."

"I hate that she and I have been bumping heads lately. That's going to make it even harder to get through to her but I can't let her bad behavior slide. If I don't tighten the reins now I know she'll be completely out of control."

"And you're right. You have to stay steady the course and do what you know is right for her. You have to be her father first. She doesn't need you to be her friend."

Contemplating his mother's words he sat in reflection for a few moments, his mind racing as he considered what he needed to do. Minutes later Malcolm and his mother exchanged a look.

"What's on your mind?" Miss Claudette asked. "You look like you have something you want to say."

Malcolm bit down on his bottom lip as he pondered her question for a brief moment. "I want you and the girls to meet my friend Priscilla. She and I talked about it earlier today and I was really comfortable with her and the girls getting to know each other. Now I'm not so sure."

"Why not?"

"If there's something going on with Cleo, I have to focus on that. I'm starting to think the timing's just bad."

His mother rocked slightly back and forth, her head nodding. "She must be very special for you to want to introduce her to the girls."

Malcolm smiled. "I really like her, Mama."

"Just how serious is it?"

He shrugged his broad shoulders but didn't bother to reply.

His mother pressed her fingertips to the side of his face. Her head bobbed slightly. "Well, I look forward to meeting this young woman," Miss Claudette said as she opened her Bible. "I'm going to read for a few minutes before I go to bed. If you're hungry, there's some baked lasagna in the refrigerator."

Nodding, Malcolm stood back up. As he moved out the door his mother called after him.

"Yes, ma'am?"

"If you are serious about this young lady then you have to consider what kind of mother she's going to be toward Claudia and Cleo. My babies need a strong female figure to look up to and they need to see you in a healthy relationship with a woman.

There's never going to be a perfect time for her to meet the girls and if she can't handle either one of them having a problem now then she surely won't be able to handle it later. You need to keep that in mind."

Malcolm stood staring at his mother momentarily. "Yes, ma'am," he said, nodding his head. He turned to make his exit, the conversation still racing through his head.

Chapter Six

Malcolm woke with a quick start. The air in the room was chilled and he realized he'd kicked his blankets to the floor. It was still dark outside, the early morning hour always perfect for his daily run. He rolled against the mattress to steal a quick glance at the alarm clock on the nightstand. Realizing that he had at least another hour before the alarm was scheduled to sound he rolled back, pulling the covers back up over his legs.

After tossing and turning longer than he would have liked he finally sat upright in the bed, rest refusing to come. He'd fallen asleep thinking about his daughters. The girls had consumed his dreams and he'd wakened with thoughts of them on his mind. Morning breath blew past his full lips as he sighed. Although his concerns about what could possibly be affecting Cleo weighed heavily on his spirit, he no longer had any qualms about Cilla meeting his children. He'd taken age-old advice from his mother and had prayed on it, dropping to his knees for answers. In that moment it had felt like everything had come together, his reasons for wanting his daughters and his girlfriend to meet outweighing any concerns about it not working out.

Thoughts of Cilla billowed through his mind. His affection for the woman had grown substantially and he realized that their friendship had quickly become so much more. Although they joked about marriage and children and a future together, Malcolm had come to the realization that Cilla was definitely the woman he could see having all that with. That understanding came with wanting them all to meet and bond.

He felt himself smile, realizing that everything about him and Cilla together felt right with his spirit. When they were together, he felt complete, having never realized just what he'd been missing until she'd come along. He suddenly imagined himself wrapped around her, wishing she were there in his bed beside him. Remembering their shared kisses and her touch made him break out into a sweat, the rise of heat moving him to kick the blankets back to the floor. As he continued to think about Cilla his body responded in kind, an erection lengthening beneath the sheets. He palmed the wealth of flesh, imagining that it was her hands kneading and caressing him so easily. A shiver raced down the length of his spine and his body shuddered at the thought.

He stroked himself easily, wishing it was Cilla who was stroking him. His hardened member twitched eagerly. Perspiration dampened his hand as flesh touched flesh, each pass of his palm shooting a current of electricity through his core. He imaged that it was her fingers gliding up and down against him.

He lifted his hips and parted his legs as he stretched his body out against the pillows. Losing himself in the fantasy, he thought about her mouth and the luscious lips that always tasted sweet. He willed that mouth to him, her damp kisses exploring, teasing, tasting. Energy surged with a vengeance as his pace quickened, his fist tightening, his strokes harder. Every muscle tightened, his whole body beginning to feel like it would combust if he couldn't have her.

His lips parted as his breath quickened, Cilla's name on the tip of his tongue. Malcolm knew that once the opportunity presented itself he would eagerly make love to her. He was almost desperate to make love to her, he thought, imagining his body delving deep inside hers. He pushed himself into his palm, over and over again, as he imagined himself pushing and pulling his whole self in and out of her body. He moaned her name over and over again as if in prayer, every thought of Cilla Jameson consuming him. As he fantasized about her warmth, moistness wrapped around him, her juices flowing as he tasted her, Malcolm felt a spasm shoot through his groin. His body pulsed and surged as he bit down against his bottom lip to keep from crying out. He rode wave after wave of pleasure before snatching his hand from his crotch.

His breathing had become a heavy pant as he gasped for air. His body was still heated, still wanting, still wishing Cilla was there to share in the pleasure he imagined between them. Desperate to shake the rising desire that refused to be abated he threw his legs off the side of the bed, moving onto his feet. He inhaled, taking a deep breath and then another. He moved toward the bathroom. Since meeting Cilla, cold showers had become a very necessary evil and Malcolm found himself excited by the prospect of leaving them behind once and for all.

Malcolm skipped into The Playground, his footsteps light as joy gleamed across his face. Despite the rough start to his morning, Cilla meeting him at the coffee shop had shifted his mood nicely. He liked starting his day with her and he couldn't stop himself from imagining what it might be like to have her wake by his side. They'd enjoyed their morning coffee before he'd kissed her good-bye, the two agreeing to meet up later in the afternoon.

Inside the building, the sound system was on low. He instantly recognized the newest release from Meshell Ndegeocello. The song managed to combine several distinctly disparate styles at once, a bossa nova foundation with a country slide guitar and slinky soul vocals. Something about her intonation and the song's melodious beat felt good, seeming to support the warmth and happiness he found himself feeling.

Romeo was sitting atop a barstool, his requisite calculator, lead pencil, yellow-lined notepad, and financial ledger sheets in hand. They paid an accountant good money to keep their books and records but every month his friend insisted on running the numbers himself as an added system of checks and balances. It gave the man a level of comfort

Malcolm didn't understand but still supported. His smile was wide as he greeted his friend.

"Hey, Rome. You find any discrepancies yet?"

Romeo laughed. "I'm still looking. How are things going with you?"

Malcolm grinned. "I have no complaints."

His buddy nodded, shifting his gaze toward the back of the room. "I hope it lasts," he said, his voice dropping ever so slightly. He gestured with his eyes.

Malcolm looked where his friend stared and felt his body tense. He bristled when he saw his ex-wife staring in his direction, Shanell eyeing him anxiously. He looked back at Romeo and nodded. "How long has she been here?" Malcolm asked, his own voice now a soft whisper.

Romeo shrugged his broad shoulders. "Ten minutes, maybe. Not too long."

Malcolm took a deep breath. He cleared his throat before moving toward the woman. As he came to the table where she sat he gave her a quick nod. "Hey, Shanell. What are you doing here?"

She shrugged, the barest of smiles pulling at her thin lips. Ages ago Shanell Cobb had been the most beautiful woman Malcolm had ever known. He had honestly believed they were going to grow old together, the love they shared so solid that no one and nothing could have broken their bond. As he sat staring he couldn't deny that those days were long gone. Shanell had found something she loved more than she had ever loved him.

Shanell's natural hairstyle was a tangled mess atop her head. She wore no makeup, her complexion sallow and blemished. Her clothes were well worn, and the hint of odor wafting off her body told him she probably hadn't bathed in days. Romeo had made her a cup of coffee and a sandwich that she'd barely touched. She had chewed her fingernails down to the quick and her hands were shaking nervously. The transformation since the last time he'd seen her was drastic, and telling. He didn't want to believe the truth but he couldn't begin to deny what was right there in front of his eyes.

He took a deep breath and held it before blowing it slowly out. Then he spoke. "You're using again, aren't you, Shanell?"

The young woman shrugged her narrow shoulders. "What I do isn't any of your business, Malcolm," she snapped.

He snapped back. "It is when it affects our daughters!"

Shanell rolled her eyes at him "Look, you called me, remember? I got your message and since I was in the neighborhood, I stopped by. But I didn't come here to get no lecture."

Malcolm took another deep breath. He had called her, wanting to have a discussion about their children. Seeing her face-to-face gave him answers to questions he hadn't imagined he'd ever again need to ask. His sigh was loud and heavy.

"Did anything happen with Cleo the last time you took them to Baltimore?" he asked.

"Anything like what?"

"I don't know, Shanell. That's why I'm asking the question." His stare was harsh and unnerving.

Shanell dropped her eyes to the table and the coffee cup between her palms. She shook her head from side to side, her gaze darting back and forth. "Nothing happened. They spent most of their time with my mama. Why? Did they say something happened?"

Malcolm shook his head, finally dropping into the seat across the table from her. "No. The girls aren't saying much at all about that trip. But Cleo's been getting out of hand lately and I'm trying to figure out why."

Shanell blew her own sigh. "Well, I don't know. They were good when they were with me. I didn't have any problems."

"Did you spend time with them at all?"

"I told you that nothing bad happened. I'm their mother and I would know," she said emphatically.

Silence washed between them, both eyeing the other skeptically. Shanell finally broke the quiet. "Since we're talking, I need to reschedule my visitation. I'm not going to be able to come get the girls for a while. I lost my job and I'm trying to find a new one."

"When did this happen?" Malcolm questioned.

She pushed her shoulders toward the ceiling for the umpteenth time. "It's been a while now and since I don't have my apartment no more things are just a little hard for me." Her eyes darted back and forth, refusing to meet his.

"What do you mean you don't have your apartment? The last time the girls were with you they stayed at your apartment! What happened between then and now?"

"I mean I got evicted!" she snapped. "Evicted! I had to get out this week."

Malcolm dragged a heavy hand across the back of his neck, rubbing the tension that had pulled the muscles taut. "Why didn't you say something *before* you got evicted, Shanell? You know I would have helped."

She lifted her eyes back to his and for the first time in a long time, Malcolm saw a brief flicker of something familiar behind the dull gaze. His own misted with tears and he turned his head away, fighting to stop them from falling.

"It's not a big deal," she said with a shake of her head. "I'm going to work it out."

Malcolm leaned back in his seat, his hands folded together in his lap. He watched as she fidgeted and shook, the first signs of her coming down from her drug high. It would only be a matter of hours, maybe even minutes, before she would need another fix.

When he spoke again his voice was soothing, his tone calm and even. "Do you want to go to rehab, Shanell? I will pay for help but you have to want it. I can take you right now. Just tell me you want to go, Shanell!"

Shanell jumped to her feet. Ire pierced her expression. "What I want is for you to get off that sanctimonious horse you like to ride and leave me the hell alone! That's what I want," she said, every muscle in her body shaking.

Across the room Romeo had turned to stare, concern flickering in his eyes. He turned back to his paperwork when Malcolm's gaze waved him down. Turning back to Shanell, Malcolm nodded.

"Fine. But the girls are off-limits until I know you're clean. Don't go to their school. Don't call them. And I mean *no* contact. Do you understand me? And I'm calling their case worker to let her know."

"I wouldn't hurt my babies, Malcolm!"

"Shanell, when you're using you will do whatever you have to do to get that next hit. You might not mean to cause them harm but you can't control yourself and you know it. I will not let you put them at risk."

Tears suddenly rained over her cheeks as she hugged her arms tightly around her torso. She nodded her head. "I love my babies, Malcolm. You make sure they know that I love them and I'm going to get help real soon. Promise me you'll let them know that."

He nodded his head in assent as he moved back onto his feet. "Where are you staying?" he asked, knowing she probably wouldn't be truthful with him.

"I have a friend I'm staying with until tomorrow, then I'm going back to Baltimore to my mama's."

Malcolm didn't reply, knowing that Miss Maxine would never allow Shanell back home as long as she was in the throes of her addiction. Shanell knew it too. Both knew the streets of wherever she found herself would soon be home for her.

"When you're ready, Shanell, you know I'll be here to help," he said finally.

Shanell gave him another weak smile. She reached for her sandwich, wrapping it in the paper napkin that rested on the serving tray. She pushed it into her pocket. Her gaze met his one last time. "I could use some money, Malcolm. Just a few dollars. I'll pay you back."

He hesitated for a brief moment, meeting the look she was giving him. Minutes passed before he finally reached into the pocket of his slacks and pulled out a roll of bills. He counted off five twenty-dollar bills and handed them to her. Her smile widened as she clutched the cash to her chest.

"I'll get help. I promise," she said as she moved toward the exit door. "Bye!" she shouted as she hurried from sight, the door slamming closed behind her.

Malcolm moved back to where Romeo sat. The two men exchanged a quick look. Rising from his seat, Romeo moved back behind the bar and poured hot coffee into two mugs. He pushed one toward his friend as he sipped from the other.

"You know she's just going to use that money to make a buy, don't you?"

Malcolm nodded. "Yeah, I do. But I hope and pray she doesn't."

Romeo nodded with him; nothing else needed to be said.

Malcolm's head hurt. He knew he needed sleep but he didn't imagine himself resting any time soon. Business had been brisk and they were still trying to get the last partygoers out of the building for the night. Two couples were standing idly in the center of the room, lost in conversation as they waited for a friend to come out of the men's room. Outside the men's room door Romeo tossed up a hand indicating that it might be a minute. Odetta shook her head, amusement painting her expression.

Moving behind the bar Malcolm switched off the sound system. Everything in the room seemed to vibrate from the infraction, every sound louder.

A young woman moved in his direction, a bright smile across her face.

"I could use a ride, handsome. I think my date abandoned me!" she said with a soft giggle. She had a cute face, an abundance of blond hair and skin the color of milk chocolate. Her dress was tight, short, and she stood easily on five-inch stilettos.

Malcolm smiled. "I can call you a cab, honey, but that's all I can do for you.

The young woman smiled back. "I promise I will make it worth your while," she said, her tongue sweeping slowly over her lips.

Odetta suddenly stood between the two of them, her hands clamped tightly against her full hips. "Girl, bye. The man already told you no."

Rolling her eyes, the woman swung her blond hair over her shoulder. She turned toward the couples in the center of the room. "Will one of you fools go see what's keeping that asshole, please. I cannot believe you'd actually fix me up with such a cheap trick," she said to her friends as she moved in the direction of the exit.

The other two women rushed to catch up to her as she mumbled and cursed her way out the door. The two men both threw each other a look, neither interested in following their friend into the men's room. With a snide comment and shrug of their shoulders they followed behind the women.

Odetta rolled her eyes, annoyance painting her expression. She moved toward the men's room and knocked against the door. "Hey! You need me to call you an ambulance?" she screamed through the vent slats.

There was a mumbled response, then she pushed open the door and eased inside. Romeo bust out laughing, his gaze meeting Malcolm's.

"I pity that poor fool when Odetta gets hold of him," Malcolm said as he laughed with his partner.

"What poor fool is that?" Cilla questioned, her warm voice coming from the entrance.

Malcolm grinned. "Hey, what are you doing here?" he said as he moved from behind the bar to where she stood, leaning to give her a deep bear hug.

She smiled back as she leaned into his side. "I couldn't sleep so I thought I'd come see my favorite guy. Looks like I'm a little late for the party though!"

Romeo laughed again, lifting his hand to give her a wave. "How are you, Cilla?"

"I'm good, Romeo. How about yourself?" She and Malcolm eased their way back to the bar. He gestured for her to take a seat on a barstool.

"Ready to get out of this crazy house," Romeo said with a warm chuckle.

There was suddenly a commotion coming from the rest room as Odetta threw the room door open. An exceptionally tall, overly thin man with a military haircut moved into the space, Odetta gently guiding him out. His eyes were narrowed, seeming as if he were struggling to keep them open.

"This one was sound asleep with his pants down to his ankles," she said, her head waving. "He actually fell off the commode onto the floor."

Romeo shook his head. "I would have gotten him, Odetta."

"I know but a girl couldn't pass up a late-night peep show!" she said with a wink of her eye.

Malcolm laughed. "I swear, Odetta, you are going to lose us our license one day."

Odetta laughed with him. "Boy, please! I didn't see much of anything at all. At least nothing worth talking about!" She held her thumb and index finger up, the space between them barely an inch apart.

Romeo's face flushed red, his cheeks heating. "Too much information, Ms. Brown. Way too much information."

The tall man suddenly stood upright, his eyes widening. "Hey," he said. "That's my date! Hey, baby! You ready to take Big Daddy home and tuck him into bed?" His words were thick and slurred like his mouth was filled with cotton. He took a step in Cilla's direction.

Cilla bristled nervously as she tossed Malcolm a look.

Malcolm took a step in front of her, easing his body between her and the stranger. "Sorry, partner, but that's not *your* girl!" he said.

The man looked confused, then his shoulders sank back down. "Gots to find my girl," he slurred.

Romeo moved to his side. "Come on, friend. I think your girl might have left you but if she hasn't there's a taxi waiting to take you right to your front door," he said as he guided the man to the door and outside.

Cilla laughed. "So, I take it that was the poor fool?"

Malcolm nodded. He turned back to her, leaning to press a damp kiss to her forehead. "It's always something around here."

Odetta chuckled. "How you doin', girlfriend?" she said, her eyes shifting in Cilla's direction.

"I'm really good, Odetta. How about you?"

"Girl, my feet hurt. I'm ready to go home," she said with a soft sigh.

Cilla nodded. "I know what that's like."

Romeo moved back inside, locking the front door behind him. "Let's blow this joint, people!"

"You get your boy a ride?" Malcolm asked.

He nodded. "His *girl* was parked out front waiting for him. Now, I'm going home to *my* girl. Odetta, do you need a ride?"

"Please. My Keith is working third shift tonight. I don't feel like waiting for him to get off."

Romeo moved to the bar and picked up his jacket, slipping it over his arm. "Malcolm, I'll take the deposits. You and Cilla can get the lights on your way out."

Malcolm gave him a thumbs-up. "Not a problem. I just need to load those last glasses into the dishwasher and we'll be right behind you."

"Y'all have a good night!" Odetta exclaimed as she followed Romeo out the back door.

"Good night!" Cilla exclaimed, waving her goodbyes.

Seconds later the club was quiet, just the tick tock of the clock beneath the counter resounding through the space. Cilla watched as Malcolm wiped down the counter. He tossed her an easy smile as he loaded the last dishes into the washer and turned it on. His eyes swept around the space one last time, insuring that nothing had been missed. When he was satisfied, he turned his attention to Cilla.

She was watching him intently, something like wonderment washing across her face. She smiled and the beauty of it warmed his spirit. She wore no makeup and he was awed by the silken quality of her crystal complexion. Her cheeks were naturally flushed and her eyes bright. He liked how she looked at him, something about her gaze seeing in him what he hadn't even known was there. As he moved to her side, her bottom lip began to quiver and so he kissed her, wanting to still the hint of anxiety that had risen within her.

"I'm glad you came," he said. His breath was warm against her mouth as he whispered softly.

She nodded. "I wasn't sure I should. It seemed a little . . . a little . . . forward?"

He shrugged. "I don't think so. I like that you don't mind stepping out of your comfort zone for me."

She giggled softly. "And only for you."

"That makes me feel very special," he said with a bright smile.

"So, are you ready to go, Mr. Cobb?" she questioned, her tone eager.

He nodded. "I just need to get some paperwork out of the office," he said.

He clasped his hand around hers and pulled her along beside him. They moved across the room toward the door with the FOR EMPLOYEES ONLY sign. Inside, he flipped on the lights, dropping the hold he had on her as he moved to the desk, taking a seat in the leather executive's chair.

Cilla's gaze swept around the space. "This is cute," she said as she took everything in. Her eyes rested on a framed poster that hung on the wall behind the desk. "Is that Piano Man Burdett?" she asked, her gaze skeptical.

Malcolm took a quick glance over his shoulder. "The one and only. He used to be our featured piano player. Do you know Piano Man?"

"I know his music. My father was a huge fan of his. He's deceased now, isn't he?"

Malcolm chuckled. "Naw! He's still alive and kicking. He's Romeo's father."

"His father?"

Malcolm nodded. "It's a long story."

"Give me the short version."

Malcolm took a deep breath as his eyes rested on hers. He leaned back in the chair and gestured for her to take a seat on the upholstered sofa. Dropping down onto the cushioned seat she pulled herself upright in the corner of the couch, drawing her long legs back against her buttocks.

"This old guy comes in one night and asks for a job. All he can do is play a piano so Romeo lets him. Turns out the old guy is none other than Piano Man, in the flesh. Before you know it, this place is blowing up, everyone trying to get in to hear him play. A few months go by and he and Romeo get really close, then one day out of the blue he announces that he's Romeo's father. The two never knew each other, in fact, Romeo's mother had told him his father was dead or some nonsense like that. Obviously, there was some drama, Piano Man takes off and then months later turns up in the hospital after having had a stroke. Romeo and Taryn have been taking care of him ever since."

"Wow! How's he doing?"

"He has some speech and mobility issues but his

mind is still sharp. Every now and then we sneak him in for a shot of scotch and the music."

"I hope I get the opportunity to meet him someday. The man is iconic. Any jazz aficionado knows what a musical genius he was."

Malcolm nodded. "I like to think he still is. He can't play anymore but you can still see that drive in his eyes." He took another deep breath, blowing it out slowly. "I look forward to introducing you. Piano Man can't resist a beautiful woman and definitely not a woman who knows his music. You'll have him wrapped right around your fingers in no time!"

Cilla laughed and Malcolm laughed with her. The wealth of it was warm and teasing, embracing them both. They eased back into the quiet, their gazes locked as they stared. Cilla felt her pulse quicken as heat blossomed deep in her core. She drew a hand to her abdomen as she inhaled swiftly, the sensation sweeping through her.

Rising from his seat Malcolm moved from behind the desk to where Cilla sat. He stood above her for a quick moment while he inhaled the sight of her, everything about her nourishing and comfortable. He bit down against his bottom lip as he felt heat rain south, hardening every muscle in his large body.

"Why are you looking at me like that?" Cilla whispered. Her eyes were wide and she panted ever so slightly.

"I could ask you the same question," Malcolm whispered back, his gaze still locked tight to hers.

He dropped one knee onto the couch, his body tilting as if to straddle hers. He leaned forward, one hand resting against the back of the sofa to her left and the other on the sofa's arm to her right. He leaned even farther and she gasped slightly as his mouth stopped a fraction from hers. Their gazes still danced together as he allowed himself to drop even closer, the heat from his large frame igniting a firestorm between them.

Cilla's lips parted slightly. She reached her hand to his chest, pressing her fingers against the faint brush of hair that teased the opening of his white dress shirt. Her other hand moved to his face as she gently stroked his cheek and then he kissed her, securing his mouth to hers. He kissed her and without any hesitation she began to kiss him back. Before she realized what she was doing Cilla pulled him down against her, wanting to feel the wealth of his weight against her body.

They were an entanglement of closed eyes, mouths wide open and hands roaming everywhere. Fingers teased and kneaded flesh, every touch extraordinary. Their tongues twisted and glided easily together, their mouths dancing beautifully against each other. Malcolm thought she tasted like warm butter and cinnamon and he found himself craving her more and more. He savored the sweetness, his hunger so intense that he couldn't begin to imagine it ever being quenched.

His kiss was possessive, claiming every nerve and fiber in her being. If there had been an ounce of doubt before, there wasn't anymore. She belonged to him, her heart and soul taken. Cilla wrapped her arms around his neck, clutching at the back of his shirt. She licked his lips, gently biting against the soft flesh. Lengthening her body against the couch she opened her legs as he nestled himself against her. She inhaled his scent, his taste, everything, unable to get enough.

Neither wanted the moment to end. Malcolm trailed his lips over her cheeks, her nose, then nuzzled his tongue into the dimple beneath her chin before moving back to her mouth. The kiss seemed to last forever and still wasn't enough to satisfy their thirsts. Cilla sank farther into the sofa, taking Malcolm with her. Both marveled at how nicely they fit against each other, their respective arms feeling like home. He suddenly pulled himself from her, gasping heavily for air as he moved back onto his feet. She drew her knees to her chest, wrapping her arms around them as she struggled to catch her own breath.

Sweat beaded Malcolm's brow as he drew his palms across the top of his head then settled them along the line of his hips. Frustration creased his brow.

"What's wrong?" Cilla managed to ask, already knowing the answer before he spoke the words.

He took one deep breath after another to steady his nerves and slow the intense beating of his heart. He focused on the stare she was giving him, sultry heat seeping from her gaze. He struggled for a brief moment, searching for the right words to convey what he was feeling.

"I want to make love to you," he said finally. He was emphatic, his tone conveying the intensity of his desire as he repeated himself. "I want to make love to you. I *need* to make love to you but it's so much more than that. You are—" He suddenly hesitated, the words catching deep in his chest. "You mean more to me than I can begin to tell you." He took another breath and held it before going on. "We need to stop. If we don't slow things down right now, I'm going to take you right there on that couch and you deserve better than that from me. When I make love to you the first time it'll be on silk sheets, in a five-star hotel after I've wined and dined you and told you over and over again how beautiful you are. There will be flowers and chocolates and I will make it the most incredible night you will ever have." He heaved a deep sigh.

Cilla took her own deep breath. A slow smile crept across her face, her eyes shimmering as they misted lightly with tears. She nodded her head slowly. "I imagine, Malcolm, that no matter where we make love the first time, and every time thereafter, it will be incredible."

He extended his hand toward her, pulling her onto her feet. He eased her into his arms and held her tightly. As Cilla wrapped her own arms around his waist he pressed a kiss to the top of her head. The scent of coconut and jasmine coated the thick strands. He kissed her a second time and tightened the grip he had around her torso. They stood together for some time trading easy caresses.

"I should be heading home," she said softly.

He nodded. "I can drive you if you want. We can come pick up your car after our morning coffee tomorrow."

She giggled softly. "If you drive me home, you and I both know what's going to happen and I don't have silk sheets on my bed.."

Malcolm chuckled softly. "We might need to do something about that," he said, with a hint of humor in his tone.

Amusement danced across Cilla's face. If only he knew, she thought. Buying silk sheets was the first thing she planned to purchase when she made it home to her computer and her favorite online shopping spot.

Chapter Seven

"So you were a booty call without being called? Explain to me how that works, please?"

Cilla shook her head. "I was not a booty call!"

"When you show up at a man's place in the middle of the night hoping you're going to get some that makes you a booty call."

"I would have been a booty call if he had called and had asked me to come over specifically to give him some. But he didn't even know I was coming."

Bianca's eyes skirted toward the ceiling in her home. "And you still didn't get yourself any."

"Girlfriend, please, you don't know what I did or did not get."

"Oh, I know. I know if you're talking to me and not in bed with him that your dry spell is still dry as hell."

Cilla laughed. "I'm not having this conversation with you, Bianca."

"Don't. I know I'm not missing out on anything because you don't have anything to tell me."

"I do have something to tell you. I think." She

paused, shifting the cell phone from one ear to the other. "I think I'm falling in love with this man."

Bianca groaned loudly. "Say it ain't so!"

Cilla could feel her grin pulling so wide that her cheeks actually hurt. She took a deep breath and shook her head. "I do, Bianca. I've never met anyone like him. He's respectful and kind and generous and he cares about me. He cares about me and he's not afraid to show it."

Her friend was shaking her head as if Cilla could actually see her through the receiver. "Take my advice, love is very overrated."

"This coming from the woman who swears by love. Aren't you the same woman who was head over heels in love with a man she'd known for how long? Less than a week? Don't I recall something about a Christmas kiss sealing the deal?"

"I fell in love with the *idea* of falling in love. I'm really not that serious about it."

Cilla laughed. "You're a liar! I know for a fact that Ethan has your nose wide open!"

Bianca grinned. "Maybe. But our situation is unique."

"Be honest with me? Do you think I'm crazy? I mean we're still just getting to know each other. And Malcolm might actually be really bad in bed."

"You and I both know that's a lie! Your man is sexy as hell. I can tell by the way he walks and how he moves on the dance floor that he is not bad in bed. In fact, I'm willing to bet that man has professional skills between the sheets."

"You don't know that."

"You might not be able to tell the pros from the

amateurs but I surely can. I'm a master at detecting things like that," Bianca said, laughter ringing in her voice.

Cilla giggled with her. "You are such a fool!" she said teasingly.

"That may very well be, but I'm not the one questioning my relationship with a really great guy. I let everyone know what a great guy my Ethan is."

"Malcolm is a really great guy, too, isn't he?"

Bianca blew a warm breath. "Girl, he's the guy fairy tales are made of. You aren't going to do much better so don't mess it up. I know how you do."

"What is that supposed to mean?"

"It means if you mess up, there are women who will gladly take your place. If I didn't already have a man you might get your feelings hurt."

"You'd do that to me? You'd break the sister code and date one of my ex-boyfriends?"

"Girl, good men are an endangered species. And I'm talking the kind of good man you want to take home to your daddy. The kind of good man Pops would want to see you married to and who would play golf with him once a week because they have so much in common. If you let a precious commodity like that go, then you better believe someone else will be there to pick him up. Who better than your best friend in the whole wide world? I'd want a good thing like that for you! No one is going to think about a code when there's gold to be had and men like my Ethan and your Malcolm are pure gold!" Bianca laughed heartily.

Cilla laughed with her as she changed the subject. "So what are you doing today?"

"Church first and then I'll probably head over to the flea market. I want to try and find myself a vintage mirror for my foyer. Do you want to come?"

Cilla paused for a brief moment. Malcolm had already forewarned her that he would be out of pocket the entire day, having plans with his daughters. Despite her wishful thinking she didn't even anticipate talking to him until later in the evening. "Yeah," she said. "And I'll even go to church with you too."

"Lord, have mercy, there must be a storm coming!" Bianca exclaimed.

Cilla laughed. "Don't even go there. You act like I never go to church."

"Oh, I know you go. Once last century and now. It's a wonder the sky hasn't started to fall."

She giggled again. "I am not that bad, Bianca!"

"You're not that good, either."

"At least I don't have a host of sins I need to confess every Sunday morning."

"I might have one or two but then I have a much more interesting life than you do."

"Says the woman whose last date was how long ago?"

"A very minor detail and only because my man is away on business."

"Pick me up," Cilla quipped. "I'll be ready."

"See you in a few," Bianca said as she disconnected the call.

Malcolm's head swung back and forth like he was watching a tennis match. He found himself thoroughly entertained as the twins shared a story about something that had happened in math class. Math was the only class the two high school freshman shared at Ravenscroft School. The two had moved him to tears with their jokes and tales about high school life. As Claudia hit her punch line the two girls laughed simultaneously and he laughed with them.

"Okay, okay, okay!" Malcolm exclaimed as he swiped a tear with his index finger. "That's just too much! You two sound like you're playing in school more than you're learning."

"We're learning," Cleo giggled.

"I got a ninety-eight on my last exam," Claudia chuckled.

"I did okay," Cleo quipped, her smile fading a smidgen.

Malcolm smiled as he looked from one to the other. "Well, I'm very proud of you both. When I went to parent-teacher conference everyone had good things to say about you and how you were performing. You know good grades make me very happy."

Cleo cut an eye at her sister. Claudia gestured with her head, her eyes wide. "Well, I didn't do so good on my English project," Cleo muttered.

Malcolm shifted his gaze toward the young girl. "What's that mean?"

The two girls exchanged a second look before Cleo replied.

"I didn't finish so I got an F and I failed my science test but Mr. Barnes said that I can retake it next week."

Malcolm leaned back in his seat. He folded his hands together in his lap. His brow furrowed as he took a deep breath. His eyes dropped to his breakfast plate for a quick second before he shifted his gaze toward Claudia.

"Sweetheart, would you do me a favor, please?"

The young woman gave him a smile. "Sure, Daddy!"

"Would you please get me some more bacon and another omelet before they close down the omelet bar?"

Claudia nodded. "Cheese and vegetables," she asked.

"Extra cheese," Malcolm responded, his smile returning to his face.

Claudia grinned back, her head bobbing up and down as she skipped away. Malcolm watched as his daughter crossed the carpeted floor of the restaurant. They were catching the tail end of the breakfast buffet at Golden Corral, one of the girls' favorite places. Despite his mother's protests they'd been allowed to plan the entire day. Both had opted to bypass Sunday school and church for the all-you-can-eat meal.

He turned back to Cleo who was eyeing him curiously. "I'm worried about you, kiddo. Something's going on and I don't know what it is. Do you want to talk?"

Cleo's eyes shifted around the room as she struggled to avoid her father's stare. "There's nothing wrong," she mumbled softly. "Everything's fine."

Malcolm nodded. "I don't agree. You've been moody and now you're telling me that your grades have dropped. Something's going on with you."

Cleo shrugged her narrow shoulders. "There's

nothing wrong," she snapped, a hint of attitude rising in her tone. She cut her eye at him then dropped her gaze back to the table.

There was a moment of pause as Malcolm sat staring at her. Cleo was the younger twin, born three minutes after her sister. Cleo had actually been born the following day at 12:01 in the morning, giving them separate birth dates. That fact always fascinated both girls, being able to celebrate the dates of their birth on different days. He remembered the exact moment his girls had pushed their way into his life. The minute the nurse had laid Claudia in his arms he'd fallen head over heels in love. In that moment he couldn't imagine himself loving anyone else as much and then they had handed him Cleo to hold. His heart hadn't been the same since.

He'd been petrified at the prospect of parenthood but his children had made him a better man. They'd become his lifeline, the heartbeat that kept him whole and standing and ultimately sober. He loved them both like he had loved nothing else before them or since.

Malcolm pushed himself up from the table and moved to the seat beside his daughter. He dropped an arm around her shoulders and pulled her to him, hugging her against his chest. He held her for a moment before he spoke. "Don't you ever forget that you can always talk to me about anything. Even if it's something that might upset me, I will still be here to support you. If you need my help don't you ever be afraid to say so. Okay?"

She nodded her head against her father's chest.

"Now, we're not done with this conversation

because I think there's something you want to tell me but you just don't know how. So you and I are going to talk again after you've had some time to think things over. Until then, you just remember that I love you, baby girl!"

Cleo reached up to kiss her father's cheek. "I love you, too, Daddy!"

"I love you and you!" Claudia said, returning with her father's omelet and bacon and a second plate piled high with fruit and chocolate-covered strawberries.

"How much do you love your old man?" Malcolm teased as he reached for one of her strawberries.

Claudia laughed. "I love you to infinity."

"I love you to infinity times two," Cleo said.

"Well, I love you to infinity times two plus infinity!" Claudia retorted.

He gave them both a dramatic eye roll. "Well, I love you both so much that after we eat I'm taking you both to the flea market!"

Both girls clapped excitedly. "Can we buy something?" Cleo asked.

Malcolm smiled as he pulled a forkful of food to his mouth. "You can buy two somethings!"

The weather was absolutely perfect for the Raleigh flea market at the historic state fairgrounds. The sun was bright and peeking high from behind a bevy of cushiony clouds. There was just enough breeze in the air to keep the rising heat at bay. A pleasant crowd of tourists and shoppers packed the aisles inside and out and the assorted items for sale ran the gamut from baseball cards to chocolate fudge.

Malcolm raced behind both girls as they jumped from one booth to another, oohing over knockoff jewelry, sun catchers, gauze tops, and all things shiny and pretty that caught their eye. In a matter of minutes he saw his promised two somethings manifest into a host of bags that he was expected to carry. He laughed as he marveled at their capacity to find a need for almost everything they laid their eyes on.

"But Daddy!" Claudia exclaimed excitedly.

"But Daddy nothing. I am not an ATM machine, baby girl, nor do I have a money tree growing in the backyard."

"But we can't go home without something for Grandma. Her feelings will be hurt," Cleo reasoned.

Malcolm rolled his eyes skyward. "Well, if it's for your grandmother why do I need to buy two of them?"

"Because we need one for Grandma Maxine when she comes to visit," Claudia insisted.

"They're really pretty, too," Cleo noted. She ran her hand across the polished wood.

Claudia had spied the rocking chairs first, both girls skipping off to inspect them. Made from salvaged hardwood, the rockers had a classic curved headboard and slat back, with pretty spindle-turned arms and base supports. Each had deep seats and were polished to a high sheen. His mother had been wanting one for the front porch since forever. He was impressed that the girls had even remembered.

With the saleswoman extolling their quality and

uniqueness and both girls batting their lengthy eyelashes at him, Malcolm found himself outnumbered, feeling as if his credit card had been talked right out of his pocket. He smiled at the delight in the twins' eyes as both claimed a rocker, sliding their lean frames into them.

"You two have cost me a fortune today," he said as he slid the purchase receipt into his pocket.

"No, we haven't," Claudia said as she rocked her torso back and forth to move the chair.

"After the movie you can say we cost you a fortune," Cleo teased.

Malcolm feigned a look of surprise, his eyes wide and his mouth open. "The movies? I have to take you to the movies, too?"

The girls giggled. "You said whatever we wanted!" they exclaimed at the same time.

The joy across their faces made the man smile. In that moment they had him completely wrapped around their little fingers. He was grateful that neither knew just how much.

"I need to go pull the car around. You two stay right here with our chairs so no one runs off with them and I'll be right back."

Both girls nodded.

"And no talking to strangers," he reiterated, shaking an index finger at the two of them.

Both girls rolled their eyes, ignoring him completely. He chuckled softly to himself as he strode quickly back to the parking lot. As he reached his vehicle he couldn't help but note how well the day was going. He was enjoying his time with the twins and made a mental note to himself to carve more time in his schedule for days just like this one.

He settled down in the driver's seat of his SUV and started the ignition. Before he put the car into gear he stole a quick glance to his cell phone. There were no missed calls or messages and though he had hoped to hear from Cilla he knew that she didn't want to interfere with his time with his daughters. He typed a quick text message to her and after pushing the SEND button, backed out of the parking space.

"Daddy won't be mad at you, Cleo!" Claudia was shaking her head at her sister. "And even if he's mad at you for a little bit, he'll be able to fix this! Because you really need him to fix this!" The young girl tossed a glance over her shoulder and around the space to see if anyone was watching. The crowd at the flea market was oblivious, everyone going about their own business.

Cleo was crying, tears streaming down her delicate face. She was visibly distressed, her face flushed a brilliant shade of red because she was crying so hard. Her slender frame shook with a vengeance, every muscle trembling. She had a tight grip around her cell phone, the device engaged as she scrolled through a text message that had been sent to her. Claudia stared over her sister's shoulder, mortified by what she was seeing.

"This is bad, Cleo. Daddy really needs to know."

Cleo shook her head. "I'll figure it out, but you swore, Claudia. You swore you wouldn't tell anyone."

"I don't know if I can keep that promise," she said, pointing to where Cleo was staring. The phone buzzed again signaling the arrival of another text message.

Cleo narrowed her gaze on her sister, her vision still clouded by her tears. She swiped a hand across her face, brushing away the moisture that dampened her view. "I swear," she suddenly hissed. "If you tell anyone I will never forgive you, sissy. Never!"

Claudia swiped away her own tear. Before she could say another word, Cleo did an about-face, rushing off in the opposite direction.

"I like the other one better," Cilla said as she and Bianca stood two steps away from a gold-framed mirror. She was studying the accent piece intently. It was a classic Louis Philippe rectangular mirror crafted with ornate beading and acanthus leaf carvings around the frame. It featured a dusty gold finish and the original aged mirror glass. "It's too gold," she concluded. "I think the silver tones in the other one will look better in your foyer with that gray slate tile."

Bianca nodded. "I think so, too," she said. "Let's get back to that vendor before she sells my mirror to someone else."

The two women took an easy stroll through the midday crowd. The flea market was a popular weekend jaunt for young and old alike and the atmosphere was easy and carefree. As the two pushed past other buyers, Cilla's cell phone suddenly beeped, a text message showing on her cell phone screen. A bright smile filled her face as she read the short message from Malcolm.

"What?" Bianca questioned, eyeing her suspiciously.

"What do you mean what?"

"I mean why do you have that stupid grin on your face?"

Cilla tilted the cell phone screen toward her friend. "He says he misses me."

Bianca shook her head. "Awww! Young love!" she said teasingly.

Cilla laughed, giggling like her first crush had paid her some attention. "Don't be jealous."

Bianca laughed with her. "Girl, please! You know I don't have a jealous bone in my body."

The two women continued their stroll, both laughing and joking easily. The two were lifelong friends, having met in grade school. They'd been best buddies since Miss Rayner's third grade class at Pinewood Elementary School. In high school they'd been cheerleaders together. After graduation Cilla had moved to Chapel Hill and Bianca had left the state, drawn by the big-city lights of New York.

When her parents had moved from their Charlotte home to Boone, North Carolina, Bianca had come back to the state, settling herself in Raleigh, and the two had picked up their friendship as if they'd never been apart. For a time they'd shared an apartment, then Bianca had bought a fixer-upper in the historic Oakwood neighborhood near downtown Raleigh. Cilla had preferred the newness of her Brier Creek townhome. Their working together at the pharmaceutical company that employed them had been a fluke and a blessing that neither had ever taken for granted.

Their conversation was abruptly interrupted when a crying teenager slammed into Cilla. Hard. Both landed harshly against the pavement, the collision startling them both. The girl's cell phone flew in the air and everything Cilla had been holding in her hands dropped to the ground as well.

"Ummph!" Cilla grunted, the abruption knocking the wind from her lungs.

"I'm sorry," the girl gushed, shock registering across her face as she looked about nervously. She stared intently, contrition seeping in with the tears in her eyes. She looked about, moving to help Cilla pick up her purse and the contents that had spilled out on the ground. "I'm really sorry!" she said again.

Bianca leaned to pick up one cell phone and then the other. The two Samsung units were identical, both even protected by the same stylish, damage-resistant cases. Without giving it any thought she passed the device that had landed closest to Cilla to her and the other to the girl.

"Are you okay?" Cilla asked, concern washing over her expression. She brushed the dust from her white shorts. "Is there anything we can do to help?" she asked as she reached into her leather handbag for a tissue, passing it to the young woman.

Cleo's tears suddenly came harder. The two women tossed each other a look. Bianca shrugged her shoulders, her expression voicing her bewilderment.

Cilla looked around, tossing a glance over one shoulder and then the other. "Sweetie, are you here with someone?"

Before the girl could answer, a man's booming voice could be heard in the distance. Coming from behind her, it grew louder, the frantic call moving the three of them to turn and stare. Recognition suddenly washed over Cilla's face. She looked from the girl standing before her to Malcolm who was rushing in their direction. The resemblance was suddenly unmistakable. She had her father's eyes and nose but her lips were full with a very feminine pout. Her hair was a thick mass of blue-black waves pulled back into a loose ponytail at the nape of her neck that hung down to her midback. She was race-horse lean with long, thin legs, no hint of curves to her hips and the faintest beginning of a bustline peeking beneath her top. Racing behind Malcolm was the child's identical twin. Both girls wore the same denim shorts. One had paired hers with a white T-shirt and floral-printed Converse sneakers. Her sister wore hers with a short-sleeved button-up blouse and sandals. A wave of anxiety suddenly pierced Cilla's stomach.

Malcolm looked from his girlfriend to his daughter and back again. Confusion shimmered in his dark eyes. He shifted his gaze to Cleo as he dropped two hands against his daughter's shoulders. "Cleo, what happened? Why'd you run off like that?"

The girl said nothing, panic shining in her eyes.

Malcolm asked again, his tone a tad more forceful. "I asked you a question. What is going on?"

"Claudia and I got into a fight," Cleo mumbled as she tossed a quick glance at her sister.

Wide-eyed, Claudia's mouth opened and then closed, her expression telling. Cilla didn't miss the silent exchange that seemed to say more than either girl had spoken.

Malcolm looked at his other daughter just as Claudia dropped her eyes to the ground, biting against her bottom lip. He heaved a deep sigh as he looked back toward Cilla.

"Hey, what are you doing here?" he asked as he leaned to kiss her cheek. He waved a hand at Bianca.

"Hey, Malcolm!" Bianca said, her singsong voice ringing through the warm air.

Malcolm could feel both girls suddenly shift their focus toward the three adults. When he looked, two pairs of eyes were studying them curiously. He heaved another deep sigh as he gave Cilla a bright smile.

"Well, I guess introductions are in order," he said, his emotions running the gamut from excitement to frustration. "Cilla, I'd like to introduce you to my daughters. This is Claudia Monet and you seem to know Cleo Michele."

Cilla smiled back. "Cleo and I actually ran into each other. Literally," she said as she rubbed a palm against her bruised hip.

"I wasn't looking where I was going," Cleo mumbled.

Malcolm shook his head, suddenly understanding. "I hope you apologized."

"She did," Cilla said quickly, she and the girl exchanging a look. "It was definitely an accident. Neither one of us was looking where we were going. We both hit the ground hard. I was just making sure she hadn't hurt herself."

Malcolm muttered a low grunt of frustration, then

took a deep breath as if to calm his nerves. "Are you okay, Cleo?"

Cleo nodded, still not saying anything.

Malcolm and Cilla locked gazes, both laughing nervously.

"Well, I had hoped to do this over dinner, but since we're all here," he said, "Girls, this is my friend that I was telling you two about. This is Miss Cilla."

Bianca cleared her throat.

Malcolm chuckled softly. "And that's Miss Bianca. She's a friend, as well."

Bianca waved. "Hi, girls!"

"It's very nice to meet you both," Cilla said. "Your dad talks about you two all the time."

Claudia's smile was bright. "Hi!"

Cleo's expression was less enthusiastic.

Cilla's own smile was nervous as she shifted her focus toward Malcolm. "Bianca and I were just hanging out. She was looking for a mirror."

Bianca suddenly jumped, remembering where they were headed. "I've got to go before she sells my mirror!" she chimed. She waved and turned. "Catch up with me when you're done," she yelled as she tossed Cilla a look over her shoulder.

Cilla nodded her head as she called after her friend. "I won't be long."

A nervous silence suddenly dropped over them. Cilla felt self-conscious under the youthful stares boring through her. Both girls were looking from her to their father and back, waiting to see what the two were going to do. She took a deep breath.

"So, have you guys been having a good time today?" she asked, her eyes shifting back and forth.

Malcolm nodded. "We have. The girls have been giving me a run for my money."

"We're going to the movies next," Claudia chimed in.

"I'm not so sure about that," Malcolm said, his brow raised as he looked at them. "I don't know that we're going to do anything until one of you tells me what you were fighting about."

That silence swelled thick and full a second time as he eyed one and then the other.

Cilla giggled softly. "Well, I'm sure you'll have fun no matter what you do."

"Would you like to join us?" Malcolm questioned, his gaze dancing back and forth across her face. "We'd love to have you."

She shook her head, the twins' gazes narrowed like daggers. "Maybe next time. I can't abandon Bianca. She gets all sensitive when we're supposed to spend the day together and something happens that we don't."

"We know the feeling," Cleo muttered sarcastically.

Malcolm's mouth opened and then closed but he didn't bother to comment. He and Cilla exchanged a look and she found herself fighting not to laugh out loud.

"Daddy's going to grill," Claudia said. "Maybe you can come eat dinner with us?"

Malcolm nodded. "I do a mean barbecue chicken if I say so myself."

Cilla smiled. "Is he any good, Cleo?" she asked.

The young woman shrugged her shoulders. "He's all right," she said nonchalantly.

Cilla met the look Malcolm was giving her. Her own gaze was hesitant.

He smiled, emphasizing his comment with the intensity of his stare. "I would really like you to come. Now that you've met the girls I want you to meet my mother."

Claudia moved into her father's side, wrapping her arms around his waist. Cleo moved against his other side, her head leaning against his shoulder. The trio stared at her intently until she finally nodded her assent. "I'd like that," she said as her eyes flitted from one face to another.

Something like joy flickered through Malcolm's eyes. His excitement washed over his expression. "Great. Will six o'clock work for you?"

She nodded. "Six o'clock is fine."

"I'll text you directions," he said, his grin a mile wide.

Cilla nodded, then before either said another word he leaned and kissed her mouth, the gesture swift and easy. With a slight wave of his hand he turned, pulling both of his girls along behind him.

As they moved off, Claudia's voice echoed in the distance. "Way to go, Daddy! She's so pretty!"

Chapter Eight

Bianca was laughing hysterically, finding what had happened far funnier than Cilla did. "If you had seen your face when you were sitting on the ground! You wanted to be mad and then you saw her boo-hoo-hooing. That soft spot of yours kicked in then!"

"What's up with that?" Cilla questioned. "Something had her seriously upset but she didn't want her father to know what."

Bianca shrugged. "Probably some boy hurt her feelings. You know what we're like at that age."

"Maybe, but I definitely got the feeling that she was hiding something and whatever it is her sister is keeping it a secret too."

"How do you know?"

"Remember how we'd do when we didn't want our moms to know what we were up to? The looks we'd exchange when we didn't have our stories straight so we'd know to roll with the lies you were telling. Well, she and her sister did the same thing."

"The lies I was telling? I never told any lies. I

might have bent the truth a little but I never lied!" Bianca laughed.

Cilla laughed with her. "Bent the truth? Girl, sometimes you'd have the truth so twisted that it couldn't do anything but break. You spun some serious tall tales."

"I had a vivid imagination!"

Cilla's eyes rolled. "Well, I hope he can get her to talk to him. These days kids have too much going on for a parent to be in the dark."

Her friend nodded. "I'd volunteer to go with you to dinner but I don't do kids. Besides, it'll give you a chance to play family and see what that's like."

"Well, I appreciate that but I don't remember Malcolm inviting you."

"And what's up with that? You let him know that wasn't cool. I like barbecue too!"

Cilla shook her head at her friend. She stole a quick glance to the clock on the dashboard. "It's getting late," she said. "I need to go get ready." She pointed Bianca in the direction of her home.

"Do you even know where you're going?" Bianca asked.

"Malcolm should have texted me directions by now," she said as she pulled her cell phone from her pocket. As she engaged the device Cilla realized the phone she had wasn't hers. There was no password on the unit and as she slid her index finger across the screen it opened to the last page Cleo had been viewing. Cilla's eyes widened, her mouth dropping open in shock as she flipped through the images on the screen.

"Oh, my God!" she gasped.

"What?" Bianca asked, glancing at her from the corner of her eye. "What's wrong?"

Cilla didn't answer as she flipped through the device, moving from one image to another. She couldn't begin to believe what she was seeing, but it was there, in more detail than she would have needed. Someone had photographed the girl and other young girls. The images were nude or semi-nude. She suddenly understood the child's hysterics, what she hadn't wanted her father to know. Tears pressed hot against her eyelids.

"I can't believe this!" Cilla exclaimed as she slapped a hand over her mouth. "Ohhh! The pictures! Oh, my God! Oh, my God! Oh, my God!"

"Who? What?" Bianca chimed as she came to a stop at the intersection, shifting the vehicle into park. She snatched the device from Cilla's hands to look for herself.

Moments later the car behind them blew its horn, the driver clearly annoyed. Bianca passed the phone to her friend before shifting back into drive and depressing the gas pedal. As the car jerked forward, both women let out loud gasps.

"I have to tell Malcolm," Cilla finally said.

"You can't tell Malcolm."

"Why not?"

"You being the bearer of bad news will put a serious crimp in your relationship. Plus, this kind of drama is going to upend that family for a good long time. There is no way he's going to take this well. And it coming from you is just going to make it harder for him to want to move forward."

Cilla shook her head. "What if she was your daughter? Wouldn't you want me to tell you?"

"That's different. I'm not interested in dating you so you had better tell me if my child were caught up in some mess like that."

"And what if I don't tell and he finds out I knew. He'll never forgive me."

Bianca blew a deep sigh. "I would really hate to be you right now because you have to tell."

Cilla turned to stare out the window. In that moment she hated the predicament she'd suddenly found herself in.

"No, no, no!" Cleo cried as she threw a hissy fit in the center of the room.

"What's wrong?" Claudia questioned.

"This isn't my phone! She has my phone!" she screamed.

Claudia shook her head. "It's no big deal, Cleo. She'll bring your phone back when she comes for dinner."

"And why did you invite her anyway? This was supposed to be *our* day with Daddy."

"Daddy wanted her to come. Couldn't you tell? He got all giggly and he seemed really happy. I like it when Daddy's happy. He's downstairs right now humming and singing. Daddy never hums! Besides, I want to get to know her."

"Well, I'm not interested in knowing her. I just have to get my phone back."

Claudia gave her sister a look. "What's on your

phone anyway? Why'd you get so upset when you looked at that message?"

Cleo shook her head. "It's not important."

"You're lying. Whatever it was made you really upset otherwise you wouldn't have gone running off like you did. You need to tell!"

"Leave me alone, Claudia!"

"I'm really tired of getting caught up in your lies. I hate lying to Daddy!"

Cleo blew a loud sigh. She shook her head, tears misting in her eyes. "I don't know what to do, sissy! It's gotten really bad and I don't know how to fix it," she said, the tears finally falling for the umpteenth time. Claudia moved to her sister's side and hugged her warmly. "It's going to be okay. But you have to ask for help. You have to!"

Cleo nodded. "I guess." She took a deep breath. "I just need some time, okay. I'll tell, I promise, but I need some time."

Claudia stood staring at her sister, trying to decide if she wanted to believe the half-truth that had just come out of her mouth. "Well, you should start by telling Daddy that you have Miss Cilla's phone. She won't know how to get here if she doesn't get the text message he promised to send."

Cleo pouted, shaking her head. "Okay, but the minute she gets here we have to get my phone from her."

Cilla was still trying to figure out what to do when the cell phone in her hand rang, some current pop song the ringtone of choice. She was only half surprised when Malcolm's smiling face appeared on the screen, indicating that he was the incoming caller. She took a deep breath before she answered.

"Hello?"

"Hey, you!"

"Hey, yourself. What's up?"

"I don't know if you noticed but you've got my daughter's phone. We have yours."

"I did," Cilla said. "Bianca must have gotten them mixed up when Cleo and I crashed into each other."

"I still can't get over the way we ran into you today."

"Me neither," Cilla said. "Is Cleo okay?"

There was a second of pause before Malcolm answered. "I think so. I get the feeling something's off but I can't figure out what it is. She's been weird all day. Hiding out in her room, locking doors, just behaving out of character. I'm thinking I might need to seek out professional help and maybe take her to a therapist if she keeps it up."

Cilla nodded into the receiver. "That might be an idea."

Something in her tone caught his attention. "Are you okay? You sound like something's bothering you?"

Cilla lied. "No. I'm fine. Just nervous about meeting your mother."

"I hope you can still come. I've already prepped the chicken," he said, his excitement rising in his tone.

Cilla found herself smiling. "I can't wait," she said. She could sense him smiling with her.

"Good," he said. "Because I really want to see you. I meant it when I texted you that I missed you."

"I missed you, too," she said.

They talked for a few minutes more and after Malcolm had given her directions to his family's home he disconnected the call. As she moved to get dressed she still didn't have a clue what she was going to do but she knew that insuring Cleo's safety had to be foremost in her decision.

Cilla's mouth dropped as she pulled her car into the driveway of the North Raleigh home. Its exclusive location with the gated entry had been impressive. The home itself took that impression a step further and then some. The traditional Georgian architecture had to have been a dream come true, Cilla thought. The extraordinary Southern estate was more house than Cilla had seen in quite some time. She'd assumed that Malcolm and his family lived well, but she hadn't imagined, with him being so down to earth and country, them living so lavishly. She suddenly wondered just what else she didn't know about the man.

As she parked her car in the empty space next to Malcolm's she saw Cleo standing in wait. The young girl jumped to her feet. She tossed a glance over her shoulder before moving toward the car, waiting for Cilla to step out of her vehicle. Cilla took a deep breath and then another before she opened the door. She pulled a smile onto her face, preparing herself for whatever might come.

"Hi, Cleo!" she said brightly.

"Hi. Can I have my phone?"

Cilla reached a hand out to brush a strand of hair from the girl's face. "Is your dad inside?"

"Yeah. Can I have my phone? Please?"

Cilla nodded. "Your dad said that you and your sister lost your phone privileges for that fight you had earlier. He asked me to return the phone to him."

Cleo twisted her face in frustration as she tossed her hands in the air. "I really need to get my phone. I need to . . . to . . . I need to get my homework assignment off of it," she said brusquely.

"What homework assignment?" a voice suddenly questioned from the entranceway.

Both Cilla and Cleo turned to see who had spoken. Claudette Cobb stood with her hands crossed over her chest. She focused her gaze on her granddaughter, waiting for the girl to answer her question. When Cleo didn't, she shook her head.

"That's what I thought. You daddy said no phone and he meant no phone. Get your behind inside and let your father know his friend is here."

"Yes, ma'am," Cleo muttered. She glared at Cilla before turning and moving back into the house.

Mama Claudette gestured for Cilla to follow her into the home. "I'm Claudette Cobb, Malcolm's mother," she said, her voice soft like cotton. "And you must be Priscilla."

"Yes, ma'am. But everyone calls me Cilla."

The matriarch extended her hand. "It's very nice to meet you, Cilla. My son has told me good things about you."

"It's very nice to meet you, Mrs. Cobb."

"Please, everyone calls me Mama."

Cilla smiled. "Yes, ma'am. You have a beautiful home," she said, her eyes swinging slowly around as she took in the décor. They'd moved from the foyer to the kitchen and family room. "It's absolutely incredible!"

"Thank you! It was a gift from my son. I'd dreamt of living in a house like this since I was a little girl down in Macon, Georgia. Never imagined that I'd ever have that chance. My husband, Malcolm's father, had bought us a comfortable bungalow when we first moved here after we married and I loved that house but this was my dream come true. After his daddy died he bought this house and moved us all in here."

Cilla smiled at the words she'd chosen—her "dream come true." Her head bobbed slowly up and down. "You're a very lucky woman, Mrs. Cobb."

"I think so. I have an amazing son who's blessed me exponentially and I'm able to watch my grand-babies grow into amazing women. Each day is one blessing after another." The woman paused in a brief moment of reflection, then rested her gaze on Cilla's face, her smile wide. She gestured for her to take a seat at the kitchen counter. "So, tell me about yourself, Cilla," she said when she finally spoke again.

Malcolm paused in the hallway, staring into the kitchen at Cilla and his mother. The two women were laughing comfortably, each seeming quite at ease with the other. Cilla stood at the marble-topped island, helping with the salad fixings. His mother was fussing over a pot of beans. Claudia had joined the two women and they were exchanging anecdotes as they got to know one another. Something about the moment moved his spirit, feeling like everything was right in his small world. He smiled, marveling at how his family suddenly felt fuller, more complete with the beautiful woman there. His thoughts were suddenly interrupted, his mother calling his name.

"I hope you didn't burn that chicken, Malcolm. Cilla didn't come all the way over here to eat bad food."

"I know that's right, Mama Claudette," Cilla said with a laugh as Malcolm moved into the kitchen space.

He placed the platter of meat he'd been holding onto the countertop. "I didn't burn the chicken," he quipped as he leaned to kiss his mother's cheek.

Claudia giggled. "Daddy's showing off, Grandma! This will probably be his best chicken ever!"

Amusement danced in Malcolm's eyes as he tossed his daughter a look. "Are you really trying to embarrass your old man?"

She giggled again as she shifted her gaze toward Cilla who was laughing with her. Cilla's eyes shifted toward Malcolm.

"What are you laughing at?" he quipped as he moved to where she stood. He eased behind her and wrapped his arms around her shoulders. He pressed his face to hers as he hugged her close. "I'm glad you came," he whispered into her ear.

Her smile was wide as she nodded. As he kissed her cheek Cilla relaxed against him for a brief second.

She felt his mother and daughter eyeing them and a wave of awkwardness billowed between them.

"Your mother was just telling me about your cooking skills. Something about beef Stroganoff gone wrong," she said.

"That's not fair," Malcolm said. He released the hold he had on Cilla as he tossed up his hands. "I'm trying to get the woman to like me and you two are trying to scare her off! What's up with that?"

His mother chuckled heartily. "I don't think you have to worry about that, son. She likes you. In fact, I'd be willing to wager that Miss Cilla likes you a lot!"

Claudia giggled in agreement.

Cilla felt herself blush, color heating her cheeks.

"Where's Cleo?" Malcolm suddenly questioned, realizing the girl was missing from the bunch.

His mother frowned. "Pouting. Again."

Cilla couldn't miss the frustration that passed over Malcolm's face.

"I'll go get her," he said.

Mama Claudette shook her head as she swiped her hands over a plush kitchen towel. "No, I'll go get her. You should show Cilla the house. Claudia, watch my beans for me, baby girl."

Malcolm and Claudia both answered in unison. "Yes, ma'am."

Cilla smiled as Malcolm reached for her hand and pulled her along behind him. They moved quickly through the family room, into the dining room, and past the formal living room.

"So what do you think?" he asked when they were out of earshot.

"Your mother's a pistol! She is so funny!"

"She definitely has her moments," he said. He finally came to a stop in the wood-paneled office. There was one wall of books and a drafting table that sat room center. Photos of him and his daughters decorated the desktop and walls. "This is my office," he said as he closed the door behind them.

"It's very nice," she said. "The whole house is beautiful!"

"It's too much house if you want my honest opinion," Malcolm said, "but it's what my mother wanted." He shrugged his broad shoulders.

"She's so proud of you."

He nodded. "I'd do anything for my mother. I love that woman to death!"

"So, you're a mama's boy through and through."

Malcolm laughed. "Guilty as charged!"

They laughed easily together, slipping into that state of balance with each other that seemed to come naturally. Malcolm was still holding tight to her hand and he pulled her against him. He eased both of his arms around her waist and pulled her closer. Dropping his mouth to hers he kissed her hungrily, relishing the softness of her lips. The connection was sweet and gentle as he reacquainted himself with her taste. The kiss deepened and he teased her lips with his tongue until she allowed him in, her own sliding easily into his mouth. She tasted sweet and citrusy like oranges and peaches. His tongue danced a two-step with hers as he tightened the hold he had around her body.

Both purred when they finally pulled away, breaking the connection. Malcolm leaned his forehead against hers. "My mother knew I wanted to kiss you, that's why she sent us away. So we could have some alone time."

"I don't think that's what your mother was thinking."

"You don't know my mother. But you will!"

Cilla laughed.

"We should go back," she whispered. "I don't want your mom thinking bad about me."

"My mom likes you. A lot. I can tell."

Cilla smiled. "Your family's very sweet. Claudia is absolutely adorable."

"I wish I knew what was going on with Cleo," he said, concern suddenly blanketing his expression.

Cilla felt herself tense. The shimmer in her eyes faded considerably. She took a deep breath and held it for a brief moment. Malcolm was staring off in thought, worry furrowing his brow. "You know, there's something I really need to . . ." she started.

There was a harsh knock on the door just before the structure flew open. Cleo stood anxiously on the other side, one hand on the knob, the other holding up the wall. "Hi," she said, looking from one to the other.

"Well, speak of the devil! Hello!" Malcolm chimed. "Did I invite you inside?"

The girl's eyes widened. "I . . . well . . . I . . ."

"That's okay. We'll talk about it later. Did you speak to Miss Cilla?"

"Hi, Miss Cilla," she said as if they had not had a conversation when she'd first arrived.

Cilla gave her a smile, the two locking eyes. Cilla didn't miss the anxiety shining in the young girl's stare. She suddenly felt an overwhelming sadness.

She struggled to keep it from showing on her face. "Hi, Cleo. How are you?"

"I'm good." She looked toward her father. "Grandma said come eat. The food is ready."

Malcolm nodded. "Thank you. We'll be right there."

Cleo stood staring at the two of them, her eyes shifting from one to the other, back and forth.

Malcolm stared back. "Yes?"

"I was just wondering if you gave Miss Cilla her phone back?"

Malcolm snapped his fingers. "I actually forgot about the phone. Thank you for reminding me," he said.

"I'll get it before I leave," Cilla interjected. "I'm actually hungry and I can't wait to taste this famous chicken your father has made." She winked an eye at him as she brushed her manicured nails across the front of his shirt. She moved toward the door. As she came to the girl's side she rested her hand against Cleo's shoulder. She smiled at her sweetly. "Everything's going to be okay," she said.

Chapter Nine

The meal went better than any of them could have anticipated. Both girls were in rare form and between Malcolm and his mother, Cilla couldn't remember the last time she'd laughed so hard. The jokes and stories were abundant, the food delicious, and the company engaging. Dinner flew by. Before Cilla knew it Malcolm was admonishing his daughters to shower and get ready for bed. They had school the next morning.

As Malcolm had cleared the dishes Mama Claudette invited Cilla to walk through her nightly ritual with the girls. Cilla didn't miss the smile that pulled at Malcolm's mouth as he feigned interest in his chore.

Bathed and dressed in their nightclothes, both girls were waiting in their grandmother's bed, tucked beneath an antique quilt that decorated the space. The room was warm and inviting and Cilla's gaze was drawn to the pictures on the nightstand; one of Malcolm as a young man, his parents' wedding photo, the twins' baby pictures.

Claudia was happy to see her there and said so. Cleo could have cared less, as disinterested in Cilla's presence as she could be. Cilla stood off to the side as Mama Claudette led the girls in their nighttime prayer. Their youthful voices were heartwarming as they prayed for their souls to be taken by God if they failed to wake from their slumber. When they were done, Claudia jumped excitedly. "Story time!"

Cleo heaved a heavy sigh. Mama Claudette shook her head as she turned toward Cilla and explained the Cobb family short story ritual.

"Before bed each night we make up a very short story. Everyone gets to add one line and one line only. Tonight will be the first time in a long time that our story will have five lines instead of four."

Cilla nodded her understanding as Mama Claudette led the tale. "Once upon a time there was a master builder, a man who'd built skyscrapers as high as the clouds."

Cleo spoke next, focusing her gaze directly at Cilla. "One day he met the woman who guarded the secrets of the kingdom, nothing ever passing her lips that was not supposed to be told."

Malcolm's voice suddenly rang from the doorway. "Together they were magic, their love bigger than the sun and the moon."

"You've used that line before," Claudia interjected.

"He always uses that line," Cleo noted.

"I can use any line I want," Malcolm said. He stuck his tongue out at the two of them.

"Let's finish up now," Mama Claudette chided. "It's getting late."

Claudia continued. "One day they shared a kiss

so magical that the secrets the woman kept spilled out in the open for everyone to see."

Everyone turned to look at Cilla for the last sentence. She smiled as she looked back at each one. Then she spoke. "But the master builder had built a beautiful box to catch them all so none of the secrets ever got away and they lived happily ever after."

The girls both rolled their eyes. Mama Claudette chuckled warmly and Malcolm laughed out loud.

"I think you're a natural," he said.

"That was fun."

Mama Claudette clapped her hands. "Off to bed you two!" She leaned to kiss one twin and then the other. Both girls hugged and kissed their father as they headed toward the door. Claudia stopped to hug Cilla and Cleo tossed up a dismissive hand.

The adults stood waiting until they heard the girls' respective room doors slam closed. Mama Claudette nodded. "Malcolm, you make sure everything is locked up downstairs. I'll see you in the morning, son!" she said. "Cilla, I hope to see you again soon. Please, don't be a stranger."

Cilla gave the woman a warm hug and the matriarch hugged her back. "Thank you for everything, Mama Claudette," she said.

Malcolm kissed his mother one more time, then entwined his fingers between Cilla's, pulling the back of her hand to his lips. He kissed it gently then guided her out of the space and back down the circular staircase.

"That was fun," Cilla said. "And you do that every night?"

Malcolm nodded. "Actually we've been doing it

since I was a little boy and my father participated. I'd like to think it'll last forever but I'm sure the girls will tell us they're too old to get tucked in and do story time sometime in the near future."

"Maybe not. Maybe they'll understand just how precious these moments are and want to keep up the tradition. You never know!"

"Let me show you something," he said as he guided her back to his office and the wall of books. His finger trailed a line of uniformly sized, hard-covered books. He pulled one from the row. "Every night my mother writes those little stories down and she keeps them. One year I gathered them all up and had them bound into a book as a Mother's Day present for her. When she started doing story time with the girls, I wanted to make sure we preserved them, so every year I publish all the stories for that year into a book. We have the big book, the first one, and now nine years' worth of stories." He passed one of the editions to her.

The leather-bound book was a collaboration of vignettes and simple line drawings. Some of the sketches were immature and childlike, the others more refined.

"This is wonderful!" Cilla exclaimed. "Who did the artwork?"

"The girls did some and the rest is mine."

"You're quite talented, Mr. Cobb."

He shrugged ever so slightly. "It's nothing really. I just wanted to capture the memories. Something for the girls to pass down to their families."

Cilla passed the book back to him. She wrapped her arms around her torso, hugging herself. "I should be going," she said.

Malcolm nodded. "You could always spend the night."

She laughed. "Uh, no! Your mother likes me. I'd like to keep it that way."

He slipped an arm around her waist and pulled her close. His kiss was teasing and Cilla felt heat soar through her midsection. They held the kiss for a good while, both knowing that it would take little prodding to move things a step further. She broke the connection abruptly, taking a step back from him. They both laughed nervously.

"Coffee in the morning?" she asked. She took a quick glance at the clock on the oversize desk.

Malcolm grinned. "I wouldn't miss it for anything in the world. Are you sure you can't stay?"

Nodding, Cilla moved toward the home's front entrance. At the door, Malcolm stepped outside, pulling the door closed behind him. They made small talk as he walked her to her car. Unlocking the vehicle, Cilla pulled open the driver's-side door. As she turned to say good-bye Malcolm eased himself against her until her back was pressed against the vehicle. Above them there was a full moon shining brightly. The stars flickered like miniature bulbs against the blue-dark canvas. Malcolm whispered her name as he clasped both hands around her face, his thick fingers pulling through her hair. Then he kissed her again, his hands dancing up and down her back. Beneath the late-night sky they traded gentle, easy caresses, losing themselves in each other's touch.

By the time she pulled her car out of the driveway, Cilla's head was a whirlwind of lustful fantasy as she struggled to regain her composure. It wasn't until she reached the second stoplight that she realized she'd forgotten to get her phone back and that Cleo's phone and Cleo's secret were still hidden in her purse.

Cilla imagined that if she looked like she felt she'd probably scare Malcolm away. It felt as if she'd only had a few minutes of sleep, having tossed and turned for most of the night. Her stomach felt like a curdled mess, her nerves completely frazzled. She hadn't bothered to dress, tossing on a pair of old sweats and a T-shirt. Her usual curls were brushed back flat against her skull and were captured in a tight bun at the nape of her neck. She wore no makeup. Anxiety creased her forehead and dark circles painted her eyes. There was nothing at all pretty about the apprehension that consumed her.

She took a deep breath and held it before stepping from her car. Outside the weather was beginning to change. The early-morning air had just a hint of chill and she shivered, wishing she'd thought to bring a sweater. But Cilla hadn't been able to think clearly about much. Between thoughts of Malcolm and his daughter and how she suddenly found herself fitting into the mix, she was completely discombobulated. What bothered her most is that she should have told Malcolm. She should never have left his home without showing him what she'd found on his daughter's phone. She was racked with guilt and it was consuming. She blew out the breath she'd been holding as she moved toward the coffee shop entrance.

Inside, Malcolm was already seated at their corner table. He'd bought the coffee, two cups sitting in wait atop the table. The expression across his face was welcoming, his smile gentle, until he laid eyes on her and then concern registered in his dark gaze.

"Hey," Cilla said as she took the seat beside him. She was gnawing nervously on her bottom lip, her hands twisting in her lap.

"What's wrong? Did something happen?" Malcolm questioned.

She shook her head. "We need to talk."

Malcolm shifted forward in his seat. His own anxiety was suddenly on overload. "Whatever you want," he said. "Just tell me what's going on. You don't look good."

Cilla sighed heavily. "I didn't sleep well. I've been thinking about you all night."

Malcolm chuckled softly. "I thought about you too but it was a good thing for me."

She shook her head, the faintest of smiles pulling at her mouth.

Malcolm smiled back. "That's much better. Now tell me what's going on." He reached a hand out and grabbed hers. She was shaking and he suddenly would have done anything to ease her discomfort.

Cilla took a deep breath. Then another as she stared into his eyes. For a brief moment she wished that she could have done anything not to stir the pot she was about to agitate.

Malcolm was still staring at her curiously, his

warm palm caressing the back of her hands. He bristled ever so slightly when she pulled herself from his touch. She reached into her handbag, searching deep in the bottom lining until she pulled out his daughter's cell phone, setting it on the table. He looked from it to Cilla, confusion washing over his expression.

"I don't understand? I wasn't worried about the phone. I knew you'd get it back to us and Cleo's still being punished so she can't use it anyway."

"You need to look through her phone," Cilla said. "I think it'll explain why she's been having such a hard time lately."

His gaze still flitting back and forth, Malcolm picked up the device from the table and engaged it. It opened to the same social network site that Cilla had seen. It took him a moment to comprehend what he was seeing and then he gasped, loudly, sounding as if he'd just been punched in the stomach.

"What is this?" he asked, his voice coming louder than he expected. He looked around the room, suddenly afraid that he had drawn attention to them. He drew his gaze back to Cilla's face and asked a second time. "Really, what is this?"

"When Cleo and I ran into each other at the fairgrounds this is what she was looking at. And she was crying hysterically. I think this is what upset her. She met me in your driveway yesterday and she was desperate to get her phone back. It was clear that she didn't want anyone to see these."

"You knew about this last night and you didn't tell me?"

"I was waiting for the right moment."

Malcolm snapped. "The right moment?"

"I was hoping for an opportunity to talk to Cleo, to see if I could find out who did this to her."

"It's not your place to talk to my child," Malcolm suddenly hissed. "You should have talked to me. You should have told me!"

Cilla nodded ever so slightly, tears welling in her eyes. "I was only trying to help, Malcolm."

"If you wanted to help you should have told me the minute you found out."

Cilla nodded again. "You're right," she said, her expression hardening. "I should have, but I didn't. Because I knew how difficult this was going to be for you and for Cleo. Most especially for Cleo and I was hoping I could figure out how to make it better before I did have to tell you."

"You didn't have any right to keep this from me," Malcolm snarled, his expression heated.

"Malcolm, there is nothing you can say to me that I haven't already said to myself. I've been beating myself up over this and I'm sorry. All I can do now is apologize to you. If you want to be mad at me, be mad. If you want to yell at me, then yell. I can take whatever you need to dish out. But whatever you need to do, however you need to take out your anger, you take it out on me before you have to confront your baby girl because she needs your support and love right now and nothing more."

Malcolm moved onto his feet. He muttered between clenched teeth. "Well, thank you for that but I think I'm fully capable of figuring out what my daughter needs." Then without another word he turned and hurried out the door.

Outside the cold air hit him like a much needed slap in the face. He suddenly felt numb and deflated, all the wind knocked from his sails. He slid into the driver's seat of his car but he didn't bother to start the engine, suddenly unsure of where he was going or what he planned to do.

Malcolm suddenly felt overwhelmed, unable to fathom the magnitude of what he had to deal with. He suddenly felt like he'd failed Cleo, not to know that this had happened to her. And he had questions. Who had done this to her, and when? And what about Claudia? Was she caught up in this mess as well?

He was still holding tight to that phone and he opened it again, scrolling through the dark images. He paused on a photo of Cleo, the hazy figure of someone in the picture with her, his hands where they should not have been. Someone had touched his baby, stealing her innocence, and Malcolm was suddenly ready to kill. Something like rage swelled full and thick through his spirit. He threw the phone, hard, and it ricocheted off the dashboard to the floorboard beneath his feet. He slammed his fists against the steering wheel, over and over, until he didn't have the strength to hit anything more. Tears clouded his vision and he slumped over the steering wheel sobbing like a baby.

Inside the coffee shop Cilla sat alone, fighting not to cry. The moment had gone as bad as she'd anticipated and she still hadn't been prepared. Malcolm had been angry, his words harsh, but beneath all that he'd been hurt. Cilla's heart was broken as she thought about the look that had been in his eyes, knowing that she had been partly responsible for putting it there.

Cilla rose from her seat. Grabbing both cups of coffee off the table she tossed them into the trash basket at the door. Stepping outside she felt numb, no longer feeling the cold morning air. Looking across the parking lot she saw Malcolm sitting in his car, his body hunched forward, his arms wrapped around his head. She could only begin to imagine the pain he was feeling.

Cilla headed toward her own car, tossing one last look over her shoulder. She'd only taken two, maybe three steps before turning an about-face. She swiped a hand over her eyes, brushing away the tears that had begun to fall. With an air of determination she strode quickly to Malcolm's car. After opening the passenger door, she slid inside. Startled, Malcolm turned abruptly. Cilla held up both her hands, the stance defensive. The two sat staring at each other, neither saying a word. Minutes passed and Cilla swore she could hear both their hearts beating harshly in their chests.

She blew a deep sigh, then nodded ever so slightly. Malcolm shook his head, his tears still flowing. Reaching her arms out Cilla wrapped them around his shoulders, pulling him to her. He fell forward against her chest, easing his own arms around her waist. They clung to each other. He cried, unable to contain the hurt that consumed him. He cried and Cilla held him, her tears finally merging with his.

* * *

"Did Daddy say why we get to stay home today?" Claudia asked.

She and Cleo were sitting at the kitchen counter as their grandmother prepared their morning meal. Fried bacon scented the air and the aroma of blueberry muffins was starting to waft from the convection oven.

Mama Claudette shook her head. "No. Your father called and just said to keep you home today. He said he would contact the school for your homework."

"Something must be wrong," Cleo muttered. She tossed her sister a look and Claudia shrugged her narrow shoulders.

Mama Claudette lifted her gaze from the bowl of eggs she was whisking. "Your father will explain when he gets here. You two don't need to speculate about his reasons for doing what he does. You just need to do what you're told. Is that understood?"

"Yes, ma'am!" both girls chorused as they stole another glance at each other.

Minutes later the three were eating, their plates filled with scrambled eggs, bacon, muffins, and hash brown potatoes. Large glasses of freshly squeezed orange juice completed their meals. When Malcolm and Cilla entered the room, laughter rang through the space, the girls enjoying playing hooky with their grandmother.

"Good morning," Mama Claudette chimed. Her smile dimmed slightly as she noticed the tension that creased her son's brow. She pulled her smile tighter as she met Cilla's stare.

"Hi, Mama Claudette," Cilla said, her voice soft and low.

The matriarch nodded. "It's good to see you again, Cilla. Did you two have a good run?" she asked, assuming that both had gotten their days' worth of exercise.

"I didn't run, ma'am."

The older woman nodded. "That coffee, huh?"

Cilla smiled. "That and your son."

Mama Claudette laughed. She stole a glance toward Malcolm who met the look. Theirs was a silent conversation as she tried to discern the look on his face, his expression less than cheerful. She rose from her seat and moved to his side, leaning up to kiss his cheek. "Can I get either of you something to eat?" she questioned.

They both answered no, Malcolm staring stone-faced as Cilla shook her head.

Despite his best efforts Malcolm was unable to hide the emotion that consumed him, the wealth of it painted across his face. Both girls were eyeing their father curiously. Cleo met the look her father was giving her and she began to shake, a wave of anxiety falling over her spirit. Her head snapped from him to Cilla and back and in that instance she knew that what she had hoped to keep secret had been exposed. An uncomfortable silence swept through the room.

Cleo jumped from her seat, spilling her juice onto the table. Tears began to stream down her face, her cheeks swelling red from her rising blood pressure. She was suddenly angry at the world. "You told!" she screamed, directing her comment at Cilla. "Why did you tell?"

Cilla's own anxiety rose tenfold. "I'm so sorry, Cleo!"

Malcolm moved toward his daughter. Resting his hands against her thin shoulders he pulled her to him, wrapping her in a deep embrace. He pressed a kiss to the top of her head, holding her tightly as she stood shaking in his arms. "We need to talk," he said softly.

"I'm sorry, Daddy! I'm so sorry, Daddy!" she sobbed, her tears dampening the front of his shirt.

"It's going to be okay, kiddo. Daddy promises. Everything is going to be okay," Malcolm said as he led Cleo from the room. He shot his mother and Cilla a quick look before the two disappeared up to the young girl's room.

Claudia swiped her forearm across her eyes, her own tears blocking her sight. Cilla took a deep breath as she moved to the table and took a seat beside the young girl. Wrapping her arms around her shoulders she gave her a quick hug, rubbing her palm gently across her back.

"Is Daddy mad?" Claudia asked, lifting her gaze to Cilla's.

She shook her head. "No. Your daddy's just worried about you and your sister." A wave of understanding seemed to sweep between them.

Mama Claudette stood watching, a host of questions spilling from her eyes. She crossed the room and joined them at a table. "Would someone please tell me what's going on?"

Cilla looked at Claudia, her eyebrows raised. The little girl took a deep breath, biting nervously against her bottom lip. She wiggled fretfully in her seat before she spoke.

"The last time we went to Baltimore with Mommy, Cleo snuck out and went to a party with Candy Man."

"Candy Man?" Mama Claudette's eyes widened.

Claudia nodded. "He let her drink and she smoked and she didn't get back until the next morning."

"And your mother didn't know?"

The girl didn't answer, her gaze dropping as if there was something she was afraid to tell. The two women exchanged a look.

Her grandmother asked about Shanell a second time. "Claudia, where was your mother, baby?"

Claudia met the look her grandmother was giving her, blowing a low breath as if to dispel the burden that hung heavy over her spirit. "Candy gave her some money and told her to go to the dope house," she whispered.

Mama Claudette bristled. "Baby girl, why didn't you tell your daddy?"

The child shrugged, tears pooling at the edge of her eyes. "We didn't want mommy to get into trouble."

"Did you go to that party?" Cilla asked softly.

Claudia shook her head. "No. That was the weekend my cycle started and I had really bad cramps. Mama gave me a pain pill and it made me sleepy. I fell asleep."

Mama Claudette nodded. "Where was Maxine?"

"Grandma Maxine was out of town that week. Mama didn't tell Daddy because she didn't want him to say we couldn't go to Baltimore with her. And he would have made us stay home if he knew Grandma wasn't there."

"So you were at the house by yourself?"

Claudia nodded.

"Did Shanell know Cleo went to a party with Candy Man?" Mama Claudette asked again.

Claudia hesitated for a brief moment before answering. "Candy Man threatened to tell Daddy something bad about Mommy if she didn't let us go to the party. He said if we went then she wouldn't owe him anymore."

"And they said all this in front of you and your sister?"

"No, ma'am. They were fighting in the bedroom and we were eavesdropping."

Cilla reached her hand out to Mama Claudette, gently caressing the old woman's shoulder. The two women exchanged a look and Mama Claudette tried to pull her full lips into a smile. She turned her attention back to Claudia.

"Did Cleo tell you what else happened at the party?" Cilla asked.

Claudia hesitated a second time then nodded. "I think it was bad," she whispered, her head shaking vehemently. "It was really bad."

Mama Claudette gasped loudly. Both of her fists were clenched tightly. Her face was flushed and she was visibly shaken. She took a breath and held it to calm her nerves. "Cilla, do you mind staying with Claudia while I go check on the rest of my family, please?"

"Not at all. We'll be fine. Take all the time you need."

"Thank you," Mama Claudette muttered as she exited the room.

Claudia turned around to stare at her. Cilla met her gaze and gave the girl a smile, hoping her expression didn't show the stress she was feeling. Claudia smiled back, lifting her lips into the slightest bend.

"Candy Man put those pictures on that website," she said, staring intently.

Cilla nodded. "Is Candy Man the man in the pictures with your sister?"

She shook her head no. "His name's Nikko. But Cleo doesn't remember what happened. She thinks they put something in her drink. I should have told. I made it worse, didn't I?" Claudia dropped her gaze to the floor.

Cilla reached out to give the girl another hug. "No. You didn't do anything wrong. You were trying to protect your sister."

"I just think we made a mess out of everything."

"You and your sister can't blame yourselves. And your dad is going to get it all fixed. But you and your sister need to trust him. If anything like this ever happens again, you have to tell him. And if you can't tell him, you need to talk to someone."

The girl nodded. "What's going to happen now?"

Cilla paused, uncertain herself about what was going to happen next. She lifted her eyes to find Claudia staring. "Right now, you and I are going to clean the kitchen up for your grandmother. After that, we'll see!"

* * *

When his mother entered the room, Malcolm had been standing at the window, his arms wrapped tight around his torso. Cleo sat on top of her bed, curled in a fetal position, tears still raining down her cheeks. He'd been fighting to contain his anger but as his daughter had spilled every last dirty detail he found himself wanting to rage.

Mama Claudette shifted her gaze from him to Cleo and back. He shook his head, unable to verbalize what was on his heart. She sensed his distress but she didn't say anything. Moving to the bed she eased her plump body next to her granddaughter's and pulled the young woman into her lap, gently caressing her hair.

No one spoke for minutes, the quiet in the room feeling thunderous. Both Cleo and Mama Claudette sat waiting for Malcolm to give them direction, neither knowing what was going through his head, unable to gauge his emotion. He finally cleared his throat as he moved to where they sat, coming to a stop at the foot of the bed. "I think you girls should call Grandma Maxine and head up to that shopping outlet. She needs a break and I think spending time with all of you would do her some good."

"That sounds like a good idea," Mama Claudette said. "I'm sure we'll have a good time."

Cleo sat up, staring at her father. She rubbed the tears from her eyes, brushing her fingers across her cheeks. "Do you hate me, Daddy?"

His expression was incredulous. "Of course not!"

He cupped her face between his palms. "Baby girl, Daddy could never hate you! I love you more than anything else in this world," he said emphatically. "Don't you ever forget that!" He pressed his lips to her forehead. "Now, why don't you go find your sister so you two can call your grandmother Maxine. And let me speak to her before you hang up, please."

Nodding, Cleo slid her thin frame off the bed. She turned to give her grandmother a quick hug. As she passed her father she threw herself into his arms, wrapping her own around his thick neck. He held her tightly, wishing for a brief second that she were five years old again when everything about her small world was good. When ugly and evil had just been words she didn't understand. He kissed the side of her face and gave her a tap across her backside as he shooed her out the door.

For a brief moment Malcolm and his mother stood staring at each other. Both were struggling with a wealth of emotion that neither could comprehend. Mama Claudette finally broke the quiet between them.

"Was she . . . ?" The old woman bit down against her bottom lip, afraid to say what she'd been thinking. She took a deep breath. "Did he violate her?"

Malcolm shook his head. "I don't know. She says that she drank and she smoked marijuana. She remembers someone taking off her clothes and she knows there were pictures taken. She says some man told her she was going to be a movie star. But she doesn't remember anything else. At least not anything she's comfortable telling me."

"I think I need to call Dr. Smith and make an appointment for her to be checked. We need to have

Cleo examined to make sure she's okay. So we know exactly what we're dealing with."

Malcolm nodded. "Tell him it's an emergency. The sooner he can see her the better. Hopefully he'll have an appointment this morning before you leave. If not, then definitely as soon as you get back."

His mother leveled her gaze on his face. "What are you going to do?" she asked.

Malcolm met the look she was giving him. "I'm going to Baltimore to get some answers."

Chapter Ten

"What now?" Cilla asked, repeating the question Claudia had asked of her.

He was pulling his car out of the driveway, easing the vehicle into midday traffic. The morning had flown by since their encounter in the coffee shop and the drama that had ensued. Cilla thought back to everything that had transpired since. She blew a low sigh, still waiting for him to respond.

They'd spent the afternoon helping his mother while she ran Cleo to their family doctor. It had devastated Malcolm to think his little girl might have to be further traumatized by a pelvic exam, be checked for STDs or given a pregnancy test. She was barely a teenager and he found it all too much for him to handle. But relief had come when the doctor had confirmed that she was still a virgin, the violation not the worse that they'd imagined. But Malcolm was still angry that he'd been unable to keep her safe and someone had tried to take advantage of her. His mood had shifted and Cilla could see the beginnings of a downhill spiral.

To give them all a hand Cilla had helped Claudia pack for her and her sister and had arranged for a car service while Malcolm coordinated their schedule with their Baltimore relative. Cleo had been cordial to her at best, still clearly miffed that Cilla was even breathing, least of all, in their home trying to help. Cilla knew that it was going to take some time for Cleo to warm up to her. Under their current circumstances she figured she could endure the hostility for a while longer.

When Malcolm didn't respond she asked a second time. "So, what do you plan to do now?"

He stared at her. "I'm going to drop you back off to your car. You're already late for work and I can't impose on you any longer. Then I'm going to Baltimore."

"I've already called my job and told them I'm not coming in for a few days. You're not going to Baltimore by yourself. That's not happening."

"You need to stay out of this," Malcolm retorted. "It's not your problem."

"That's not going to happen either," Cilla snapped.

He shook his head. "Why are you doing this?"

There was a moment of hesitation as she pondered his question. Cilla shifted in her seat, turning her body to face him. "I love you. That's why."

Malcolm's head snapped in her direction, the car slowing abruptly. She continued before he could respond.

"If we're going to Baltimore I need to go pack a bag. My car can stay where it is for now."

With nothing else to say, Malcolm nodded, accelerating the vehicle as he turned his attention back to the road. Minutes later he sat in Cilla's living room, waiting as she grabbed a quick shower and tossed clothes into an overnight bag. With everything spinning through his head he was finding it difficult to focus.

The sound of running water echoed in the distance as he sat in a stupor, thoughts of the woman tripping through all the other muddled mess in his mind. She loved him. Her speaking the words had surprised him and only because he had not expected them to be spoken when they had. The moment they'd passed her lips he'd felt it with every fiber in his being. It had been on the tip of his tongue to say them back, the emotion deeply embedded in his heart, but the trauma of his other issues had held them in check. For the first time in a long time uncertainty had rippled through his system.

He was suddenly aware of movement in the other room. From his seat on the sofa he could see through the partially closed door into Cilla's bedroom. She was naked and as she moved past the door's opening he caught a quick glimpse of her bare assets. His breath caught deep in his chest as he held an inhale of air in his lungs.

Every dip and curve was stunning. Her breasts, hips, and thighs were thick and full, complemented by the cinch of her waistline. Cilla was so beautiful that he felt like the luckiest man in the world. He shifted forward in his seat, talking himself out of going to her. He was suddenly caught off guard when she stepped out of the room, a silk bathrobe tied loosely around her waist.

"I'm sorry," she said, smiling sweetly. "I promise I won't be much longer. I had to make a few phone calls and now I just need to grab some clothes from the washroom."

"You're fine," Malcolm mumbled, clasping his hands together tightly in his lap.

She smiled again as she swept past him toward her kitchen. She returned a moment later with a small pile of clothes in her hands.

Malcolm moved onto his feet, blocking her path. His breath was heavy as he panted ever so slightly. They locked gazes, staring intently. Malcolm eased both of his hands beneath her robe. When his fingers touched bare flesh she gasped, his heated touch trailing around her waist to the lush curve of her buttocks. He stepped against her, pulling her close as he dropped his mouth to hers. The kiss was easy and gentle, the lightest touch against the softest skin. He trailed his hands across her back, her robe pulling open enough to expose the black lace bra and panty she'd slipped into. Her skin was damp and warm, still heated from the hot shower she'd taken. The kiss deepened, her tongue searching his as their lips danced sweetly together. Her own hands were still holding tight to the laundry she'd claimed from the dryer.

His mouth tangoed a minute longer against hers before he broke the connection. He continued to hold tightly to her, the embrace feeling like the sweetest balm as he nestled his face in her hair, feeling his heartbeat sync in time with hers. He took a step back, allowing his arms to fall back to his sides, his hands folded into tight fists. For a brief moment they stood staring, there being no need for words. Malcolm shifted his body, taking a step back out of her way. Cilla continued toward her bedroom. Minutes later she returned wearing well-worn jeans, a novelty-printed T-shirt, and high-heeled boots.

She paused at the front door, gesturing in his direction. "I'm ready, baby," she said softly.

Malcolm smiled back, rising slowly to his feet. Uncertainty flickered in his dark stare. Although the words were unspoken, Cilla could see that he really wasn't sure whether or not he would ever be ready.

Cilla didn't recognize the woman standing in the center of the nightclub with Romeo. She did however know the man who stood in conversation with them. Special Agent Randolph Taylor was still tall, dark and handsome, not looking as if he'd aged at all since they'd ended their two-year relationship five years ago. She didn't miss the lift to his eyes when he spied her coming through the door ahead of Malcolm. Neither did Malcolm as he took note of the stranger's presence. Cilla could feel him tense as they all turned to stare, their chatter coming to an abrupt halt.

"Hey, what's up," Malcolm said as the two of them moved to join the others. He shook Romeo's hand then leaned to hug the woman at Romeo's elbow.

When Cilla walked into the other man's outstretched arms, hugging him warmly, the jealous expression across Malcolm's face was noticed by them all. Malcolm extended his hand in introduction.

"Malcolm Cobb, and you are?"

"I'm Special Agent Randolph Taylor," he answered, shaking the man's hand.

"Special Agent?"

Cilla nodded. "Randolph and I are old friends. I called and asked him to meet us here."

Malcolm's gaze narrowed. His jaw tightened as he clenched his teeth tightly together.

"Hi, you must be Cilla. I'm Aleta Bowen," the other woman said, introducing herself. "I've heard a lot about you."

"Good things I hope," Cilla smiled.

"Very good things."

"Aleta is my godmother and a really good friend to us all," Romeo explained.

"So what's going on here?" Malcolm questioned, looking from one to the other.

Romeo dropped a heavy hand against his friend's shoulder. "Cilla called and told me what was going on. I called Aunt Aleta to come watch the club for us while we're in Baltimore."

"Priscilla called me as well," the special agent interjected. "I actually came to advise you against going to Baltimore."

Malcolm shot the man a hostile look. "What's it to you?"

"I work the sex crimes unit out of the FBI's Raleigh field office."

A flash of anger washed over Malcolm's expression. He cut a narrowed gaze toward Cilla, heat flushing his dark cheeks. Hearing a stranger verbalize what had happened to his baby girl as a sex crime was suddenly debilitating, every ounce of his internal fortitude feeling as if it had been shattered. He broke stance, striding abruptly to the bar. They all watched as he pulled a bottle of vodka from the shelf, dropping it and a shot glass onto the counter.

He stood staring at the drink, every muscle shaking with indecision.

"Why don't you all sit down," Aleta said softly. She moved to the back of the bar where Malcolm stood, dropping her palm against the back of his hand. She shook her head as Malcolm met the look she was giving him.

Romeo had moved to the bar as well, standing on the other side. "You don't want to do that," he said, his comment directed at Malcolm. "You're going to be no good to us if you take that drink."

Cilla called his name from across the room. "Please, don't," she said. "Think about the girls."

He took a deep inhale of air, releasing his grip on that bottle as Aleta took it from his hands. He moved around to the front of the bar to Cilla's side. She grabbed his hand, kissing the back of it as they both took a seat across from her old friend.

Agent Taylor looked from one to the other. His gaze rested on Cilla's face for a second longer than necessary. He forced himself to turn his eyes back on Malcolm as he spoke. "Cilla sent me the links to the website where your daughter's photos were uploaded. My team has already shut it down and we're working on tracing it back to its owners."

"So no one can see those pictures now?"

"Not on that site, Mr. Cobb, and we're tracing whether or not they were uploaded to any other internet sites. Unfortunately, the nature of the sex trade business is that a new internet site pops up as fast as we can get them taken down. Their IP addresses are wide and sweeping."

Malcolm's sigh was heavy. He nodded his understanding. "So now what?" he asked, suddenly grateful that someone else might have the answer to that question.

"Now, you let us handle this. Cilla says your daughter identified two of the men. The one in the picture with her and the other who was responsible for her being at the party. Is that correct?"

Malcolm shook his head. "She told me who took her to the party. His name is Bynum. Ray Bynum. They call him Candy Man. He's been dealing drugs on the streets of Baltimore for years. But she didn't say anything to me about who the guy in the picture was. She said she didn't know him."

Randolph tossed Cilla a questioning look.

She took a deep breath, realizing that the information Cleo had shared with her father lacked some of the details Claudia had shared with her. She felt both men eyeing her, waiting for her to comment.

"Claudia told me the man in the picture is named Nikko."

Malcolm bristled. "Nikko Prince?"

"She didn't tell me his last name."

"Do you know him?" Randolph questioned.

"Nikko Prince is my ex-wife's current boyfriend. He's the lowest form of scum there is."

"What's your ex-wife's name?"

"Shanell Cobb. She sometimes uses her maiden name. Perry."

They all watched as the agent jotted notes into a lined notebook. Malcolm suddenly slammed a fist against the wooden table. Everyone in the room held a collective breath.

Randolph leaned back in his seat. "Mr. Cobb, I don't have any children of my own so I'm not going to sit here and pretend that I know how you feel or that I understand what you and your family are going through. But I deal with this every day. That's why I'm asking you to trust me. Let the bureau handle this. Please. You don't need to take matters into your own hands. All that's going to do is make my job harder and risk you or someone else getting hurt. Your girls don't need that. Right now they just need you to be their father, not a vigilante."

When Malcolm didn't bother to reply, the man continued. "Before I leave here, Mr. Cobb, we'll already have warrants issued for both men. The Baltimore field office will execute those warrants as quickly as possible."

Malcolm nodded, grinding his back teeth.

"We're also going to need to interview your daughters. If you have a family attorney, they can be present and because of the sensitive nature of the crime we'll make sure a female agent does the questioning."

There was a moment of silence as Malcolm reflected on the man's words. He finally nodded his head. "The girls are headed to Potomac Mills with their grandmothers. I can make arrangements for you to talk to them when they get back."

"Would you agree to allow one of our agents to meet them in Virginia later today? The sooner we can talk to them the better."

"Why the rush? You already have the names of the two men involved."

Randolph paused. He tossed Cilla a look before focusing back on Malcolm. "This case is bigger than you might realize. We've linked this site and others to a string of child abductions and sex trafficking cases that cross five states that we're aware of. Your daughter is one of the few young girls we've been able to identify who might have information that can point us in the right direction. She's also one of the lucky ones. This is very important because most of these children aren't so fortunate."

Cilla squeezed his hand. Malcolm blew another heavy sigh.

"Yeah, all right," he said with a quick nod. "But their grandmothers need to be there with them. I don't want any agent talking to either one of my daughters without them there."

Randolph extended his hand, shaking Malcolm's in agreement. "I'll be touch," he said, rising from his seat.

Cilla stood with him. "I'll walk you out," she said. She avoided the look Malcolm gave her as he shifted his gaze between the two of them.

Outside Randolph hugged her again, his embrace lingering. "I've missed you," he said as she pulled herself from his arms. "I was surprised to hear from you."

"I needed your help and I know you're the best."

The man nodded. "Your friend seems like a good guy. But I did some digging. He's got a past."

Cilla gave him a look, her brow furrowing with annoyance. "We all have a past, Randolph. And there's nothing you can tell me about Malcolm that I don't already know."

Randolph nodded. "Well, just try to rein him in. He doesn't need to do anything stupid."

"He won't."

"You hope not."

Cilla pulled her gaze from his, turning to stare down the empty sidewalk.

Randolph drew his hand across her cheek, the gentle caress reminding them both of their good times together.

She cut her eye back in his direction. "I need to get back inside. Thank you again for everything."

Randolph nodded. "There's not much I wouldn't do for you, Cilla. That's the only reason I'm here now. I hope you know that."

Turning an about-face, Randolph headed in the direction of the parking lot. Cilla watched until he was out of sight. Then she headed back inside the nightclub.

Despite their best efforts neither of them had been able to convince Malcolm to stay in Raleigh. The man was determined to go to Baltimore, claiming he needed to find Shanell for some answers. Cilla was grateful for Romeo, the man joining them on the trip. They'd been in the air for less than an hour and Malcolm had barely spoken ten words to her. He was angry and she knew he needed to process the emotion before they discussed it. Romeo tossed her a sympathetic look as Malcolm made his way to the bathroom, securing the door behind him.

"You did the right thing," he said.

She blew a loud sigh. "I hope so. He's not happy with me right now though."

"He cares about you. And he knows you care about him. This is just hard for him. I imagine it would be hard for any man."

"I can only imagine," Cilla said softly.

Romeo shook his head. "I don't know what I'd do. If someone hurt my son it would probably take an army to keep me from seeing red and not acting on it."

"I'm glad you came. I don't know if I can help if anything jumps off."

"We're not going to let anything jump off. I promise that."

"He's lucky to have you for a friend."

Romeo shrugged his broad shoulders. "I'm the lucky one. Malcolm got me through a really rough time last year. I don't know if I would have made it without him. I owe him and there's nothing I wouldn't do for him."

Malcolm's voice suddenly rang from the back of the plane. "You two could at least wait until we land before you start to talk about me."

Romeo laughed. "At least we were saying nice things about you."

Malcolm dropped back into his seat. "So you say."

"I got your back, bro!"

The two men exchanged a quick look between them that made Cilla smile. For a split second Malcolm actually smiled back and then he closed his eyes and took himself a quick nap.

Chapter Eleven

Shanell Cobb sat in an old building, on an old sofa, both of which had seen better times. The room was dimly lit, the air putrid and dank. Another couple lay curled around each other on a small loveseat and a man cowered in the far corner, rocking his large, naked body back and forth. He swatted imaginary flies from around his head, spittle seeping from the corner of his mouth like water from an open spigot. Shanell didn't know any of them and didn't care if they knew her.

Her hand was shaking as she placed two tic-tac-sized chunks of black tar heroin onto a silver spoon. She squirted a minute amount of water on top of it and then flicked a lighter across the spoon's bottom to dissolve the combination. When it was ready, she rolled a wad of cotton into a small ball and dropped it into the drug, watching as it puffed up like a sponge.

She carefully pushed the tip of a syringe into the center of the cotton and pulled the plunger back slowly until all of the substance was sucked into it, the cotton filtering out any trash. She cast her gaze back toward them, smiling ever so slightly as recognition washed over her.

She'd already tied off her arm with a rubber strap, a good vein protruding against her warm caramel flesh. The rest of her journey would be all uphill, Shanell mused as she inserted the needle into the length of her vein, insuring that it was where it needed to be.

Seconds later there was a surge of euphoria and she suddenly felt like all was well in the world again. It was a cheap but effective high. Minutes passed and her mouth was dry, her skin flush with heat. Her limbs felts heavy and her thoughts were finally clouded. Soon she was on the nod, alternating between a state of wakefulness and drowsiness. She was grateful for it, welcoming the deep sleep that she knew would soon consume her.

As she slowly drifted into a world of her own making, Shanell suddenly thought of the man standing there in her dreams, a wealth of sadness seeping from his eyes. She wished she'd had an opportunity to tell him something that could have taken that sadness from him. A story that would have soothed his heartache. And then just like that she couldn't think of anything else, all of her senses flying like the blackbird in one of her favorite songs.

Cilla was exhausted but she didn't complain. She'd been struggling to keep up for the last few hours as Malcolm and Romeo had hurried from one spot to another. At every stop there was someone who knew Malcolm or whom he knew, yet no one had seen his ex-wife or had any knowledge of where she might be. Until the last stop.

The building looked condemned, an empty shell of a space that held nothing good for anyone. The man at the door had recognized Malcolm, posturing slightly as he barred them from entering. They had only been permitted inside when Malcolm had palmed a twenty-dollar bill into his hand and Romeo threatened him.

Shanell sat on a dirty sofa in a drug fueled stupor. An older version of her twin daughters, it wasn't too difficult to understand Malcolm's attraction to the woman. Her hair was disheveled and it was clear that she hadn't had a bath in days. Dirt caked her fingernails and the thin sundress she wore was tattered. But even in her disarray her good looks shone through.

Cilla struggled not to cry, her emotions suddenly on sensory overload. Two steps ahead of her Malcolm came to an abrupt stop, his gaze like a laser focusing on his ex-wife. He called the woman's name and she shushed him. He called it a second time and she held up her hand, giving him her palm. Annoyance painted her expression as she struggled to get her hit. Behind him Cilla and Romeo could only stand and watch, all of them feeling like they'd been dropped dead center into a bad movie.

Cilla felt Malcolm cringe as he stood staring and she hung back, suddenly feeling like she was intruding on a private moment between the two of them. Romeo sensed her rising anxiety and he pressed a gentle hand against her back as they waited to follow Malcolm's lead. Once again the two men exchanged a look and Cilla couldn't help but sense them having a silent conversation that she wasn't privy to.

"Shanell!" Malcolm called out her name. "Shanell! Wake up!"

With a groggy stare Shanell lifted her head from the coffee table, struggling to focus. A wide smile suddenly pulled at her mouth as she jumped to her feet, throwing her arms around Malcolm's neck.

"Malcolm!" Despite the gruff, cracking tone, excitement rang in her voice. "I missed you!"

Malcolm grabbed her arms and pulled them back down to her sides. She fell back into her seat laughing foolishly. "Have a drink with me," she said, gesturing for an imaginary bartender.

Malcolm took the seat beside the woman. Romeo and Cilla remained standing. Shanell looked from one to the other, her eyes squinting. She swiped her hand across her face, brushing snot from her nose onto the back of her hand. She wiped her hand onto her dress. "You don't want a drink?" she whined, pushing her lips into a pout.

"No, Shanell. I need to talk to you."

She blew a gust of air past her lips. "What now? Don't you spoil my good time 'cause I'm having a really good time."

Frustration painted Malcolm's face. "Did you know about Candy Man taking Cleo to a party the last time the girls were with you?"

Shanell rolled her eyes. "I don't owe Candy nothin'! I settled my debt!"

"Did you give him our daughter for payment?" Malcolm spat, venom punctuating each word.

A look of confusion washed over her expression.

"I . . . no . . . I . . ." She suddenly got angry. "Why are you bothering me? Leave me alone!" she exclaimed, her voice rising.

The man in the corner suddenly stopped rocking, tilting his head in their direction.

Romeo shook his head. He pressed a large hand to his friend's forearm. "Malcolm, we should go. You're not going to get any answers here."

Shanell shifted her eyes. Her smile returned bright and full. "Rome! Hey, Rome!" She leaned in his direction. "You want to buy me a drink?"

"Not today, Shanell."

The woman sucked her teeth, her eyes rolling toward the back of her head. "Tch!" She suddenly caught sight of Cilla, her gaze narrowing considerably as she looked her up and down. "Who are you?"

Cilla tried to force a smile onto her face, the slight bend to her lips looking more like a grimace. "I'm Cilla."

Shanell looked from Cilla to Romeo and back. "This ain't your wife!"

Malcolm took a deep breath. "Cilla is my friend."

Shanell's gaze narrowed even more but she didn't say anything. She cut her eyes back at Malcolm. "What do you want?"

"Where's Candy Man?"

"You wanna buy? I can take you to him. Candy Man's got good candy! We can get some good stuff, Malcolm. It'll have us feeling real good!" The woman's excitement seemed to return with a vengeance.

Malcolm nodded. "Yeah! Where can we find him?"

"He's down at Hollins. Hollins, that's where

he's at," she said, referring to the marketplace on Arlington Avenue.

"What about Nikko? Where's your boy at?"

"Nikko?" She looked confused again.

"Yeah, where's Nikko. I need to holler at him."

She shook her head. "I need some money, Malcolm. Can you lend me some money?"

Malcolm rose from his seat, Cilla and Romeo following his lead. He shook his head. "No. I don't have any money, Shanell."

And then he turned, heading toward the exit. Behind him Shanell called his name.

He turned around, meeting the look she was giving him. "What, Shanell?"

She screamed. "Keep that Cilla bitch away from my babies, you hear me! I don't want her nowhere near my girls!"

With a shake of his head, Malcolm slipped his arm around Cilla's waist. Together they exited the building as quickly as they'd entered.

Minutes later they found themselves at the two-story marketplace in southwest Baltimore. A typical row-front neighborhood bordered the old shopping center that housed an assortment of vendors hawking everything from fresh meat, seafood, and produce to baked goods, crafts, and clothing.

Nothing about the neighborhood was what Cilla was expecting. Children played along the sidewalk. Families sat out on stoops. Music sounded from someone's home. Corner storefronts boasted designer coffee and African artifacts. Cilla had expected dingy and dank, someplace that invoked fright and alarm, but there was nothing there that gave her that feeling.

Romeo pulled the car into a parking spot not far from the market entrance. Outside the front door a few men and boys were gathered in conversation. A woman pushing a stroller while her toddler clung to her pant leg hurried by, rushing to catch the MTA bus sitting at the corner. Cilla was content to sit and people watch until Malcolm reached into the front glove compartment and pulled out a gun. He pulled back the slide and looked down the chamber, checking to see that it was loaded.

"Why do you have that?" she suddenly questioned.

When he didn't answer immediately she asked again. "Malcolm?"

"Cilla, please!" he snapped.

Romeo tossed her a look.

"But you have a gun!" she snapped back, shifting to the edge of her seat.

"I also have a Maryland state conceal and carry license to own this gun," he said.

Cilla was suddenly on edge. "You don't need a gun, Malcolm. This isn't what I was expecting."

Malcolm and Romeo exchanged a look.

"It's just in case," Romeo said as he turned to meet Cilla's anxious stare. He tried to reassure her. "We don't know what we're dealing with. These men aren't necessarily on the up and up."

She looked into the rearview mirror to see Malcolm staring back at her. He tucked the weapon into the waistband of his pants, pulling his shirt to cover it. She heaved a nervous sigh.

Malcolm suddenly jumped. "That's him," he said, his eyes focused on a Bill Cosby look-alike.

Before Cilla or Romeo could respond Malcolm

was out the car and gone. Romeo jumped out behind him. He pointed a finger at Cilla. "Call your FBI friend and get some help. Tell him where we are. Tell him if he hurries he'll find Candy Man here or at Johns Hopkins Hospital if he takes too long."

"But he's in Raleigh!" Cilla quipped, her eyes wide.

"Call someone!" Romeo yelled. "And now!"

Shaking, Cilla's gaze followed Malcolm and Romeo into the building. When the door closed behind them she dialed 911.

Ray "Candy Man" Bynum was waiting for an order at Chuckie's Chicken when Malcolm caught up to him. With one hand he spun the man around, his gun aimed at his head. Candy Man was caught off guard, his eyes wide with fear.

"Hey, hey, hey, now! We ain't got no problems here!" the man sputtered, his hands up, palms forward.

"That's where you're wrong," Malcolm snarled.

Recognition suddenly swept over the old man.

"You . . . you . . . you kin to Miss Maxine, right? What you got me hemmed up for, man? I ain't do nothin' to you!"

Malcolm shook his head. "No, but you did something to my daughter. Maxine's granddaughter. You remember her? Shanell's baby girl?"

Something like real fear suddenly crossed the man's face. "'Dem twins! I know dem girls. I ain't touched neither one of dem girls!"

"But you know who did and you know who took pictures, don't you?"

Candy shook his head from side to side. "I don't know nothin'! I swear! I just drove her to meet her mama's boyfriend. I didn't do nothin' else."

Malcolm cocked the gun. Behind him Romeo called his name. The smell of warm urine suddenly punctuated the air, a puddle of moisture pooling at Candy Man's feet.

"Where can I find Nikko?" Malcolm snapped.

Candy Man was suddenly a blubbering mass of doughy flesh. He was visibly shaking, the gun pressing against his temple feeling very final.

Romeo called Malcolm's name a second time, his gaze sweeping over the crowd that had gathered to watch. "We need to go," he snapped, spying the security guard who was pointing two Baltimore police officers in their direction. Neither moved with any sense of urgency.

"I'm only going to ask you one more time," Malcolm said.

Candy nodded. "Club . . . Club . . . Club Mercury," he finally muttered.

With that Malcolm slammed his fist into the man's face, sending him to the floor. He hovered over him for a brief second before he secured his gun and adjusted his jacket, then just like that he and Romeo slipped through the crowd and away. As the cops helped Candy to his feet, slapping handcuffs on him, the two men eased their way right out the market's front door.

Cilla was standing nervously outside the car, wringing her hands anxiously. A wave of relief washed over her as the two men approached the vehicle, gesturing for her to get back inside. Romeo took the driver's seat, pulling into traffic, tossing one last look behind them.

"Club Mercury," Malcolm stated.

His friend shook his head. "No."

"What do you mean no?"

"I mean no. We're not going to that club. The police will be there soon enough. We're not going to try to beat them there."

"I'm going to that club."

"There's nothing there waiting for you but trouble, Malcolm."

"I thought you had my back?"

"I do but I'm not going to let you do anything stupid and you're walking a very fine line."

"I'm going to that club," Malcolm repeated.

"Over my dead body," Romeo quipped.

The look Malcolm gave his friend was chilling. "Whatever it takes," he said, his tone lashing.

Romeo laughed. "Give it your best shot, bro."

From the backseat Cilla watched the exchange as if she were watching a tennis match. A blanket of silence fell over the car, neither of them having anything else to say. Cilla was anxious to know what had happened back at the market but she didn't ask, not sure she could handle the answer.

An hour later they were checked into the Renaissance Baltimore Harborplace Hotel. Both men walked her to her hotel room door, wishing her a good night. Malcolm had the adjoining room next door. He disappeared inside, clearly distracted. Romeo headed down the hall to his own room.

As Cilla moved into her own space she didn't know what to think. Everything with Malcolm seemed to have gone from bad to worse and since the encounter with his ex-wife he'd become a thread shy of hostile, barely speaking to either of them. She stood at the door between their respective rooms. Her ear was pressed tight to the structure hoping to at least hear him moving inside. They needed to talk and she imagined that with his current state of mind she was going to have to initiate that conversation.

As she stood contemplating what she needed to do next there was a knock on her room door. Romeo stood on the other side, his gaze seeping with frustration.

"What's wrong?" Cilla asked, already knowing the answer before the man spoke.

He shook his head as he stepped past her, moving to the entrance between her room and the next. She shifted her gaze toward the connecting door, pushing past the man as she rushed to open it. Undoing the latch she stepped over the threshold into the other room. Malcolm's bag sat on the floor in the entrance, everything else in place as it had been when they'd checked in.

Romeo tossed up his hands. "He's gone!"

It was some ungodly hour in the morning when Malcolm finally returned to his hotel room. As he entered he came to an abrupt stop, surprised to find Cilla sound asleep in his bed. The door between his hotel room and hers was wide open, every light illuminating the two spaces.

She lay in a fetal position, her body tense. Even in her sleep he could sense that he had put her through an unnecessary amount of stress. He was suddenly kicking himself for being so insensitive. He blew a deep sigh as he eased his body down onto the foot of the bed. He rested his elbows on his thighs, dropping his head into his hands.

He didn't have any excuses for his bad behavior. He had known better. He should have done better. He'd gone on the offensive, then he'd built a wall between them, shutting her out. He'd not been at his best. He would understand it if Cilla never wanted to have anything else to do with him but he hoped she'd be able to see past his momentary indiscretion and give him another chance. Then again, he wondered if their roles were reversed if he could be as forgiving.

He sat in reflection for a good while, thinking back to everything that had happened, how his life had suddenly changed. Then he sat in prayer, needing guidance and strength. Malcolm knew beyond any doubt that if he were going to be a pillar for his daughters he was going to need some divine intervention to see him through. Easing off the bed so he didn't disturb Cilla's rest he dropped onto his knees in prayer, his hands clasped together in front of his face. He prayed like he had not prayed in a very long time, wanting more than anything to be able to get both of his girls past their trauma and help his family find the healing they were all going to need.

With the final amen he sat back on his haunches, his gaze shifting up to where Cilla lay staring at him. She met his eyes with her own concerned stare. She lifted her body upright, shifting back against the headboard. A slight smile pulled at her full lips and he could see it in her eyes that she was relieved to see him.

"Hey," he whispered.

"Hey yourself," she whispered back.

"I'm sorry," Malcolm said softly. "I just . . . I . . ." He blew a loud sigh. "I have no excuses."

Cilla nodded. "I think I understand. I really do."

"I wish I did. I just don't know anything anymore."

Malcolm rose off his knees, climbing into the bed. He pulled himself up till his back was against the headboard, his body resting beside hers.

"What happened, Malcolm?" she asked. "Did you find that guy at the club?"

He shook his head. "No. I waited but he never came. Then your friend called me. They actually found him down in South Carolina. He'd been picked up there last week on another charge. Your buddy Randolph didn't give me the details but it sounded like this guy's been doing a lot of dirt."

"So where've you been all this time?"

Malcolm heaved a deep sigh. "Fighting the urge to take a drink. I sat at that bar and all I wanted was to make it all go away. I figured one drink and I'd be able to numb all this hurt."

"But you didn't."

"No, I didn't," he said, shaking his head. "I thought about my mother and my daughters and I thought about you. And I knew it wasn't worth it."

"I was so worried about you and that damn gun and knowing how angry you were. . . ." She paused, fighting to make her words make sense. "I just . . ."

Malcolm reached for her hand, entwining her

fingers between his own. He squeezed it gently. "I'm so sorry," he said.

She gave him another look, cutting her eyes in his direction. "What would you have done if you'd found him, Malcolm?"

He looked back at her, pondering her question. "I don't know," he said, his answer as honest as he could muster. "Cilla, I have never been as angry as I am now over this mess. That bastard put his hands on my baby girl and I wasn't there to protect her. I wanted to hurt him the way he hurt her. I want him to suffer like she's suffered. I hate to think that I'd be capable of harming another human being but I'd be lying if I told you I wouldn't have killed him. Because I really wanted to see him dead. I still do."

"At least you're being honest with yourself."

"I have to be honest. My integrity is all I have."

"Romeo was worried about you too."

"I know. I called him. He helped talk me down. But he also knew that I had to work through it on my own."

"Well, I'm not going to lie. I was afraid you were going to shoot someone. You have a gun, Malcolm!"

He chuckled softly. "I have a few guns, but they're all legal and I know how to handle them."

"That may be an issue. I don't like guns. They scare me."

"That's fair but let me teach you how to handle one before you count them out."

Cilla paused. "Okay," she said, "but only if we do something about that bad attitude of yours. You're moody. And you shut me out. That was not good."

He paused, ruminating on her comment. "I agree," he said finally. "And I'm willing to get some help. I've decided that the girls and I need to go back to family counseling and I'm willing to do couple's counseling if you want me to. Because I want us to work, Cilla." He squeezed her hand tightly. "I love you, too, and I don't want to lose you."

Cilla squeezed back, his words warming her spirit. She took a deep breath and blew it out slowly. "I didn't know that things with your ex-wife were as bad as they are."

His sigh was heavy and void of any emotion. "Neither did I. I thought she might be using again but I wasn't sure. When I said something she denied it and child services never found anything when I complained to them. Until she showed up at the club the other week I had no idea that she'd gone downhill as badly as she has. And knowing that she purposely put our child in harm's way? I can't tell you what that did to me!"

"Was it that bad when your marriage broke up?"

He started to shake his head in response, then he paused. "That's a lie. It was that bad and I should have known better. Shanell hurt my heart. Bad. I understood that her addiction was an illness. I got all that. But I wanted to believe that her love for me and the girls was bigger than her love for the drugs and it wasn't. When it got really bad I knew that I had to leave if I wanted to survive. So this time I shouldn't have missed the signs. I shouldn't have trusted her. But I did and now Cleo's paying the price. I failed her."

Cilla could feel his pain, the knife in his chest feeling as if it had pierced her own heart. She would have done anything to take that hurt from him. She eased into his side, leaning her head on his shoulder. They sat together for a few more minutes, neither saying a word. Malcolm broke the silence.

"So what's the deal with you and agent man?"

Cilla laughed, her head waving. "No deal. He's just an old friend. I trust him and I knew he could help."

"He still loves you."

She shook her head. "He never loved me. He loved what he wanted me to be in his life. He never bothered to know me."

"So how long has it been since you two were last together?"

"You mean when did we break up?"

Malcolm smirked. "Yeah, that too."

"Randolph and I dated for two years. We both realized that we wanted different things so we parted ways but we remained friends. He moved to Charlotte. Until yesterday it had been five years since we last saw each other. I didn't even know he was back in Raleigh. There's nothing for you to be jealous about."

"Who said I was jealous?"

"I know you were worried."

He shook his head. "Nope, I'm very secure in our relationship."

"So we have a relationship?"

"You're my girl. We better have a relationship."

Cilla giggled as Malcolm wrapped both arms around her torso and hugged her to him. He nuzzled his face against her neck. They both felt comfortable in each other's arms, the sensations sweeping between them akin to a lost soul finding its way home.

Their lips met in the sweetest kiss and it felt as if fire had erupted from a volcano. Their kiss was pure bliss. Her supple lips were sweet against his and he felt her body melt easily into his. There was a purity to their kisses, rising emotion fueling the experience, the erotic moment telling as their mouths tangled.

Cilla's eyes were closed, her whole body falling into a heavenly ride as she imagined the possibilities, her body betraying her feelings. She wanted him, was ready to open herself to whatever he was willing to give. The moment felt like forever as his mouth danced brilliantly with hers.

The sun was just beginning to rise when the conversation and the kisses between them fell into a lull, Malcolm drifting off to sleep first. His body was curved snugly against hers as he finally succumbed to the exhaustion. Every one of his hardened muscles fit her to perfection as if they'd been perfectly sculpted for each other. He was strong and solid and she felt secure in his arms, grateful for the moment that had brought them even closer to each other. He snored softly, his breathing the sweetest timbre and before she knew it Cilla slipped into slumber with him.

Chapter Twelve

Bianca stood with her arms crossed over her chest and her head waving with amusement. The expression across her best friend's face made Cilla laugh.

"I really don't see what you find so funny," she said. "And you used to complain that I had too much drama going on in my life!"

Cilla giggled. "I know, right. But I think everything's going to work out. Unlike your drama which usually just ends in a hot mess."

"That has yet to be seen."

Cilla shrugged. "Well, I think we're on the right path. Malcolm and I are talking so that's half the battle."

Bianca nodded. "How's his daughter?"

"She's getting there. She's been seeing a therapist for the last few weeks and that's a good thing. I think it's just all a little overwhelming for her. Malcolm's not sure what to do so his answer is to just keep her busy. I imagine when they get back to a normal schedule things will get better."

"Can you be normal again after something like that?" Bianca asked.

The two women exchanged questioning stares.

Cilla inhaled, a deep breath filling her lungs. "I wish I could do something to help her," she said softly.

Rising from her seat Bianca moved to the refrigerator and pulled out a bottle of cheap wine. She took two glasses from the cupboard and filled them both and moved back to the table, setting one in front of Cilla as she took a gulp of the other. She sat back down meeting her friend's eye.

"I'm sure you being there is a big help. Malcolm knowing he can lean on you has to be a comfort. And you doing everything you can for him and his girls, well . . ." She shrugged. "He knows you love him."

"I do love him, Bianca. It's crazy just how much that man means to me."

"I want it on the record that I am not wearing taffeta, crinoline, or anything poufy at your wedding."

"But I want taffeta and crinoline!"

"You want your best friend at your side. My ass is wide enough. I can't have you put me in a dress that's going to make it look wider."

Cilla laughed as she took a sip of her own wine. "I think we're having a moment, Bianca."

Bianca laughed with her. "I know we are!"

The two women sat in conversation for a good hour. Cilla looked down to her watch. "I have to run. I promised Malcolm I'd meet him at the club. He and his attorney were meeting with the district attorney's office this afternoon."

"Why didn't you go with him?"

"I still have to pay my bills," Cilla said matter-of-factly. "I've about used up all my vacation days and I don't have any personal days left."

Bianca nodded her understanding. "Well, call me when you can."

Cilla headed toward the front door of her friend's home. "Don't I always!"

Malcolm hated that he could quote statistics on child abuse. He also hated knowing that the numbers reported probably didn't begin to paint a full picture of the problem because so many crimes against children went unreported. But what broke his heart, what absolutely crushed his spirit was knowing that his child was now one of those statistics. And despite knowing Cleo's story had a happier ending, he couldn't help but think of all the sons and daughters in the world who weren't as fortunate. Children whose innocence had been stolen with no regard. He blew a heavy sigh.

He'd spent the afternoon learning how technology was now a predator's wet dream come true. With an estimated ninety percent of teens and young adults online and just as many trolling social-networking sites, the victim pool was endless. The child sex trade was just another horror Malcolm couldn't fathom, the commercial exploitation bigger business than he had ever imagined. Discovering that Nikko Prince was a big fish in an even bigger pond made Malcolm's blood boil. Any other time in his life and he would have done everything he could to give Nikko a wealth of hurt the man would have never recovered from. If he only had himself to think about, then the repercussions would have been worth the crime.

Despite what he would have liked to do Malcolm had to consider how the consequences of his actions would have impacted his family and what he most wanted was for them all to find healing. Just days earlier he learned that Prince had taken a plea deal, avoiding a trial and eliminating the need for Cleo to testify. Knowing that Cleo would be close to fifty years old if Prince ever saw the light of day again was a small victory and he was grateful. Knowing that Prince still had to face charges in four other states and would likely live out his old age behind bars was icing on some very bitter cake.

Malcolm suddenly realized he was still sitting in the driveway of his home. With the air-conditioning turned off the heat inside had begun to rise. Perspiration beaded across his brow. He blew another heavy sigh as he opened the door, the barest hint of an early autumn breeze billowing inside. It was only then that he noticed Cilla's car parked at the curb.

Inside the house his mother called out his name, waving him into the family room. She sat in front of the large-screen television, watching an episode of *General Hospital.*

"What time is it?" Malcolm asked, looking from the television program to his wristwatch.

Mama Claudette laughed. "You're on time. I recorded my stories earlier. I had a moment to myself so I thought I'd catch up."

"Where are the girls?"

"Claudia's at dance class. Mrs. Winters, her friend Tara's mother, is going to bring her home."

"What about Cleo?"

"Cleo is in the kitchen with Cilla. They're cooking dinner for us all tonight."

Malcolm smiled. "How's she doing today?"

His mother smiled back. "Moody as usual. But that's just her personality. Your daughter has a lot of attitude."

"That's a good thing, right?"

"It is a good thing," Mama Claudette said.

Malcolm dropped into the seat beside his mother. He paused, staring at the television screen as the character Sonny Corinthos was pleading his case to yet another blond bombshell. Malcolm shook his head, in awe that his mother was still watching the same soap opera after so many years.

"Sonny hasn't changed a bit, has he?" Malcolm said, the statement more comment than question.

Mama Claudette laughed. "Don't you worry about Sonny. He's handling his business. You need to be handling yours."

Malcolm cut an eye at the woman. "Excuse me?"

"I'm talking about Cilla."

Malcolm blinked. "What about Cilla? Things are good with us."

Mama Claudette smiled. "I think they are and I'd like to see things continue to be good. So you need to handle your business."

"I thought I was doing that."

His mother blew a soft sigh. "At some point, son, you're going to need to let us all get back to being normal." She emphasized the word "normal" with air exclamations, her fingers flicking along the sides of her gray head. "You've been hovering over Cleo for weeks now. She is never going to know just how strong she is if you continue to hover over her likes she's going to break."

"I'm not hovering."

"Yes, you are, and you're treating her like she's damaged. She is never going to move past what happened to her if you don't stop. And you being so focused on Cleo has you ignoring Claudia. That's going to cause a whole host of other issues that we don't need."

Malcolm bristled at his mother's comment. "I don't . . ."

Mama Claudette held up her hand, stalling his denial. "You've got to start living again, Malcolm. If you don't get back to the business of living your life and doing what you need to do for you, then neither will the twins. You and Cilla were building a beautiful relationship. You need to get back to that before what you started falls by the wayside and you don't have anything."

Malcolm shook his head in disagreement. "Cilla and I are fine. We're happy."

Mama Claudette met his gaze, denial puddled deep in the corneas of his eyes. "When's the last time you and Cilla had a conversation that wasn't about the girls or the case or what you learned about crimes like Cleo's or . . ."

A wave of understanding suddenly washed over Malcolm's spirit. He held up his hand, his expression dropping. "I get it."

"You know from experience that you can't ignore your relationship no matter what hand life deals you. You have to stay focused on keeping your foundation solid if everything else is going to stand up to what gets thrown at you. Not only for each other but also for your children. A woman needs to know that even when times are hard and things get rough she's still a priority in your life. If she trusts that then she will always have your back."

Malcolm sat in reflection for a good while, pondering his mother's words. It wasn't until two commercial breaks later that Mama Claudette spoke again.

"Maxine is coming this weekend to spend some time with us. We're going to make it a granny and girls weekend. You might want to disappear for a few days."

A momentary wave of confusion washed over Malcolm's face. "Disappear? Where . . . ?"

Mama Claudette laughed. "Boy, I didn't raise you to be so slow!" she chuckled.

Malcolm suddenly found himself laughing with her. "Oh, okay, I get it!"

The matriarch shook her head, her eyes shifting back to the television. "I always wanted your daddy to take me to Sea Island and that Cloister hotel. But we could never afford it, bless his soul! I hear it's a very romantic spot for couples."

"You don't wear a lot of makeup, do you?" Cleo asked, turning her gaze toward Cilla.

The woman shook her head, her eyes shifting from the onion she was chopping to the young girl's face. "No, I don't. I learned many years ago that less is more."

Cleo's gaze narrowed, confusion shimmering in her eyes. "Huh?"

"The less makeup I wear, the better I look, and the more I don't need it."

"Oh!" Cleo said. "Grandma Claudette doesn't wear a lot of makeup either. She says too much makes you look cheap."

"That's why your grandmother has such beautiful skin."

Cleo went back to mixing the batter for the cornbread Cilla was teaching her how to make. "My daddy likes your butt. 'Cause it's so big! He's always staring at it when you walk away."

Cilla laughed heartily, her cheeks flooding with color. "Well, the next time you catch him staring you tell him to stop, okay?"

Cleo smiled back. "It's really not that big," she said. "I mean it's big but it's not, it's . . ."

"I know what you mean," Cilla said. She changed the subject. "How are things going at school?"

Cleo shrugged her narrow shoulders. "They're okay. I hate my science class. The teacher is stupid and he's always yelling at people."

"That's not good," Cilla said.

Cleo nodded. "Supposedly he had a nervous breakdown last year. The seniors started throwing erasers and wet tissues at him and he snapped. The vice principal had to come escort him away. So now some of the kids in the class throw things at him to try and make him cry. So he yells a lot."

"Would you like the class more if you had a better teacher?" Cilla questioned.

Cleo shook her head no. "Science is crazy. I just don't like it and we had to dissect a frog! It was so gross!"

Cilla shuddered. "I remember doing that when I was in school. I hated it too."

"Claudia always gets A's in science. She likes it."

"There's nothing wrong with that. You like math, right?"

"Yeah!"

"And you're good at it. That's your strength. That's why you always ace your exams."

"How do you know I get good grades in math?"

Cilla laughed. "Your dad is always bragging about it. That's how I know."

Cleo blushed, color tinting her cheeks. "He's such a goofball!"

"He's proud of you."

Cleo paused to think about that comment for a moment, not saying anything at all. When she returned to the conversation it was to ask Cilla what to do next, her cornbread ready to go into the oven.

Standing in the doorway, Malcolm watched as Cilla and his daughter shared time and space together. The energy between them was nowhere near the easy dynamics Cilla shared with Claudia but there wasn't that noxious tension that had been there weeks before. He attributed that to Cilla's patience. From start to finish she'd allowed Cleo to build their bond at her own pace, letting the young girl know she was there to support her and be her friend.

It had been a challenge but Cilla had insisted he stay out of it, to let them find their way on their own. Despite his wanting to intervene a time or two when Cleo had gotten out of hand, he'd let Cilla take the lead, trusting that she knew best. And she had. He could see it as Cleo eagerly worked alongside the woman to prepare the evening meal. She looked comfortable, even excited, and her smile was wide. It had been some time since Malcolm had last seen her smile so brightly.

What his mother had said really did click. Cleo would heal once they all stopped treating her like something was wrong with her. It had also been too long since he'd last told Cilla he loved her, imagining after having only said it one time that the beautiful woman might find it difficult to believe. His whole family would be fine once he relaxed and allowed them to be. He nodded, suddenly feeling like a weight had been lifted from his shoulders.

Clapping his hands excitedly he moved into the room. "Hello, hello, hello! Something smells good in here!" He moved around the counter to give his daughter a hug, then eased his way to Cilla's side, wrapping his arms around her waist as he pulled her close. He pressed his mouth to hers in an easy kiss.

"Hi, Daddy!" Cleo chimed. "I made the cornbread and Cilla's making the chili. We're having a chili and cheese fiesta. It's Cilla's recipe!"

He winked an eye at the woman in his arms before releasing the hold he had around her body. "Well it smells delicious. I can't wait to taste it. And you made the cornbread all by yourself?"

"Cilla showed me how."

"Your daughter is quite the chef," Cilla said. "She even put the dessert together!"

"It's peach dump cake," Cleo said, her eyes wide with excitement. "You just 'dump' all the ingredients into one dish. It's super easy! It'll go into the oven while we eat dinner so it's ready when we're done. Right, Cilla?"

The woman nodded as she turned back to the chili that had begun to simmer on the stovetop. "That's right. We should be ready to eat once Claudia gets home from dance class."

Malcolm nodded. "Did you finish your homework, young lady?"

Cleo nodded. "Cilla helped me with my English assignment."

"They're studying modern and contemporary poetry," Cilla said. "And I'm a big fan of Walt Whitman and Emily Dickinson."

"A poetry buff! I'm impressed."

Cilla smiled.

"It's just a whole lot of words to me," Cleo said, "but Cilla told me to just think of it as rap music without the music. Then it made sense. I like Emily Dickinson's love poems."

"Well, I am impressed," Malcolm said, his own smile canyon-wide.

Cleo nodded. "I'm going to go check on Grandma. You two can play kissy-face until I get back."

Cilla laughed. Malcolm shook his head.

"Thank you," he said. "We appreciate that!"

Cleo grinned as she turned and headed toward the door. Before she made her exit she gave Cilla one last look. "Cilla, are you staying for short story time tonight?"

Cilla tossed Malcolm a quick look. "I can."

Cleo smiled. "Good," she said before she disappeared out the door.

When the girl was out of sight Malcolm pulled Cilla back into his arms. "Hey, you!"

"Hey, yourself!"

He dropped his mouth to hers and kissed her, his desire searing her lips with heat. They held the connection for a good minute before he let her go. "I wasn't expecting to find you here."

"Neither was I but your mother called and asked if I could come give her a hand with a few things."

Malcolm chuckled, the riff coming from deep in his gut. Cilla eyed him questioningly.

"My mother's concerned about our relationship. I think this is her way of intervening."

Cilla smiled. "What did she say?"

"She basically told me that I don't show you how much I love you nearly enough."

Cilla reached up to kiss his mouth, pressing her lips to his. "So you do love me?"

"I love you more than you know, woman!"

"You'd do anything for me?"

He nodded, allowing his lips to dance over her one more time.

She smiled. "Then set the table. Dinner is just about ready."

Malcolm laughed but before he could say another word, his family bombarded the room, Claudia and Cleo racing ahead of their grandmother, their excitement and chatter like the sweetest sound to his ears.

Chapter Thirteen

The four-hundred-mile ride from Raleigh, North Carolina, to Sea Island, Georgia, was a leisurely seven-hour jaunt with the top down on Malcolm's Mercedes SL Class Roadster. A mix of cool jazz played on the CD player. As the wind blew through her hair, Cilla adjusted a silk scarf around her head. With her dark glasses she exuded a Grace Kelly flair, her vibe confident and sexy. Both enjoyed savoring the quiet between them, nothing really needed to be said as they enjoyed the experience and each other's company. Above their heads the sky was a brilliant shade of blue and the hint of sunlight peeked from behind a wealth of billowy white clouds. The moderate temperatures were perfection and both were glad for the chance to steal away.

Malcolm reached out and clasped his hand around Cilla's. Her palm was soft against his and he found himself craving more of her touch. He shifted his gaze in her direction and she met his stare with the sweetest smile. "I'm glad you could get away with me," he said.

Cilla pulled the sunshades from her face and gave him an easy wink of her eye. "I wouldn't want to be anyplace else," she responded.

Conversation between them was easy and casual. Laughter was abundant, both carefree and flirty with nothing on their minds but each other. They took in the sights, stopping here and there to explore one small town after another. It was the most relaxed either had been for a good long while.

The Cloister hotel was one of the most stunning places Cilla had ever seen. The five-star, Mediterranean-inspired resort sat on a unique natural setting with exclusive access to five miles of private beach. The gardens were a horticultural dream come true and the two-hundred-room hotel an architectural masterpiece. It was the lap of luxury defined by legendary elegance and a discriminating clientele.

The service was hands above any Cilla had ever experienced before and she was in awe as a bellhop led them to the suite that Malcolm had reserved for the weekend. The two-bedroom suite was extravagant with dark woods, robust fabrics, and classic furnishings. From the living room's balcony they had a magnificent view of the marshes on the Black Banks River.

Malcolm thought the only thing more beautiful than their surroundings was Cilla's expression as she took it all in. And he said so after he tipped the bellman and closed the door behind the man. "You are so gorgeous!"

Cilla smiled. "You are sweet. But I'm sure I need a good shower after our ride."

"Shower, no shower, you are still the most gorgeous thing in this room right now."

Cilla moved to where he stood and eased herself into his arms, laying her head against his chest. He wrapped himself around her, hugging her tightly. The sweet scents of his cologne and her perfume melded together in an olfactory delight. She inhaled him, breathing him in like he was oxygen. The heat between them was simmering and Cilla felt herself break out into a sweat, perspiration beginning to trickle in unexpected places. She inhaled another deep breath.

Malcolm relished the feel of her in his arms. Just her touch had him heated as he felt a quiver of electricity shoot through his southern quadrant. He shifted his weight from one leg to the other, desperate to stall the rising tremor of muscle between his legs. He suddenly took a step back, dropping his arms and hands to his sides.

He pointed toward the larger bedroom. "Why don't you go grab that shower? Maybe get yourself a quick nap? I have a few things I need to take care of and when I get back we can get dressed and head to an early dinner."

Cilla nodded. "That sounds like a plan."

Malcolm leaned to kiss her cheek, allowing his lips to linger there briefly. Then he turned and exited the room. Outside the suite door he took a deep breath and then a second, calming the shivers that had rushed across his spine, out into his limbs. He wanted her and it was getting harder to hide that desire. Most especially since he was certain she wanted him just as much. Malcolm was anxious and nervous. Cilla deserved only the very best from him so he was determined to make their first moment together memorable.

The water was heated, the shower massage head feeling like a trillion small fingers kneading her flesh. Thoughts of Malcolm and the sensation of the moisture raining down on her had her feeling like mush, every muscle quivering like jelly. Cilla spun her body from one side to the other, twisting the tightness out of her spine. After a few more minutes she imagined that Malcolm would soon be looking for her. She didn't have a clue how long she'd been there but she knew it had been a good while. The rumble in her tummy was motivation to get moving as well, her hunger rising rapidly.

She swiped her loofah sponge across her skin one last time, savoring the feel of the body wash across her flesh. Minutes later she was wrapped in an oversize plush white towel, her body sprawled across the king-size bed as she flipped though her cell phone. Her shower had taken thirty minutes longer than she'd expected. She typed a text message to Malcolm, wanting to check their schedule, then pushed the SEND button. His response came back quickly, taking mere minutes to turn around. Cilla smiled at his reply, the man's brief message mysterious and teasing.

She could hear him in the other room, the echo of his footsteps loud and clear. Rising from the warmth of her bed, she stretched her long limbs outward, reaching for an imagined fixture in the ceiling. Her cell phone suddenly vibrated, calling for her attention. Another message appeared on the screen, bringing a second bright smile to her face. She blew a deep sigh as the thought of him beckoned her to rise and dress. Throwing her legs off the bed she wrapped a plush, terry bathrobe around her naked body and slipped her pedicured feet into her bedroom slippers, then headed toward the closet to retrieve her clothes.

It took no time at all for her to get ready, slipping into a form-fitting, black cocktail dress. The lace number was cut low in the back, showed an ample amount of cleavage, and stopped just above her knees. The heels were cobalt blue, a thigh-high Grecian-inspired cage sandal. Feeling no need to blow dry and straighten her hair she'd allowed the strands to air dry, natural curls framing her face in a wealth of defined ringlets.

Moving from the bedroom back to the living space she found Malcolm standing in the center of the room. He held a beverage glass in his hand. Cilla's eyes widened at the sight of him. He was dressed in a black suit, white dress shirt, and a red necktie. He was freshly trimmed and shaved and Cilla imagined that he could have easily modeled for the cover of *GQ* magazine. She thought the man looked absolutely divine.

"Wow!"

Malcolm laughed, amusement painting his expression. "I take it you approve?"

She nodded. "Most definitely. You look very nice, Mr. Cobb."

"I have to agree," he said as he trailed his thumbs down the length of his lapels.

Cilla giggled.

Malcolm extended his elbow. "Shall we?"

Sliding her hand through his arm, she nodded. "We shall!"

Malcolm had made reservations at the Georgian Room, the only Forbes Five-Star restaurant in Georgia. They were greeted by a tuxedoed host who led them to a table in front of the fireplace, a stately structure with a carved stone mantel. Above their heads the chandeliers were gold and crystal, exquisite light fixtures that epitomized the lavishness of the setting. From start to finish the Georgian Room was an exceptional dining experience. Everything about it was magical.

Malcolm had preselected the chef's tasting menu, a decadent presentation of locally sourced Southern cuisine. It was a six-course presentation of indulgent fare served on hand-painted china with silver flatware and European linens. They dined on prime rib tartare, Maine lobster and chilled corn soup, loin of lamb with twice-baked, caviar-topped potato, goat-cheese crème brulee with peach compote, and meringue-topped sorbet and berries. Every bite was a melt-in-your mouth flavor-fest that teased the senses.

They could have talked for hours, enjoying each other's company as much as they were. It felt good and both were completely enamored of each other. They traded easy caresses and flirted shamelessly. Innuendo was abundant, fueling the sexual tension between them. With the last bite of dessert Malcolm and Cilla knew they wanted more, the sugar and sweet they craved not found on the restaurant's dessert tray.

Malcolm stared into her eyes, unable to put words to the desire that had surged with a vengeance.

He'd been wanting her since the first day he'd laid eyes on her and as they'd grown closer his desire had manifested into a need so magnanimous that he felt as if his whole world suddenly revolved around him having her.

He pushed himself up from the table and extended his hand toward her. Cilla's gaze was still locked with his as she entwined her fingers between his fingers. His palm kissed her palm, his touch warm and gentle. It was the sweetest of caresses as he pulled her along beside him, guiding the way back to their suite. Once inside the room, Cilla's eyes widened in awe.

Their hotel room had been completely transformed, bouquets of red roses adorning every flat surface. Candles in varying shapes and sized shimmered through the space, their light casting a sensuous glow around the room. A bottle of champagne, two crystal flutes, and an oversized heart shaped box of expensive chocolates rested on the coffee table. She smiled, knowing that the bed had been made with silk sheets. With the door secured behind them, there was nothing that could have kept them from each other.

Cilla moved to the center of the room. She turned to face him, the sweetest expression across her face. Her smile was warm and welcoming and everything good about the two of them shimmered like the brightest light from her eyes. She beckoned him to her with her index finger, her seductive expression hardening every muscle in his body.

He strode slowly in her direction, shedding his suit jacket and tie along the way. When he reached her side Cilla turned her back to him, her head tilted just so as she eyed him over her shoulder. With nothing said he pulled at the zipper that closed her dress, slowly exposing inch after inch of warm flesh. His fingers danced against her skin, his touch like hot embers igniting a serious fire through her feminine spirit. He slid his hand through her hair, releasing the strands to her shoulders. Gently pushing her head forward he pressed a damp kiss to the back of her neck. He trailed his tongue across the soft flesh, pausing at the lobe of her ear. Where his lips led his tongue followed, tasting the salt and sweet of her skin.

Cilla stood relishing the intensity of his touch. Every pass of his mouth against her flesh left her breathless. She turned in his arms, taking a step away from him. Meeting the look he was giving her she found herself falling headfirst into the depths of his dark eyes, sheer lust seeping past his lashes. With a seductive striptease Cilla slid the dress from her body, the garment falling to a puddle at the floor beneath her feet. She wore more lace beneath her dress, her bra and panty a brilliant shade of fire-engine red. The delicate design looked like intricate paint against her brown skin.

Her breasts were full and lush and they made his mouth water with anticipation. The arch of her waist accentuated her full hips and her buttocks were two magnificent globes that had him literally standing at full attention. She bit down against her bottom lip, her intoxicating stare leaving him drunk with desire.

He took a quick step toward her drawing her

into his arms. He captured her mouth, his kiss a passionate tongue-entwined melding that had her weak in the knees. With his body wrapped tightly around hers, he savored the sensation of her skin pressed to his. He gasped as her hands suddenly danced between them, pulling at his belt and zipper to release him from his clothes. Touch was suddenly urgent as they snatched the last of their clothing away, both standing naked together.

Unable to contain his enthusiasm Malcolm swept her into his arms and carried her to the bedroom. With one hand he snatched the bed covers, tossing them to the floor. He gently rested her against the mattress top as he eased his body above hers. Their mouths were still locked in that kiss, lips dancing, tongues lashing. She tasted sweet, like honey from a freshly broken comb.

Cilla was suddenly sprawled open against the bed top, panting heavily as Malcolm broke the connection, moving to his toiletry bag. He searched anxiously for a condom, finally dumping its contents to the floor until one was found. He sheathed himself quickly before falling back against her. Their connection came swiftly as he eased himself inside of her, every part of her body welcoming him in. She gasped loudly as the fullness of him found its way. When he was nestled tightly against her they both paused, relishing the intensity of the sensations sweeping between them.

Cilla wrapped her arms around his torso, her nails raking the length of his back as he began to slowly drive himself in and out of her. Every nerve ending was firing, electrical shimmers exploding with a vengeance. The connection was sweeter than anything either had ever known before.

Malcolm could barely contain himself as her liquid warmth enveloped his favorite body part. Being inside that warm sheath was unfathomable, better than he could have possibly imagined. She was tight, fitting him like a glove and with each stroke her muscles suctioned him harder and harder as she drew him in deeper and deeper. Their loving was intense as he pressed himself into her over and over again, grinding in circles back and forth.

Beneath him Cilla moaned and groaned and panted, murmuring softly. Her hips thrust upward, meeting him stroke for stroke and then she screamed his name over and over again as if she were in prayer. He filled her, the connection deep and intoxicating. She marveled at how her own body seemed to crave more and more of him, her inner lining hugging him intently. And then she screamed, her back arching with pleasure.

They came at the same time, both falling together off the edge of ecstasy. As his body exploded Malcolm cussed, speaking in tongues as his words spilled past his lips in a rush of air. His eyes rolled back, light searing his view and his head spun, the vertigo like nothing he'd ever experienced before. He screamed with her and as his body spilled into hers, her taut muscles milked him dry, pulsing over and over again.

Spent, Malcolm fell against her and Cilla drew him closer, her body melting like butter into his. In that moment both knew there was no turning back. They were linked forever and neither one would have it any other way.

Neither Cilla nor Malcolm could get enough of the other. Their loving continued into the early morning hours, even sleep unable to keep them from each other. The sun was just beginning to rise when both their bodies surrendered, nature having finally failed them. Malcolm had curled his body around hers, nuzzling his face into her hair and neck as he finally drifted off to sleep. Cilla was still too wired to rest, every nerve ending in her body amped. That spot between her legs ached sweetly, a hurt that made her feel alive and invigorated. Malcolm had loved her with a veracity that she'd never known from any man. Just thinking about it, and him, moved her to tears.

She shifted slightly and he threw a leg around her waist, almost unwilling to let her go. The gesture made her smile as she nestled herself closer to him, her hands gently caressing his arm and leg. Cilla loved the place she found herself in. There was nothing but love between them, the magnitude of it fueling every hope and dream she had for their future together.

Their weekend excursion flew by. Malcolm couldn't begin to imagine them ever having to leave but time had slipped by quickly. And he still hadn't accomplished what he had initially intended to do.

Seriously distracted he silently kicked himself for the failing.

Cilla was sleeping peacefully. Since their arrival they'd spent more time in bed than out of it, stopping only for sustenance when the need had arisen. But food and drink didn't begin to measure up to the bond that had completely sealed their fates. What he found himself feeling for the woman was immeasurable, which made what he needed to accomplish even more important.

He slowly eased his large body off the bedside. Throwing a quick look over his shoulder to insure Cilla hadn't wakened, he moved to his leather attaché and the small ring box hidden inside. Flipping the top open on the container, he stared at the diamond and platinum trinket inside.

The engagement ring had been his mother's, the one his father had put on the woman's hand to proclaim his love and adoration. And Marcus Cobb had loved his mother with everything the man had in him. That ring symbolized everything the two had believed in and had fought for until the day a pulmonary embolism had taken his life. His father had replaced the original ring set a few years before his death but his mother had held on to the original band, declaring that one day it would be gifted to her future daughter-in-law.

Malcolm had never understood her refusal to part with it when he'd married his first wife. Not until she'd slipped it into his hand the night before he and Cilla were scheduled to leave for their trip. That simple gesture had acknowledged her approval, Mama Claudette believing in the two of them as much as she had believed in his father and their love. She had never believed in him and Shanell and hindsight showed him he should have trusted his mother's instincts.

Malcolm saw proposing to Cilla as a simple formality, the next step to the inevitable. Every fiber in his being already saw her as his life partner, the woman he would grow old and cranky with. She had his heart like no other woman did and he knew that her carrying his name and partnering with him would be one of the greatest gifts life could bless him with. But he wanted the actual act of asking Cilla to marry him to epitomize his desire to make her his wife. His mother's ring was just the beginning.

An hour later Malcolm nuzzled Cilla awake. She slowly opened her eyes, the lids blinking rapidly as she focused. Seeing Malcolm's smiling face was exhilarating and she felt her own smile widen brightly. She stretched her arms out, wrapping them around the man. Everything about waking with him was a sheer joy and Cilla couldn't begin to imagine going back to the life she'd had without him.

As she sat upright in the bed Malcolm set a wicker tray onto her lap. A single rosebud sat in a crystal vase, decorating a breakfast plate of malted Belgian waffles topped with fresh fruit, slices of thick-cut bacon, an oversize goblet of freshly squeezed orange juice, and a hot mug of coffee.

"Mmmm, breakfast in bed!" Cilla purred. "A girl could get used to this."

"I hope *my* girl gets used to this because *my* girl

deserves all this and more!" Malcolm gave her a wink.

Cilla leaned forward and pressed a sugared kiss to his mouth. "Your girl feels very special."

Malcolm took a deep breath, his stomach suddenly flipping with anxiety. "I hope so. I hope you know just how much you mean to me. You've made such a difference in my life I don't know what I'd do without you."

She gave him a bright smile. "Awww! That's so sweet!"

He suddenly set a box of Cracker Jack caramel popcorn onto the tray, his gaze locking tight to hers. Cilla looked from him to it and back again.

"What's this?"

Malcolm blew a low sigh. "Let me tell you a story about Mama Claudette and my father. My mother came from a very small town in Georgia, right outside of Columbus. My father was born in North Carolina. Dad never finished school. He came from a large family. He had nine siblings and he was the only boy. By the time he hit his teens he had to help support the family so he went into the military. He was eventually stationed at Fort Benning and that's where he met my mother. He and a group of his buddies had leave one Sunday and they went to her church to get the free meal after service. Dad said he knew the minute he laid eyes on her that she was going to be his wife. Mom said she wasn't so sure. She was in school, studying to be a teacher, and she didn't see herself married to a soldier. But Dad was persistent and every chance he could get he showed up at church to talk to her.

"One day, they'd gone walking and Mom was

talking about all her dreams and the things she wanted to do in life and Dad dropped down onto one knee and swore that if she'd be his wife he would make every one of those dreams come true. And my mother said no. Dad got a little prickly because he thought she said no because he didn't have a ring when he asked her. But Mom told him she didn't need a ring. She said no because he hadn't come correct. He hadn't asked her father for his permission.

"So Dad regrouped, came back a few weeks later, walked her home from church, and asked to speak with my grandfather. And my grandfather gave them his consent with one stipulation and that was he had to ask my mother when he did have a ring to give her. Well, Dad didn't have any money. He was sending the few dollars he was making back home to help take care of his sisters. But one Sunday they'd spent the afternoon together and Dad had bought them a box of Cracker Jack to share. Well, when they got to the prize in the bottom, there was a plastic ring and my father got down on one knee a second time and asked my mother to be his wife and he put that plastic ring on her finger. And he swore to her that if she said yes that one day he was going to replace that plastic ring with one that had a diamond in it. And he did. On their twenty-fifth wedding anniversary my father gave my mother another box of Cracker Jack and inside was her ring. He died three days later."

Cilla clasped her hand over her mouth as tears suddenly sprang to her eyes. "Oh, Malcolm!" she gasped. "Your poor mother!"

Malcolm nodded as he reached for the box of

caramel corn and tore open the top. Passing it to her he gestured for her to empty the contents. Cilla gently shook the filling out onto her empty plate. She'd emptied half the contents when a small velvet bag fell onto the tray. She gave Malcolm a look, her eyes widening with curiosity.

Malcolm continued his story. "The day we buried my father my mother took off her ring and she put it away. She never wore it again."

"She didn't want to wear it?" Cilla questioned.

He shook his head. "She said that it was that plastic ring that best represented what she and Dad shared. We had it encased in acrylic and it sits on her dresser with their wedding photo. She said that one day she hoped to see that other ring on the hand of her daughter-in-law or her granddaughter. But when I married Shanell, my mother refused to let it go. She said it didn't feel right to her and she stuck to that. And then you came into my life."

Malcolm pulled the drawstring on the bag and took out an exquisite princess-cut diamond in a bright white platinum setting that featured three rows of channel-set diamonds in an eternity band. Cilla gasped, the ring one of the most beautiful pieces of jewelry that she'd ever seen.

Pushing the tray aside Malcolm grabbed Cilla's hand and gently pulled her to her feet. Dropping onto one knee he extended the ring out to her, his eyes brimming with joy. "Priscilla Jameson, I love you with everything I have in me. I want to give you the world. To make all your dreams come true. Would you do me the honor of being my wife?"

Cilla nodded, tears streaming over her cheeks. "Yes! Yes! Yes!" she said excitedly as Malcolm slid his mother's ring onto her ring finger. She threw her arms around his neck, dropping to her knees with him.

His kisses rained over her face, her cheeks, her nose, her lips. "I love you, Cilla!" he muttered over and over, his own tears mingling with hers. "I love you so much!"

Cilla hugged him tightly, everything about the moment fueling her spirit with joy and happiness. "I love you, too!" she said. "I love you, too!"

Chapter Fourteen

Planning a wedding came with challenges Cilla had never expected, the least of which was the where and the when. It didn't bother her to take things slow and simply be engaged for a while, to just enjoy the beauty of knowing they would eventually merge all aspects of their lives. Malcolm was on board with whatever, just wanting her to know that he would marry her tomorrow or be content with doing it months later if that was what she wanted.

It was everyone else testing the solvency of their relationship, wanting to see them walk down the aisle sooner than later. Mama Claudette and the twins had already picked out their dresses. Every day with Bianca was a lecture on the merits of eloping versus a very traditional union with a hundred bridesmaids. From one day to the next Cilla wasn't sure what Bianca wanted more: to see her married or on the Vegas strip celebrating the bachelorette party.

Cilla sat on the end barstool as Malcolm poured

drinks for a party of six on the other side of the room. The Playground was packed, the staff entertaining a full house. Romeo's wife, Taryn Marshall, sat by her side, the two women bonding over cups of hot coffee. Since becoming acquainted the two had become fast friends and both women liked that they got along so well since their very favorite guys were best buddies.

Taryn eyed Cilla curiously. "So, what are you going to do?"

Cilla shrugged. "I don't know. But I'm starting to feel pressured."

"By Malcolm?"

"Oh, no!" Cilla answered, her expression incredulous. "Malcolm has been amazing. He's said he'll do whatever I want to do but that's the problem. I don't know what I want!" She tossed up her hands in frustration.

"You do want to marry the man?"

Cilla's smiled was canyon-wide. "More than anything else in this world. That's the only thing I'm sure of!"

Taryn smiled with her. "Okay. I just want to make sure we got that clear."

"Malcolm is what I'm most certain of. I love him to death. I think it's just all the hoopla surrounding the commitment that's got me out of sorts. Everyone we love wants to have a say in how we get married."

"You just have to figure out what you want and do that. Nothing else. Romeo and I eloped."

"Yes, we did," Romeo interjected, coming to join the conversation. "Taryn and I had gone away for an extended weekend and we just did it."

"We were in the mountains, in Brevard," Taryn added.

"We just felt like it was right for just the two of us. But it made a few people mad," Romeo said, gesturing with his head toward Aleta and Odetta who were standing on the other side of the room.

"That's what I'm worried about," Cilla said. "I want everyone to be happy for us, not upset about how we get married."

"But they will be happy," Taryn said. "And you will be happier. I wouldn't change a thing about our ceremony. We married on the shores of Lake Toxaway, with the waterfalls as our backdrop. It was gorgeous."

Romeo nodded. "And two strangers stood up as our witnesses."

"You didn't want Malcolm or Aleta or the girls there?"

"I wanted Taryn to be my wife and I wanted it to be perfect for just us two. We celebrated with the rest of our family when we got back. It was all good!"

"What are y'all talking about?" Malcolm asked, leaning over the bar to join in.

Cilla smiled. "We were talking about you!"

The man laughed. "I thought I felt my ears burning."

"I was asking your fiancée if you two had picked a wedding date yet," Taryn said, her eyes wafting back and forth between him and Cilla.

Malcolm nodded. "I'm leaving all those details to her," he said. He reached for Cilla's hand, squeezing her fingers between his own.

"You're not going to be a groom-zilla?" Romeo said with a deep laugh.

His friend rolled his eyes. "Boy, you know me better than that. I'm as easy as they come. Now my mother on the other hand . . . !"

They all laughed.

Cilla shook her head. "I love Mama Claudette to death but she is definitely trying to go all out for this wedding."

"Yeah," Malcolm said with a low sigh. "I'm going to have to rein her in."

"She's just trying to live vicariously through you both," Taryn said with an easy smile across her face.

"She can live through the twins when they get married," he said. "Right now she's starting to look like one of those in-laws from hell!"

Laughter rippled between them all again.

"She's not that bad!" Cilla exclaimed. "She's excited and she's just trying to help."

"She's that bad," Malcolm said, grinning. "It's okay, baby. You can say it. She's my mother and I know how bad she is."

Cilla laughed. "Well, I don't want her or the girls to feel left out of the planning."

Malcolm leaned over the bar to kiss her lips. "See why I love her so much!"

Romeo wrapped his arms around Taryn's shoulders. He leaned to kiss his wife's cheek. "Well, my only suggestion is that you two do you even if that means just going down to the courthouse to tie the knot 'cause no matter what you do, it'll all work out."

Taryn nodded in agreement. "And if push comes

to shove just let Mama Claudette plan the whole thing and you two just show up."

Cilla laughed. "You might actually be onto something!"

The last customer had closed down The Playground an hour earlier. Cilla had been sitting patiently in wait as Malcolm and Romeo tended to their last shred of business. Taryn had left earlier, needing to relieve the babysitter and put her toddler son down for the night. The other employees had followed on her heels. The room was quiet save the soft vibe of Bob Marley's "Redemption Song" playing over the sound system.

Allowing herself to fall into the sweet lull of the reggae beat, Cilla swayed easily in time with the song. Her thoughts were muddled, so much on her mind that she could not focus and so she released it all by concentrating solely on the music. Minutes later Romeo's deep voice broke through the stillness, him wishing her a good night.

She tossed up her hand to wave as he exited the building, locking the door behind himself. She shifted her gaze to stare at Malcolm who was watching her from his seat across the room. His smile was easy and sweet, everything in the look he was giving her feeling like a cashmere blanket around her shoulders. He nodded in her direction and she smiled back.

Moving onto his feet Malcolm strolled to the center of the dance floor and turned toward her. As she sat watching him he seemed even taller with his head lowered just so and his gaze skewering. With his wide shoulders, trim waist, and chiseled features, Cilla imagined that he would have made Michelangelo weep. His presence was commanding and he seemed to exude power from every pore in his body. Cilla thought she could sit there watching him for hours, fighting not to drool.

He extended both of his hands in her direction, calling her to his side with the deep stare he was giving her. As she reached where he stood the last strands of Miles Davis shifted to the pulsating drumbeat of Sade's "Soldier of Love." Allowing the beat of the music to guide her, Cilla gyrated her hips from side to side as Malcolm eased his body against hers. He held his hands up as if in surrender, his own pelvis moving in sync with hers. Cilla slid her palms against his as Sade's haunting vocals took them both to another place.

Their sensuous connection as they danced was erotic and teasing, both moving with the music as if it were seeping out of their bodies. Malcolm felt himself harden in his slacks, a lengthy erection pulling taut between his legs. Cilla gyrating against that hardness soon had him ready for more. There was no denying the sheer magnitude of the desire they had for each other. Just thinking about the extraordinary woman raised his blood pressure. The barest touch moved his heart to beat as if it were trying to get out of his chest and each orgasmic ending when they made love was beyond words.

He leaned his forehead to her forehead, caressed her cheek with his cheek. Their hands were clasped tightly together, their torsos still parted as their pelvises shifted one against each the other. She suddenly pressed her mouth to his, kissing him passionately. In the distance the lull of someone's jazz celebrated the moment.

Pulling her lips from his, Cilla stared into his eyes. Neither spoke, their breathing heavy. The pink of her tongue pushed past the line of her snow-white teeth to lick her lush lips. A wave of heat coursed in Malcolm's midsection at the sight. He opened his mouth to speak when Cilla shook her head, pressing her index finger to his lips. A ripple of excitement suddenly had him sweating.

Cilla dropped slowly to her knees, her gaze still locked tightly with his. Her mouth was parted ever so slightly and unadulterated lust pierced her gaze. Malcolm felt himself begin to shake in anticipation. She slowly fumbled with the belt around his waist, releasing the buckle that held it closed. He gasped as she undid the snap to his jeans and eased the zipper downward, never taking her eyes from his stare. With both her hands she pushed his pants and briefs to the floor in one sweeping motion, exposing his manhood. His member twitched and pulsed, seeming to react on its own accord. His skin tingled, his breath hitched, and heat pooled.

Cilla pressed a kiss to Malcolm's abdomen, her chin brushing against his manhood. He was large and heavy, his organ throbbing as his blood pulsed fervidly. A flash of desire made them both shudder, Cilla's own body responding in kind as she felt her panties dampen, her juices seeping. Looking up into Malcolm's dark eyes, his lids heavy, she felt her own desire surge with a vengeance.

Malcolm gasped, his breathing fueled with want as he murmured her name. "Oh, Cilla!"

She took him into her mouth like he was a piece of candy, hungrily, her mouth heated. Malcolm moaned loudly as she swirled her tongue swiftly around the head. His blood surged and he felt himself harden even more.

"Oh God!" Malcolm exclaimed.

Cilla pulled her mouth from him, wrapping one hand around his shaft. She began to stroke him slowly, each finger feeling like its own massage unit. She reached her other hand underneath him to grab his balls. They were full and swollen in her hand. She kneaded them between her fingers, enjoying the feel of him in her small hands. She trailed a manicured nail across the curve of one and then the other. Malcolm was suddenly so overwhelmed by the sensations that his knees began to quiver unabashedly.

She slowed the motion of her hand as she felt his muscle tighten even more. It rose upward in front of her face, like the hand on a clock pointing to eight. His member was utterly beautiful, the skin dark and flawless. She dropped her eyes to stare in awe, wanting to remember every detail. With a slight smile on her face she began to stroke him faster, her grip tightening. Malcolm braced his hands against her shoulders, fighting to keep his legs from buckling and sending him to the floor. And then she took him back into her mouth.

Cilla ducked her head back down and started feasting on his shaft like it was a melting ice cream cone. She lapped at the head, suckling him hungrily. Malcolm moved his hands to her head, grabbing her hair as he started to thrust himself in and out of her mouth, hard and fast. Cilla took him all in, aroused by the sensation of having him slam back and forth over her lips.

Malcolm was lost in the moment, moaning with pleasure. Cilla had him feeling all kinds of good. He grunted, his hips thrusting back and forth. Sweat beaded across his brow and stained his shirt. The music playing in the background had been one seductive love song after another. Her mouth and hands wrapped around him were heated, making his blood boil. And then he orgasmed, the eruption through his body volcanic. "Oh, shhh . . ." he screamed, biting down hard against his bottom lip. "Cilla, yes! Oh, yes!"

Cilla clutched his buttocks with both hands, holding him tightly to her. His body convulsed, his muscles jerking. She continued to suck him into and out of her mouth, her tongue lashing. The moment was surreal and Malcolm was completely overcome. When Cilla finally released the hold she had on him, he fell to his knees before her, his body shivering and shaking, every ounce of his control lost. Every moment with Cilla was an awakening for him, and even in those moments of vulnerability Malcolm couldn't imagine life being sweeter.

After quick trips to the rest room to freshen up, it had been another thirty minutes of them kissing and caressing before Malcolm finally locked the doors to The Playground. After leaving the club Malcolm declared himself starving and in desperate need of nourishment. "That was a workout,"

Malcolm teased. "You can't do that to me and then not feed me."

Cilla laughed. "I'm not cooking."

He blew an exaggerated sigh. "You won't cook for your man?" he asked, giving her puppy-dog eyes. He batted his lashes in her direction.

"I'm not cooking for my man at three o'clock in the morning! But I will buy you a meal from the Waffle House so you can build your strength back up."

Malcolm laughed. "Sounds like you have plans for me."

Cilla grinned, her eyes wide. "Yes, sir, I do!" she exclaimed.

He stole a look at his wristwatch, the diamond-encrusted timepiece striking against his dark complexion. "At this rate it looks like you and I are going to be up all night long."

"It does. Especially once I get you nourished back up!" Cilla laughed.

Malcolm leaned across the car's center console and kissed her. "Then you're buying an extra side of bacon," he said with a straight face.

"Whatever you need, baby!"

"I need you."

Cilla smiled. "You already have me, sweetheart."

Malcolm kissed her again, then started the car's engine.

The ride to T W Alexander Drive and the twenty-four-hour Waffle House was short and sweet. Their laughter continued as they enjoyed an early morning meal of scrambled eggs, hash brown potatoes, smothered and diced, extra bacon, and large glasses of orange juice. It didn't stop until they found themselves back at Cilla's home, naked in her bed atop the new silk sheets she'd bought online. And even then they continued to tease each other, giggling like schoolkids.

Sleep came almost as soon they laid their heads down, Cilla drifting off first and Malcolm soon after. Outside the sun had just begun its slow ascent. Thick gray clouds filled the early morning sky, the billows voluminous and heavy with precipitation. A storm was brewing, something dark and ugly coming in their direction. As Malcolm's eyes blinked open once and then again, he smiled, tightening the hold he had on the woman in his arms. As his lids closed for the last time, he smiled, not caring at all if it rained. In that moment, nestled lovingly against each other, neither he nor Cilla had a care in the world.

When Cilla opened her eyes, the dark sky outside felt more like late evening than mid-afternoon. She'd wakened earlier, just long enough to call in sick to work, planning to spend the day in bed doing absolutely nothing but catering to every one of Malcolm's whims and fantasies and one or two of her own. Falling back to sleep for another few hours had been just enough to revitalize her energy.

Malcolm slumbered peacefully, slipping into and out of sleep as he rode one dream after another. The warmth of Cilla's naked body was holding him hostage in the bed and he had no desire to ever move from that spot. Side by side they shifted back and forth against each other easily. At one point he heard Cilla whisper his name, mumbling incoherently, and he imagined that he'd mumbled back. Unable to decipher what was being said he slipped back to sleep, savoring the sensation of her hands caressing his body.

Cilla leaned up on one elbow, eyeing him from head to toe. He was sporting a healthy length of morning wood, his erection protruding like a steel rod toward the ceiling. The sheets were tangled at his feet as he lay with one foot hanging off the side of the mattress, the other bent against his calve. His breathing was static, just an exhale away from being a snore. Morning stubble blessed his chin and his dark complexion had a hint of sheen from the warmth in the room. Watching him sleep had quickly become one of her favorite things to do.

She drew her fingertips against his skin, teasing the flesh against his arms, across his torso, down the length of his abdomen. She circled her pinkie in the well of his belly button and smiled as he shifted ever so slightly. She trailed her hand farther down until the length between his legs twitched and jumped. She cupped her hand over him, enjoying the feel of his hardness in her hands as her fingernails lightly grazed his balls. Her smile widened as Malcolm responded by pushing his hips upward against her palm.

Cilla's eyes suddenly widened, a lightbulb moment shooting a current of electricity across her spine. She reached behind her, pulling open the drawer of her nightstand. She pulled a vibrator from inside and engaged it. The sudden hum pulled Malcolm from a light sleep and he jumped, turning his head toward her abruptly. Before he could say anything she placed the vibrator against his manhood, rolling it along his shaft to the underside of its engorged head. She let the pulsating machine tease the hardened muscle as she began to stroke him with her other hand.

The sensations sweeping through him were overwhelming. Malcolm could feel his orgasm rising with a vengeance, ready to erupt. He moaned, spreading his legs farther apart as she teased and taunted him, jacking him slowly, then faster, then slowly again.

Cilla was completely enamored of his anatomy, marveling at the perfect symmetry of his manhood. His erection was brick hard, the length and width of him full and solid. She loved the strength and power and the mystery of his maleness. She resisted the urge to put her mouth and lips against him, instead wanting to watch as she pleasured him with her hands. She continued to explore him, her nails gently brushing the dark skin as she stroked him easily.

"Oh, God, that feels good," Malcolm moaned as his hips gently thrust upward. And then Cilla trailed the vibrator lower, pressing it between his butt cheeks.

Malcolm jumped as he grabbed her hand and rolled her quick and fast onto her back, his body hovering above hers. His eyes were wide as he shook his head. "Hey, what are you doing?" he chirped, his voice pitched higher than normal.

Cilla laughed. "No anal action?"

"That's not funny, woman!"

"Your expression is hilarious. What? Nobody ever play with your stuff back there?"

"No. Not now and not ever!"

Malcolm eased a hand between her legs, trailing his thick fingers over her clit. "Anyone ever play with your stuff back there?"

She gasped, his touch unexpected. She clamped her legs tightly around his hand. Lifting her eyes to his, she gave him a teasing look. Malcolm felt himself harden even more, the blood surging back in his erection.

"Can I play with your stuff back there?" he asked, his voice dropping an octave as he trailed his fingers back in the other direction.

Cilla laughed again. "Oh, you want to do me but I can't do you?"

Malcolm didn't answer, instead kissing her neck, gently nibbling and sucking on her skin. Cilla moaned softly as he pulled just the hint of her skin between his lips before releasing it and repeating the motion mere millimeters away. She purred softly as he shifted his body closer to hers. With apt precision he slowly explored her shoulders and her collarbone, his lips leading where his tongue followed. Crawling up onto his knees he continued to assault her skin, relishing the soft, salty sweetness as his hands roamed over her taut stomach and up to her breasts.

He suddenly lifted his head to stare down at her. "Promise me you will never wear clothes to bed with me."

Cilla met the intense look he was giving her.

"Promise me," he repeated. "I want to always be able to get to you like this."

She nodded as he tweaked a nipple between his thumb and forefinger then dropped his mouth back to her chest. He cupped the lush fullness with both hands, letting the nipples slide between his fingers. Her areolae were dark, the nipples looking like chocolate kisses against mocha pudding. His hands alternated between lightly brushing over them and gripping and pinching them. Then he flicked her nipple with his tongue and she gasped, the movement unexpected. She pressed her hand against his head, gently trying to pull him closer to her.

Removing his hands from her breasts Malcolm suddenly rolled her onto her stomach. The gesture surprised her as he slipped an arm around her waist and lifted her up onto her knees. He pressed a palm against the center of her back and pushed her torso forward. The motion rewarded him with a bird's-eye view of her succulent globes, the round of her ass like two full moons. The muscles rippled as she clenched her backside tightly, a wave of nervous energy sweeping through her.

He trailed his hands up and down her legs, lightly caressing her skin as he explored every muscle and sinew. He pressed his lips to the exposed skin, lightly biting the flesh of one curve and then the other. His hand ventured back between the intersection of her legs as he gently traced her slit with his middle finger. She pushed her sex toward his hand, her moistness coating his fingertips. Cilla moaned lightly, luxuriating in the sensations he was eliciting from her body.

As Malcolm continued a slow, leisurely exploration of her body, Cilla trembled with excitement. His touch was heated, his fingers and hands igniting a raging flame through her. He suddenly eased her over, rolling her back so that she lay flat on the bed. She inhaled swiftly, holding a hot breath.

The first taste was teasing as he dipped his tongue into her navel. Cilla squirmed beneath him. He kissed a slow path toward her most private spot, his lips moist and hot, gliding like silk against her skin. He lifted one leg and then the other over his shoulders, his hands beneath her buttocks as he pulled her toward him. Her unique scent teased his nostrils. She had a neatly manicured landing strip and he'd teased her about it, offering to landscape her pubic bush himself. He trailed his fingers through the slick curls, his touch like the gentlest breeze. Cilla blew a low breath past her thin lips.

Malcolm kissed her ankles and goose bumps blossomed all over her legs. He kissed and licked and trailed his fingers and tongue against her bare skin. He blew warm breath along her inner leg, leaving damp kisses across her knees, trailing his mouth and tongue over her inner thighs. As he drew closer to where her legs met they spread wider.

Warm breath blew like a gentle breeze across her sweet spot. Cilla shivered and the goose bumps that had receded from her skin reappeared. She'd lain still as he'd explored her legs but when he finally pressed his mouth against her sweet spot, she jerked like she had been electrocuted. Malcolm lifted his eyes to hers. She'd risen up on her elbows to stare down at him, wide-eyed excitement on her face. He trailed his tongue across her slit, savoring the taste of her.

He gently sucked the intimate lips into his mouth. He licked her up and down, intentionally avoiding touching her clit, wanting to wait till just the right moment to increase her pleasure. He licked her again, a little more urgently, and she pushed her hips forward, thrusting herself against his mouth. He slowly inserted his tongue through the door of her private place, probing as far as he could. He suddenly felt her hand on the back of his head, pulling him tightly to her. He began to lick in earnest, exploring every inch of her.

Cilla's breathing was shallow, excitement building as she drew close to her orgasm. And then he trailed his tongue across her clit, rolling the hardened bud between his lips. Malcolm used his lips, tongue, and teeth to stimulate the sensitive button and Cilla bucked hard, grinding against his face. Her climax came abruptly. In an instant she went from grinding wildly against his mouth to every muscle in her body tensed, her body planking as every nerve ending fired heat. She tried to pull herself from him, but Malcolm held her tight, his mouth still clamped over her as his tongue lavished lick after lick against her.

Satisfaction radiated across her face, her hair in a wild halo around her head. Her skin glistened from the perspiration that beaded her brow. Her entire body felt like Jell-O and she found herself unable to lift even a finger to move. Malcolm licked his way back up her body, kissing his way past her belly button, pausing to kiss each nipple and nuzzle her neck one more time. Cilla was panting, still catching her breath when she realized his cock was still erect, tapping against her sweet spot.

Cilla spread her legs even more to welcome him in. He slowly rubbed the tip of his organ up and down her glistening slit. She encouraged him with her eyes as he pressed himself past her engorged lips, their melding the sweetest intrusion. Malcolm leaned into her, slowly pushing himself inside of her. Her juices dripped over his cock as he thrust himself deeply into her. Cilla threw back her head, her eyes closed, pleasure dancing across her expression.

He held still, watching her face as her body adjusted to his size. He pushed slowly forward, then drew back and pushed forward again. He held her hips, steadying himself as he began to thrust earnestly. Cilla met him stroke for stroke as they fell into an easy rhythm with each other. Their pace increased. The sound of skin slapping skin, grunts and whimpers slipping past parted lips, breathing thick and raspy filled the air.

Malcolm drove into her and moved a hand to her chest, rubbing her nipples until they were hard and puckered. She was hot and tight and as he danced inside her he drew his thumb across her profile, slipping it past her lips into her mouth. Cilla began sucking it, as he plowed harder and harder. She sucked one finger then another into her mouth until she was practically fellating his entire hand. Her muscles suddenly tightened around his dick as she locked her muscular legs around his waist, holding him tight. A scream caught in her throat as her second orgasm hit hard. Her inner lining convulsed over and over again and then his own climax wracked his body. The moment was explosive, each screaming the other's name.

Muscles tensed as they rode wave after wave of sheer pleasure. Neither could imagine anything being better, marveling how intensely each intimate encounter consumed them. Every coherent thought was lost, both blinded by the intoxicating sensations. It was gratification unlike anything either had ever experienced. Holding tight to each other they slid easily into the afterglow. Malcolm cupped her buttocks, his body still lost deep inside hers. He held her close, as he whispered softly.

"Next time," he said, squeezing each cheek as he trailed his fingers between them.

Cilla giggled softly, her eyes closing as she felt the first realm of sleep beginning to take hold. She nodded. "Promises, promises," she said.

He chuckled with her. "Oh yeah," he said, slumber pulling him hard. "Oh, yeah!"

Chapter Fifteen

Malcolm's flight to Baltimore had been in the air for some fifteen minutes and he was still grinning like a Cheshire cat. His time with Cilla had gone by faster than either would have liked. Before he knew it he'd had to get out of her bed and back to work. It had been two short days and most of it they'd spent wrapped around each other. When they weren't making love, they were making plans for their future, still uncertain about the details of their wedding.

Checking in on the girls had been easy, the twins too distracted by all their stuff to have even missed him. Checking in on his mother had been something else. The matriarch had actually scolded him and as he thought back on it he couldn't help but smile. Although he was used to his mother's puritan standards, her old-fashioned morality still came at the most inopportune times. For a brief moment he'd thought about reminding her that he was a grown man who paid his own bills, and hers, too, but he'd bit back the words. Her being concerned didn't warrant his disrespect even if he did think it wasn't any of her business whose bed he slept in at night. He blew a low sigh as he thought about his beloved mother. He and Cilla were going to have to marry soon if there was going to be any peace in their home.

Leaving her had actually been one of the most difficult things for him to do. He'd bypassed his usual morning run to dance between her legs instead, his body craving hers. And then he'd wanted to linger there as if he had nothing else to do. The memory pulled his smile wider.

As he'd risen from the bed Cilla had narrowed her gaze, eyeing him seductively. There'd been the sweetest pout pulling at her mouth.

"Stay," Cilla had said, leaning up on her elbow.

He'd laughed as he shook his head. "I can't and you can't either. You have to go to work too."

Cilla had sighed, her eyes rolling as she threw her body back against the mattress. "Don't remind me," she'd whined softly.

"I need to get ready," he'd said, smiling down on her. "Care to join me?" He held out a hand, gesturing for her to take the lead into the bathroom.

Rising, Cilla had given him a slight curtsy then had wiggled seductively past him. Malcolm had followed quickly behind her. Inside the tiled bathroom Cilla turned on the water, waiting as it warmed. When the first rise of steam began to fill the room she stepped into the shower. Malcolm followed her, closing the shower doors behind them.

Standing in the dry end of the shower he watched as she turned to face him, leaning back in the hot water with her eyes closed, her naked body like a vision to his lustful eyes. Water cascaded over her head and face, down across her skin. As she swept her hand through her hair, drawing the thick strands down her back, his manhood had hardened, surprising him. He'd been in his teens the last time he could get erection after erection with ease.

Cilla had opened her eyes to look at him, allowing her gaze to drift downward. Her gaze was appreciative, her smile yearning. She lifted her eyes slowly back to his, crooking her finger in a *come hither* gesture. With his own seductive stare Malcolm had complied, joining her under the stream of hot water as he wrapped his arms around her waist. He kissed her deeply, warm water dripping like rain over them both.

With no further invitation needed he'd pushed her back against the tile of the shower wall. His left hand slipped down to the back of her upper thigh, pulling her leg upward. Cilla instinctively wrapped it around him, drawing him closer. They stood at the perfect angle for him to enter her warm channel one more time.

In no time at all he was buried deep inside of her. As he began to stroke in and out, he lifted her up by her ass, moving her to wrap both of her legs around him. Using the wall to hold her up he took her as if he were on a mission, his speed and aggressiveness a pleasant surprise. Amazement danced in Cilla's eyes. Minutes passed and despite the intensity of his previous orgasms Malcolm had felt another eruption rising with a vengeance. He stroked her harder and faster, over and over again. Neither of them lasted long, their coupling explosive. The intensity of his climax sent Malcolm to his knees, fighting to keep them both from falling. Her body shuddering, Cilla cried out, biting her bottom lip. She had clung to him and he'd held her, the shower's spray beating down against their flesh. Everything between them had felt like heaven.

All of Malcolm's memories were sweet. One incredible moment after another. Life with Cilla was more than he could have ever anticipated and with every day they shared together he wanted ten more. Even in their few moments of disagreement he felt good about the two of them together. He'd hit the jackpot and he wasn't willing to let the prize go.

As the plane landed Malcolm shook the fog from his head. Taking a deep breath he made a concerted effort to focus. He was so love-struck that it was like he was some pimply-faced teenager and not a man who'd lived a lifetime. A man who had loved hard and had lost love once before. He straightened his shoulders and cracked his neck, twisting his head from one side to the other. Cilla would be there at the end of the week when he flew back. She'd be waiting, her love for him as intense as his own. He trusted that. Until then he had business that needed to be handled.

Maxine met him at the door with her exuberant smile and his requisite cup of coffee. Despite the bright smile on her face she looked weary, as if the weight of the world was bearing down on her shoulders. He didn't need to ask her what was wrong, already knowing who had put that worry in her eyes.

"She's out of control," Maxine said after they'd gotten past the small talk. "I had to go downtown and ask for a restraining order against my own daughter. It just doesn't make any sense to me."

Malcolm shook his head, just as baffled as his former mother-in-law. "I don't understand what's gotten into her."

"Them locking up that no-good boyfriend of hers just sent her right off the deep end."

Malcolm's own good mood had taken a nosedive. "I'm sorry you have to go through this, Miss Maxine."

She shrugged, her narrow shoulders jutting upward. She drifted off into thought, her eyes glazing. That moment of quiet was almost haunting before she spoke again.

"You always have such high hopes for your children. From the moment they draw their first breath we start planning their futures and dreaming big dreams for them. We hope and pray that as they grow older our dreams will become their dreams.

"I lost all my boys to these streets and just when I thought she was on the right track, these damn streets came back to claim Shanell, too." She'd been staring out the window at the streets below and turned to meet Malcolm's eye. "Don't you fail Cleo and Claudia the way I failed my children. Do whatever you have to do to keep them from this madness," she said, before shifting her back to stare out the window.

Malcolm moved to her side, pressing a large hand against her shoulder. "You didn't fail them, Miss Maxine. You did everything you were supposed to do and more. There's no one around who'd ever say you weren't a good mother. You sacrificed everything you had for Shanell and her brothers. What happened to them they did to themselves. Their bad decisions and poor choices took them from here. You didn't have anything to do with their failings."

Miss Maxine blew a heavy sigh. Everything in her head told her Malcolm was right. Everything in her heart wasn't quite so sure. She nodded, forcing that bright smile back onto her face.

"The girls are very excited about you getting married," she said, changing the subject. "And your mama is just beside herself. Claudette really likes this young woman."

Malcolm smiled back. "Cilla's very special. She makes me incredibly happy."

"I hope I get to meet her soon."

"You will. I was hoping she could have come with me on this trip but she had to work." His eyes suddenly widened, his brows shifting upward. "Hey, maybe you can come down to North Carolina this weekend? The girls would love to see you and it'll be a great chance for us all to spend some quality time together."

Maxine nodded. "I'd like that. I'd like that a lot."

"Good, because you and I are still family and it's important to me that you like Cilla."

"I'm sure I'm going to love her."

Malcolm moved back to his desk. "We really need to talk about the new office in North Carolina. I'm hoping you'll think about moving and come help me run things from there."

"Are you thinking about closing this office?"

He shook his head. "No, ma'am. We have more

than enough business that it only makes good business sense to keep them both up and running."

Miss Maxine proffered her agreement. After reviewing his schedule and sliding a half dozen checks across the desktop for him to sign she headed toward the door. She came to an abrupt stop, her hand on the doorknob. Turning back to face him she met Malcolm's stare.

"What's wrong?" he questioned.

She blew another heavy sigh. "Watch your back, Malcolm. My daughter's not herself and she's blaming you for her all her troubles. I tried to talk some sense into her but that was like talking to a brick wall. Those drugs have her all messed up and I'm afraid of what she might do."

Malcolm gave her a slight smile. "Don't you worry about me. And don't you worry about Shanell. She did her worst when she put Cleo in harm's way. I won't let that ever happen again. You can trust that."

With one last nod Miss Maxine exited the room, leaving Malcolm to his own thoughts. Staring after her Malcolm couldn't miss the heaviness that bore back down on her posture. Despite his assurances she was still burdened with worry. And suddenly, so was he.

Cilla missed Malcolm something fierce. They'd spoken a few times since he'd gone to Baltimore and hearing his voice had her wishing he was back home by her side. Mama Claudette didn't miss the expression that crossed Cilla's face as she disconnected Malcolm's call. The matriarch laughed heartily.

"You two are funny to me," she said with a deep cackle.

Cilla laughed with her. "Are we that bad?"

"You're in love. You're worse than bad."

"I do love your son. He means the world to me."

Mama Claudette nodded. "He feels the same way about you."

Cilla smiled. She had welcomed the opportunity to spend time with Malcolm's mother and his daughters without him. It was important to her that they build a relationship aside from the bond she and Malcolm shared. She knew that to do that meant them sharing time and space together that had nothing at all to do with the man they all loved.

This day was her time with her future mother-in-law. She'd spent the previous evening with the twins. Picking the girls up from school had been an experience, Cilla thought, reflecting back to the previous day. Both girls had been excited about her coming. There'd been rolling jokes about her having to wait with the other parents in the kiss-and-go pickup lane. After a trip to the public library to finish off their homework, they'd gone for an early dinner at Fat Daddy's, then had walked the stores of Crabtree Valley Mall.

Earthbound Trading Company had been Claudia's favorite store. Spencer's had been Cleo's. One purple rock and a Bob Marley T-shirt later and the girls had been over-the-moon happy. Cilla's on-sale finds at Belk's had her on cloud nine as well. By the time they'd finished testing makeup samples at MAC and grabbing dessert from the Cheesecake

Factory, the three were better than good with each other.

Both girls had been animated, eagerly sharing their lives with her. The laughter had been abundant and their teasing made her feel like family. They'd had a great time together and Cilla was hopeful for the same with Mama Claudette.

"So, where are we off to?" the older woman questioned, pulling Cilla back to the conversation. "Because I don't usually wear gym clothes out in public."

Cilla laughed. "I thought you and I could do something totally out of character for both of us. We're going to a pole dancing class."

There was a brief moment of stunned silence. Wide-eyed Mama Claudette turned to look at her. "Pole dancing?"

Cilla nodded, a nervous giggle easing past her lips. "Yes, ma'am. My friend Bianca takes lessons at a studio off of Glenwood Avenue. They throw introductory parties once every month and I thought it might be fun for the two of us."

Mama Claudette paused for a brief moment before a wide smile filled her face. She laughed, the wealth of it warm and endearing. Her gray head bobbed against her thin neck. "Pole dancing! Well, I'll be damned!"

The dance studios at Turn Me Loose Fitness featured women of all ages and sizes participating in traditional and nontraditional classes. The pole dancing, twerk fitness, and Zumba classes were all filled to capacity. Once they were inside and Mama Claudette was introduced to other women of her generation she cast aside her preconceived notions of them going to some dimly lit hot spot where there was going to be gyrating and booty popping. The entire atmosphere was slanted toward more of a G rating than an X rating.

Their pole dancing involved performing aerobic moves on a vertical pole. The women who were proficient at it included spins and inversions in high heels. For their beginners' class Cilla and Mama Claudette started with a warm-up and stretching, then moved on to several arm, leg, and ab moves that evolved into a short routine on the silver-toned floor-to-ceiling rod. After the cool down they moved on to wine, cheese, and conversation with the other women, everyone joking and laughing about the good time they'd had.

Cilla was beaming as Mama Claudette enrolled in a series of twelve classes, excitement flooding her face as she wrote them a check. She was still laughing as they made their way back to Cilla's car.

"I'm so glad you had a good time, Mama Claudette! I was nervous!"

"So was I but that was just so much fun!"

Cilla nodded. "I don't know about you but I've worked up an appetite. Would you like to grab something to eat?"

"I have never eaten sushi before. Do you think we could go get sushi for dinner?"

"I know a great sushi place," Cilla said, smiling as she started her engine.

Thirty minutes later they were sitting at a table at Chopstix, a local Asian restaurant and sushi bar on Creedmoor Road. Mama Claudette was still extolling the merits of her good time, the dance experience more than she could ever have anticipated.

"Thought my hip was going to give out when we had to do that shimmy, dip, and roll!" she said.

Laughter rang between them. "Those leg extensions almost did me in!" Cilla exclaimed.

Mama Claudette took a sip of her plum wine. "I'm so glad we did that. I would never have thought about doing something like that on my own. I can't wait to tell Malcolm."

"I can just imagine what he's going to have to say."

A brief moment of quiet passed between them as the waitress placed the first tray of their order onto the table. Cilla had started them with a sashimi appetizer. It was three kinds of raw fish: tuna, salmon, and yellowtail, sliced into thin strips. A petite bowl of soy sauce, a dab of wasabi, and slices of pickled ginger rounded out the condiments.

Mama Claudette's first bite was hesitant as she tasted the salmon, adjusting to the texture against her tongue. "It's sweet," she said, a hint of surprise in her tone.

"I really like the tuna," Cilla said, the fish melting like butter against her tongue.

Mama Claudette reached for the last piece on the plate, a smile pulling at her thin lips as she savored the flavor.

Cilla couldn't help but smile with her. "I think we have a new sushi fan!"

"It's better than I expected."

"You're really going to like the other dishes," Cilla said as their waitress rested one tray after another onto the table. "Thank you," Cilla said, meeting the woman's eye.

Mama Claudette leaned back in her seat. She

crossed her hands together in her lap. "Cilla, you have been really good for this family. The twins adore you. They couldn't stop talking about you last night and you've done wonders for that son of mine."

Cilla smiled.

Mama Claudette continued. "I can't remember the last time I saw Malcolm so happy. It's like he's a different man. He won't admit it but after his divorce he stopped living life. He was going through the motions, doing everything he was supposed to do but he wasn't really happy. There was no joy there and he worked very hard to hide that from me and the girls. But since meeting you there's light back in his eyes."

"Shanell really broke his heart, didn't she?"

"Shanell almost destroyed my son," she said matter-of-factly. Mama Claudette blew a heavy sigh, her eyes shifting back and forth in thought. "One day you and Malcolm might have a son of your own and you'll understand how I feel. You want only the best for your children and when you know in your heart that something or someone isn't good for them, you want to protect them. And you can do that when they're young but then one day you realize they're all grown up and you can't run interference anymore.

"I couldn't run interference and save my son from that girl. I didn't like her and I knew she was bad for him. Then I made the cardinal mistake of showing and telling him and her how I felt. That pushed them closer together. Malcolm was hell-bent on proving me wrong and Shanell wanted to show everybody that he loved her more than he loved his mother. My dislike for Shanell put Malcolm in an awkward spot. It made it harder for him to see what we were all trying to tell him."

Tears suddenly misted the woman's gaze. Cilla reached across the table and gently squeezed the woman's hand. Compassion blanketed her expression.

Mama Claudette suddenly shook her head. "Let's change the subject. I purposely don't talk about Shanell. She's the mother of my grandbabies. I don't have to like her, but for Cleo and Claudia's sake I respect how they feel about her. She's their mother and despite everything she's done, the girls do love her. So I won't talk badly about her, no matter how I feel."

Cilla nodded. She changed the subject. "So, have you ever been scuba diving?"

Mama Claudette laughed. "No, I can't say that I have."

"I think you and I should put scuba diving on our bucket list of things to do together."

The older woman nodded her head slowly. "That might be doable."

Cilla gestured toward the dragon roll, picking up a piece with her chopsticks. "This is really good," she said. "You have to try it!"

Following her lead, Mama Claudette relished the delicate flavors, approval shining in her eyes. "Cilla, something tells me you're going to be good for me, too!"

* * *

Malcolm had tried to call his family but no one was answering their phone. All of his calls had gone to voice mail, neither Cilla, his mother, nor either of his daughters picking up their phones. His anxiety level was just about to shoot up a notch when he stepped into his home and no one was there to greet him. The house was quiet, not a sound coming from any room.

He took a quick glance at his watch. He couldn't begin to know where they all were. School was out and any other time they would all be getting ready for the next day. He was just about to go scour the neighborhood when he heard the garage door rising and his mother's SUV pull inside. Their laughter was loud and raucous as they all came in through the utility room door. The twins led the way, Mama Claudette and Cilla on their heels.

"Will someone please tell me what's going on?" he asked, relief wafting in his tone.

"Hi, Daddy!" the girls chimed in unison.

"Hey, Son-shine!"

"Hi, honey!"

"We weren't expecting you back until tomorrow," his mother said, moving to drop her shopping bags onto the table.

"Is that why none of you was answering your phone?"

The girls all shot each other a look, erupting in a fit of giggles.

"Sorry about that, honey," Cilla said. "That was my fault."

Mama Claudette pointed at Claudia. "Baby girl, go get all the phones out of the glove compartment, please."

Confusion washed over Malcolm's face.

Cilla laughed. "We were in a no-phone zone. I took the girls to the food bank to volunteer this afternoon and we weren't allowed to have our phones. Then we went shopping for toys to take to the women's shelter for their kids."

Cleo interjected. "We forgot all about 'em!"

He nodded, taking a deep breath. "Well, it sounds like you all had a good day."

"We had a great day!" Claudia exclaimed, moving back into the room. The young girl dropped all the phones onto the kitchen counter.

"We picked up Chinese food for dinner," Cilla said. "I hope that's okay."

Malcolm nodded. "What's not okay is not one of you has given me a hug or kiss. Didn't anybody miss me?"

A round of laughter rang between the women a second time.

Malcolm tossed up his hands, a wide grin pulling at his full lips. "Really? This is how you all treat me?"

"I told you he was spoiled," Mama Claudette said, gesturing toward Cilla with a nod. "He was a titty baby, you know!"

Malcolm's expression was incredulous. He looked from one to the other.

"It's okay, Daddy," Cleo said. She gave him a serious look. "We'll work on that self-confidence together."

Claudia nodded in agreement.

"You'll get over it," Mama Claudette admonished, a hint of humor in her tone.

Cilla chuckled softly. "I didn't know you were so sensitive, honey."

His eyes widened. "Sensitive?"

"His daddy was like that," Mama Claudette said, her head bobbing. "Just as sensitive as he could be. Worked my nerves sometimes!"

"It really is an unattractive quality in a man," Cilla said.

Malcolm tossed up his hands. "Okay, who are you people and what have you done with my family?"

Malcolm peeked in on the girls, both sleeping soundly. His mother had retired for the night as well. He and Cilla were left to lock up for the night. He smiled as he stood watching one twin and then the other. It had been a good night. They'd gotten a good laugh at his expense, their teasing planned as they'd pulled into the driveway. Once they'd gotten a rise out of him the girls admitted their ruse.

"You should have seen your face!" his mother had laughed, hugging him warmly.

"I thought you were going to cry," Cilla teased as she kissed his mouth.

Even the twins had laughed at him thinking it hilarious that they'd been able to poke fun at him.

Back downstairs Cilla was wiping down the table and counters. She'd brewed two cups of hot tea for them and had spilled a smidgen of sugar in the process. She smiled when he entered the room. "Is everybody okay?"

He nodded. "The girls are knocked out."

"They had a full day. You would have been so proud of them."

"I'd never thought about having them volunteer

before but I think it was a great idea. I'm glad you did that."

"Well, they had asked me to take them to the movies after school but I was already committed. Then they asked if they could tag along. I didn't see any reason not to let them go and your mother thought it would be good for them too."

Malcolm smiled. He grabbed both cups of tea, leading her into the family room. He turned on the television and lowered the volume. Jimmy Kimmel was just finishing his opening monologue. They sat side by side on the loveseat, Cilla leaning easily into his side.

He kissed her cheek. "I missed you."

"I missed you more," she replied, lifting her lips to his. The kiss was sweet, an easy, gentle connection. They relaxed against each other, their back and forth caresses the gentlest exchanges.

"So, the girls told me you all had a slumber party while I was gone."

"We did. Pajamas, popcorn, *Twilight* movies, the works! We had a great time."

He trailed his fingers across her thigh. "Do we get to have a slumber party tonight? Are you going to stay over again?"

Cilla laughed, looping her arms around his neck. "Nope! I'm going home."

He shook his head, blowing a loud sigh. "We need to pick a wedding date. And I vote for tomorrow. I'm tired of you going back across town every night. I want you here in my bed tonight. I want you there every night."

"We do need to pick out a date. In fact, I think we should get married on the first of the month."

"Really? On my birthday?"

She nodded. "Or we could wait until next year and get married on my birthday."

"I'm not waiting. I actually like that idea. Will that give you enough time to do everything you need to do?"

She nodded. "Yes. I know exactly what I want now and I think it'll make you happy too."

He kissed her mouth. "Marrying you will make me very happy. I don't care how we do it."

"Well, it was the girls who came up with the idea and I think it'll be perfect."

Even with the late-night hour the two sat talking, oblivious to time. Cilla was excited to share the ideas for their wedding. Malcolm's excitement soon matched hers, the man pleasantly surprised to discover that the women in his life had come together in such a special way.

As Cilla described every detail he could actually picture the moment the two of them would exchange their vows. If he were honest he was more than ready, not needing to wait until his birthday to make Cilla his wife. He couldn't stop himself from saying so.

She pressed her mouth to his, kissing him passionately. "The first will be here before you know it, baby, and then you're going to be stuck with me forever."

Chapter Sixteen

Cleo and Claudia were trying on their wedding dresses for the umpteenth time. Both girls absolutely loved the vintage design that Cilla had selected. The color was blush, just the barest hint of pink to complement their warm complexions. The gowns were Chantilly lace with dainty bateau necklines and wrist-length sleeves. The styling was demure and age-appropriate, stopping at their knees.

"I'm wearing my hair down and I'm going to ask the hair stylist to put rollers in so my curls are better," Claudia proclaimed, staring at her reflection in the full-length mirror.

"I want braids," Cleo said. "Miss Cilla said I can do braids."

"Do you think I should do braids too?"

Cleo shrugged. "I think you should do you. Miss Cilla said even if we wear the same dress that we can always find ways to show our different personalities."

Claudia nodded before easing herself onto the

bed. She crossed her legs and rested her hands into her lap.

Cleo sat down beside her. She turned her body just enough to face her sister, consternation tinting her eyes. She chewed her bottom lip nervously. "Do you think Daddy and Miss Cilla will ever get divorced?"

"That's stupid, Cleo! They're not even married yet. Why would you be asking about them getting divorced?"

"I just . . . well . . ." She hesitated, wanting to find the right words to voice her thoughts. She took a deep breath. "I like Miss Cilla and I don't want to like her too much and then she and Daddy get divorced and we can't love her anymore."

Claudia nodded her understanding. "Even if they did get divorced Daddy would let us still be friends with her because she's a nice person. He wouldn't want us to be mean to her or anything."

"I guess you're right."

"I don't know why you're worried, Cleo. Daddy and Miss Cilla love each other. They're just like Romeo and Juliet."

"Like Jay-Z and Beyoncé!"

"Do you think Grandma will let us wear makeup for the wedding?" Claudia jumped up to eye her face in the mirror. "I hope we can wear makeup. At least some eye shadow and a little lipstick."

"Grandma will let us if Miss Cilla says we can. But I just want to wear lip gloss."

"You want shiny, bubblegum lips!" Claudia said, giggling.

"Shiny, orange bubblegum lips!" her sister added, giggling with her.

Claudia tossed herself back onto the bed. "Well, I don't know about the makeup but Miss Cilla told Daddy that she was going to take us to get manicures and pedicures. And we get to buy new shoes, too."

"I want four-inch heels!" Cleo exclaimed.

"Daddy is not going to let you wear four-inch heels."

"He might if Miss Cilla says it's okay."

"Miss Cilla won't say four-inch heels are okay. She doesn't even wear heels that high."

Cleo shrugged. "After they get married what are we going to call her?"

"I was wondering that too. Will we have to keep calling her 'Miss Cilla'?"

"That would be weird. I mean she'll be our stepmother. We can't call her 'Miss.'"

"Should we call her 'Mom'?"

The two girls locked gazes.

"Mommy would be really mad if we did," Cleo said. "Really mad!"

"I just think we should ask Daddy. He'll tell us what to do."

"Ask your daddy what?" Mama Claudette questioned, startling them as she came into the room. She looked from one to the other. "Why do you girls have them dresses on? Are you trying to get them dirty?"

Both shook their heads no.

"We just feel pretty with them on," Claudia said.

Mama Claudette smiled. "You girls are beautiful no matter what. Now change out of them and come get your dinner, please." She moved to unzip one and then the other. She waited until both dresses were back on their racks and in their dress bags hanging back in the closet.

Cleo and Claudette were still chatting back and forth, their conversation shifting from curious to serious to random. Their grandmother listened with one ear, pleased to hear them so happy. She moved toward the door, her hand on the knob when Cleo called her back.

"What, baby girl?"

"Grandma, how come you don't have a boyfriend?"

Mama Claudette laughed. "What do I need a boyfriend for?"

"To take you dancing," one twin chimed.

"And to dinner and the movies," added the other.

"I can do all that without a boyfriend."

"But you'd have more fun."

"And you can play kissy face like Daddy and Miss Cilla."

"I am too old to be playing kissy face. Besides I'm old and old men my age don't have teeth. Who wants to be kissing on a man with no teeth!"

The girls laughed hysterically.

Mama Claudette gave them both a bright smile. "Come on now so we can eat. That's enough foolishness for one day."

Malcolm sat alone in his office. The house was quiet, everyone sleeping. He leaned forward to tie his running shoe. Despite his best efforts he was feeling the exhaustion, wishing he could crawl back into his bed for one more hour, or even two, of sleep. But sleep wasn't an option. He needed to get his run in and then meet Cilla for their morning coffee. There was much he had to share with her.

Heading toward his car he thought back to the dinner conversation from the night before. Cleo and Claudia had announced that they didn't want to call Cilla by her first name once the couple was married. According to them all the important grown-ups in their life all had some sort of title, pointing out that they called the neighbors and casual acquaintances "Miss." The two girls had deemed Cilla deserving of much more. The two had tossed around ideas, finally proclaiming that they just wanted to call her "Mom."

Thinking about Shanell gave him reason to pause. Despite his argument that they still had a mother the girls had argued back that they would still call their mother "Mommy," their way of distinguishing one from the other. Thinking about it Malcolm knew that if the shoe were on the other foot he wouldn't be thrilled about his daughters calling someone else "Dad" even if he was "Daddy." He also knew, without saying it out loud, that for them to call Cilla "Mom" would be a problem for his ex-wife, even if she was temporarily missing in action. If not now, then definitely later. But there was no arguing that the woman he loved and planned to make his wife had made quite an impression on his family.

His daughters had been on a roll, surprising him with some of their comments and observations. Even his mother had been impressed but not enough to offer any advice. "Talk to Cilla about it," she admonished, "then both of you talk to the girls. You'll figure it out."

Malcolm trusted that they would figure it out and that in the end his daughters would be happy. But he also knew that he would have to talk to Shanell about it at some point. Despite the tension currently between them he didn't want her blindsided. No matter what he felt about the woman he knew he couldn't do that do her.

An hour later he was sitting in Starbucks waiting for Cilla. She had the sweetest smile on her face when she came through the door, waving at him excitedly.

"Hey, you!"

"Hey, yourself," Cilla answered. She leaned to kiss his mouth, wrapping her arms around his neck to hug him. "How was your run?"

"It was good. You really should run with me sometime."

She tilted her head slightly as she gave him a look.

Malcolm laughed. "Or not!"

Cilla took the first sip of her coffee. "Everyone okay at home?"

"Ahhh, those daughters of mine!" he extolled.

"What did they do?"

Malcolm repeated the previous night's exchange between him and the twins. Cilla's eye widened, shock registering across her face.

"Where did that come from?" she questioned.

He smiled. "My girls love you and I think this just lets us know how much."

Cilla sat back in her seat, drifting off into thought. She and the girls had grown closer. They'd been spending much time together and she enjoyed those moments when they were silly and having fun. She was comfortable with their curiosity and knew they trusted her enough to share their secrets and ask her questions about everything from boys to their bodies. Their friendship was special and belied the original tension that had started their relationship. She loved them as much as she imagined herself loving a child of her own.

Malcolm watched her for a brief moment before speaking again. "Have you ever thought about what the girls should call you?"

She shifted her eyes back to his, shrugging her shoulders. "In all honesty, I really hadn't thought about it, Malcolm."

He nodded. "Neither had I but clearly it's been on the girls' minds."

The two continued the conversation as Malcolm voiced his concerns, thoughts of his ex-wife on his mind. She could feel his apprehensions, even agreeing with his reluctance.

"I can see how this could turn out badly. I don't know if I would want my child to call some other woman 'Mommy,' no matter how genuine her intentions are," she said. "I wouldn't blame their mother if she gets upset. I think we can figure something else out."

"Well, I think I'm going to let you and the girls work this out," Malcolm concluded. "Let me know what you come up with."

Cilla laughed. "I see how you work!"

"Yep!" He leaned forward to kiss her mouth. "What time do you have to be at the office?" he questioned.

Cilla grinned. "What did you have in mind?"

Malcolm skidded his chair closer to hers. He leaned his face close to hers, his cheek brushing against her cheek. He whispered in her ear and she blushed profusely. When he leaned back he lifted his eyebrows at her suggestively.

"Mr. Cobb!" she exclaimed, her voice dropping low.

He shrugged his shoulders and leaned forward to whisper in her ear a second time. His words were suggestive and sexy, dirty innuendo filling his comments.

Cilla's eyes skated back and forth, looking to see that no one else had heard him. Her seductive smile lifted easily. She stood up, pressing her hands against his shoulders as she leaned to whisper back into his ear. "Let's go back to my house."

Shanell Cobb had been sitting in the parent parking lot of Ravenscroft School every day for weeks, watching as her daughters came and went. In the mornings they'd skip off bus #437 or from their grandmother's car. But in the afternoon it was Malcolm's new girlfriend who sometimes picked them up.

She sat watching as the girls rushed to their father's car, he and that woman standing in conversation with two other parents. A tear fell from Shanell's eyes. That was supposed to be her standing at Malcolm's side holding his hand as he laughed happily. It was supposed to be her that their daughters ran to, excitement painting their expressions as they showed off homework and test scores. It was supposed to be her but it wasn't. She sighed, the weight of it toxic to her spirit.

As they all jumped into Malcolm's car and pulled

off she thought about following but she didn't. The last of her high was starting to wear away and she knew that the drop would be monumental if she didn't get a quick fix soon. Her hands were beginning to shake and that twitch was back, her eyes watering and the left one flicking erratically. She swiped at her face with the back of her hand, sweat beginning to run profusely in spite of the car's air-conditioning blowing on high.

Flipping through the car's ashtray she found the remnant of a cigarette butt and lit it, taking a deep drag of the nicotine. A sudden rap on the driver's-side window startled her and her head whipped left to see who it was. One of the school's uniformed security officers was eyeing her critically. He gestured for her to roll down the window.

"Excuse me, ma'am, but you can't park here."

Shanell swiped her hands across her face a second time. "Oh, sorry," she muttered. "I didn't . . . I didn't know."

"Yes, ma'am, this is the loading zone only. But you're welcome to pull your car over to the other side." He gestured with his hand, pointing to a row of empty parking spots.

She nodded. "Okay," she said as she dragged her palm through her tangled hair.

The security guard was still staring. "Are you okay, ma'am?" he questioned, concern shimmering in his eyes.

She nodded. "Yeah," she said, a bald-faced lie passing over her lips. "I'm just great!"

Starting her car's engine she tossed up a hand in

the man's direction, pulling her car out of the lot and into the early evening traffic.

The twins sat at the kitchen table finishing homework. Malcolm and Cilla were preparing their evening meal and Mama Claudette was in the adjoining space reading a book. No one expected the doorbell when it rang, everyone looking about in surprise.

"Are you expecting someone?" Cilla asked.

He shook his head. "It's probably a Girl Scout with cookies," he commented.

"I'll get it," Mama Claudette said.

"If it is a Girl Scout," Malcolm added, "buy some Thin Mints."

Cilla rolled her eyes. "I thought you were eating healthy?"

He grinned. "You're eating healthy. I don't have a wedding dress to fit into!"

Cilla laughed. "I will have no problems fitting into my dress, thank you very much!"

He shrugged, his broad shoulders pushing toward the ceiling.

They were all startled when Mama Claudette suddenly called Malcolm's name, panic ringing in her tone. "Malcolm! Malcolm! Come quick!"

His eyes widened as he suddenly bolted out the room.

Cleo and Claudia jumped to follow before Cilla stalled their steps. "You girls stay right there," she admonished. "Let your father handle whatever's going on."

"But what's happening? Who is it?" both exclaimed simultaneously.

Hearing the raised voices Cilla had her own questions but insuring the girls were safe took precedent over her curiosity. She took a deep breath. "If your dad needs us he'll let us know," she said, pointing them both back into their seats.

Mama Claudette rushed into the room. She tossed Cilla an anxious look as she wrung her hands nervously together.

"You two stay here with your grandmother," Cilla snapped as she headed toward the front of the home.

Malcolm stood in the doorway, his cell phone pressed to his ear with one hand, the other holding tight to the front door. Shanell stood in the doorway, barring him from closing it. She was drunk and sloppy, her arms flailing, slurring her words.

"Those are my damn kids," Shanell was spitting, slapping a heavy palm against her chest. "I wanna see my babies!"

"There is a restraining order against her," Malcolm was saying, clearly speaking to a 911 operator. "She's intoxicated and she's being violent," he added as he ducked, Shanell taking a swing at his head.

"I'm not 'toxicated!" Shanell snapped, swinging a second time. She lost her balance for a brief moment but came back throwing her petite frame at the door as she tried barreling her way inside.

There was suddenly a piercing shriek vibrating through the whole house as Shanell screamed loudly for both girls. "Cleo! Claudia! Where are you! Where are my babies?"

Cilla heard the girls racing toward them before their grandmother could stop them. "Claudia, stop!" she said as she grabbed the girl by her shoulders. Cleo stopped on her own accord, coming to an abrupt halt at Cilla's side.

"Mommy?"

Malcolm tossed a quick glance over his shoulder. Frustration creased his brow, a level of anger in his eyes that the girls had never seen before. It was almost frightening. Cilla drew both girls to her. Behind her she could hear Mama Claudette breathing anxiously.

"Upstairs! Now!" Malcolm snapped, looking from one child to the other.

"But Daddy, it's just . . ." Claudia started, hot tears suddenly welling up in her eyes.

"Claudia, please! You and Cleo get upstairs now!" he ordered, his tone brusque.

Mama Claudette grabbed both girls by the hand. "Come with me," she said, pulling the two along with her.

Shanell was still screaming in the doorway, trying to push her way inside. "I wanna see my babies! Let me see my girls!" Her tone shifted from begging to angry. "Cleo! Claudia! Get over here! You hear me? Get over here now!"

The two women suddenly locked gazes. Venom pierced the stare Shanell gave Cilla. She was suddenly even more frantic, punching and slapping at Malcolm as she tried harder to force her way inside. Profanity spilled past her lips as she called Cilla everything but a child of God. In the distance they could all hear the sirens turning into the drive. Flashing blue lights flickered against the darkening sky. And then Shanell fell to the ground sobbing. As the first police officer stepped onto the porch Malcolm's ex-wife was inconsolable.

Malcolm was still filling out a report with the local police department when Cilla climbed the stairs to check on the girls. Both stood at the front window in Cleo's room staring out to the line of patrol cars in the driveway. Their mother sat handcuffed on the manicured lawn as two EMS officers checked her vital signs and the injuries to her arms and hands from the strikes she'd thrown.

"What's wrong with her? Why did she do that?" they asked, throwing questions at Cilla faster than she could answer them.

"Let's come away from the window," Cilla said, gesturing for them to sit beside her.

Both girls sat reluctantly, turning their tear-streaked faces toward her. She sighed, air blowing past her lips. "I'm really sorry that you girls are upset," Cilla said. "Your mom and dad didn't mean to scare you."

"She's drunk, isn't she?" Cleo snapped, a hint of attitude in her tone.

"She's been drinking and she's not herself right now."

"I hate her," Cleo said, tears streaming over her cheeks.

Cilla shook her head. "No, you don't and don't you ever say that again. Your mother has an illness and she's sick. When she gets like that she doesn't know what she's doing. But she loves you."

"No, she doesn't."

"Why would you say that, Cleo?" Claudia cried.

"Because it's the truth," Cleo snapped back.

Cilla took a deep breath. "She does love you and you both love her. Your mom is just going through a bad time right now. It won't always be like this."

"Do you promise, Mimi?" Claudia asked, calling her by the name they had finally agreed on. Mimi, close to Mommy but not too close. Just the next best thing.

Cilla nodded. "I promise that your daddy and I will both do everything we can to help your mom."

Both girls moved back to the window, staring back out as Shanell was moved from the grass to the backseat of a patrol car. Outside the door Malcolm stood listening, still trying to come to grips with all that had happened. He slid down the wall, drawing his knees to his chest. Mama Claudette stood against the other wall, both she and her son eavesdropping on the conversation as Cilla promised something neither was sure they could make happen.

"I don't know what to do," Malcolm said, throwing his hands up in frustration.

Cilla drummed her fingers against the table. "Well, we need to do something. She needs help and support and we have to find a way to make it better. And we have to make it better because if we don't it will destroy the girls."

"Shanell is not my responsibility. Her problems are not our problems."

"Shanell is the mother of your daughters. And

your daughters are both of our responsibilities. That makes Shanell our problem."

Malcolm closed his eyes, leaning back in his seat. He sat with his head bowed, his thoughts racing. Cilla was right and he knew it but it didn't make it easier. He felt her hand on his shoulder and he reached up to press his palm against the back of her fingers. Cilla kissed the top of his head.

"So what do you suggest we do?" Malcolm finally asked.

"Talk to the prosecutor. Instead of pressing charges against her see if they'll negotiate her going to a treatment program instead. See if the courts can force her to get help. Start there."

He sighed. "I'll think about it."

"Malcolm, you can't just think about it. You need to act. The girls can't go through another episode with their mother like this last time. They can't. It's not fair to them."

He nodded. "You really are a great Mimi," he said, lifting his eyes to hers. "And I have no doubts that you are going to make one incredible mommy when we have those sons of ours!"

"One step at a time," she said. "Right now Mimi has two girls who need cheering up. So I'm spending the night and we're all going to have a slumber party."

Malcolm leaned back. "You're actually sleeping over before we're married? What will my mother say?" he said facetiously.

"It was your mother's idea actually. She's making popcorn. I'm about to whip up some chocolate brownies and we're watching the old *Nutty Professor* movies. I hear that Eddie Murphy is someone's favorite."

Malcolm laughed. "And I wonder who you heard that from!"

"Cleo says you do an impressive Professor Sherman Klump impersonation. Claudia likes your impersonation of the grandmother better. I can't wait to see them both."

His laugh was gut deep, relieving the previous tension that had swept through the air. "I'm only doing my impersonations under one condition."

"And what's that?"

"Once the girls go to sleep you have to show me something."

Cilla giggled. "Can't do that. We're all sleeping downstairs in the family room together. All close and comfy."

"How close?"

"Very close and very comfy! With your mother and your daughters. All of us together, one big happy family in one big room."

Malcolm pulled her down into his lap. He pressed his palm to her face and kissed her mouth. His tongue trailed across her lips, sliding past the line of her teeth. He kissed her eagerly, capturing her mouth with his own. One hand trailed the length of her back, the other pressed warmly against her abdomen. His kiss was deep and passionate and lingering, building to the sweetest crescendo. When he finally broke the connection, letting her go, both were panting heavily.

His salacious stare was piercing. "We'll figure it

out," he whispered, winking one eye at her. "'Cause I'm still getting some. As soon as everyone's asleep!"

Cilla was lost in the depths of a sweet dream when she felt someone shaking her awake. A gentle hand clutched her shoulder, pulling her from the pink sand and blue ocean she was tripping through. When she opened her eyes Malcolm was kneeling at her side, an index finger pressed against his lips.

Rising up on her elbows she brushed the sleep from her eyes and took a quick glance around the darkened room. The television was still playing, the volume turned off. Mama Claudette lay on the sofa, her backside facing outward, her face lost between the upholstered cushions. The twins lay side by side in their sleeping bags, both sleeping soundly. She smiled as she connected her gaze with Malcolm's. There was a wide smile on his face. He gestured with an index finger, beckoning her to follow behind him.

Grabbing his hand Cilla moved onto her feet, tiptoeing behind him as he led the way to his office. Once inside he closed and locked the door, turning back to face her.

She shook her head. "You're trying to get us in trouble," she said.

"Shhh!" Malcolm intoned, pulling his finger against his lips again. "They might hear you," he whispered.

She shook her head, her smile seductive. "If

anyone can hear us then we definitely shouldn't be here doing this," she said, whispering back.

Malcolm nuzzled his face against her neck. "We're not doing anything," he said, blowing warm breath past her ear. He trailed his tongue across her earlobe, the gesture teasing.

Cilla relished the sensations sweeping through her. "It feels like something," she muttered. "It feels like a whole lot of something."

Malcolm continued trailing his mouth across her skin as he navigated her back against his desk. With one hand he pushed the contents lying atop the wooden surface aside. Papers, pencils, and pens flew and folders dropped to the floor. They both came to an abrupt halt, hoping the noise hadn't been loud enough to wake anyone. Seconds later Cilla giggled softly and Malcolm chuckled with her. He kissed her mouth, stalling the sounds that billowed through the room.

With one swift move, Malcolm dropped his hands to her waist and lifted her off her feet. He sat her atop the desk and eased himself between her parted legs. He felt warm and snug as he cradled himself tightly against her, moving her to wrap her arms around his neck and her legs around his waist.

Their loving was quick and easy, a sweet and gentle connection. With everything that had happened Malcolm needed her touch, needed it like he needed to breathe. He craved the heat from her skin, her breath billowing against his flesh. He yearned for that intimate connection, his body possessively marking hers. That moment when he could be afraid and vulnerable and just the nearness of her made everything well and good. His need was urgent and demanding and almost obsessive and he clung to her and she to him as if their lives depended on it. Loving Cilla felt like bliss.

Chapter Seventeen

"We should dress alike today," Claudia said, her mouth filled with syrup-soaked pancakes. "It would be fun." She licked the taste of maple from her fingers.

"As long as you don't pick out some dumb dress," Cleo responded, swallowing her own bite of sausage.

Claudia nodded. "Let's wear the new jeans Mimi got us and I'll pick the shirt and you pick the shoes."

"I'll pick the shirt."

Claudia grinned. "Okay, just don't get us in trouble, please."

Cleo rolled her eyes, her own smile a bright beam in the center of her face.

Mama Claudette interjected. "It doesn't matter what either of you chooses. You still have to pass my inspection before you walk out of this house."

Both girls giggled.

"Who wants more pancakes?" Mama Claudette asked.

"I do," Claudia chimed. "Just one more, please."

Cleo shook her head. "I'm full, Grandma."

Mama Claudette nodded. "Well, you both need to finish up, clear your plates, and go get dressed. I'll drop you off on my way to the market."

"Where's Dad and Mimi," Claudia asked.

"They both had to be at work early. Cilla is going to pick you up after school today so don't dawdle around making her wait."

The two girls tossed each other a quick look.

"What?" Mama Claudette asked, eyeing one and then the other.

"It just feels like we're a real family with Mimi now."

"We like it when she picks us up and spends time with us."

Mama Claudette smiled as she reflected on their comments for a brief moment. "I think your Dad did good with that one."

Cleo and Claudia laughed. "Me too!" both clamored simultaneously.

"Go get dressed now," Mama Claudette said, changing the subject. "You're well ahead of the schedule right now so let's keep it that way."

Minutes later the twins were still chatting back and forth as they dressed. They moved between their two rooms, stealing glances in the adjoining bathroom mirror as they passed by it.

"The blue looks really good," Claudia said. "Good choice."

"It picks up the blue stripe in our shoes," Cleo said, kicking out her foot to look at the canvas Toms her sister had chosen.

Mama Claudette's voice echoed from downstairs. It was her second time calling and there was a hint of frustration in her tone.

Cleo stuck her head out the door and called back. "Coming, Grandma. We just have to brush our teeth!"

"Hurry up, please!" the matriarch called back. "You don't want to be late!"

Both girls hurried into the bathroom. After a quick brush and swish they parted in opposite directions to retrieve the last of their belongings. With book bags tossed over their shoulders, Claudia grabbed a sweater and Cleo her cell phone as they headed for the door.

Cleo came to an abrupt stop, staring at her cell phone screen.

"What?" Claudia asked, turning to stare at her. "What's wrong?"

"I got a text message from Mommy," she whispered, her voice low, tension rising in her tone.

Claudia rushed to her sister's side, pulling her own phone out at the same time. The same message was registered on her device.

The two girls stared at each other.

"What do we do?" Claudia asked.

Cleo shook her head. "I don't know."

"Should we tell Grandma?"

Cleo shook her head. "I don't think that's a good idea. She'll call the police and Mommy will get into trouble. Daddy says that she can't contact us until after she goes to rehab for her drug problem."

"Maybe we can tell Mimi. She'll tell us what to do and she won't tell if we ask her to keep it a secret."

"Daddy will get mad at her if he finds out and I don't want him to be mad at her."

"We have to do something," Claudia intoned.

"What if Mommy keeps texting us? We can't just ignore her."

Mama Claudette yelled from the bottom of the stairs. "Cleo! Claudia! Now!"

Claudia nodded. "Don't say anything. We'll figure it out."

Her sister nodded her agreement but her expression said something else altogether.

Malcolm was laughing as he disconnected his cell phone.

Romeo shook his head as his friend moved back to the table and sat down. "How's your girl?"

"Missing me!"

Romeo tipped his head toward Walter "Lightning" Lewis, the young piano player who'd been bemoaning his woes with the opposite sex. He laughed. "Young blood, you don't have any problems right now. Just wait until you get like Malcolm here. Then you'll know what real problems are."

Malcolm laughed with him. "Don't listen to him. The only issues I have in my relationship is that there aren't enough hours in the day for me to get all the time with my girl that I want."

Walter shook his curly head. "I can't be tied down to one woman. I don't know how you do it."

"Keep on living," Romeo said. "You can only do that juggling act you do for so long. Those games will wear thin quick!"

"You better listen to Romeo," Malcolm said with a nod. "He knows. Boy's been there, done that, and patented the logo on the T-shirt. Got him a doctorate in Women 101."

Romeo pointed a finger at his friend as he laughed again. "Don't listen to this fool."

Malcolm's laugh was rich and deep as it filled the room. "You better set him straight before he hurts himself." He turned his gaze to the younger man. "I can't give you any advice. I didn't have the nerve to juggle more than one woman at a time. The women I dated all scared me. I was afraid of what they might do if they caught me. But Romeo, I've seen him have three, sometimes four women sitting right here in this room while he bounces between them like a ping-pong ball."

"I was never that bad," Romeo intoned, humor painting his expression.

"Yes, you were."

"Yeah, I guess I was! But my baby changed all that. I'd never cheat on Taryn. Not in this lifetime or the next."

Walter rolled his hazel-toned eyes. "So now you're off the market. How'd you know she was the one?" he questioned.

"When a woman has your back like no other woman has ever had before. When you trust her with everything you have. You know."

Malcolm interjected. "You'll know she's the one when you stop thinking about all the others."

"Well, I guess that's my issue right now because I'm thinking about Keisha and Beverly. Trying to figure out how to get them to do a threesome with me." The young man grinned, grabbing at his crotch with one hand as he leaned back in his chair.

Malcolm laughed again. "Sounds to me like you're trying to get hurt!"

His cell phone suddenly vibrated against the

table, the ringer chiming loudly in the room. He stared briefly at the number displayed on the screen, trying to recall if it was someone he should have recognized. But he didn't. He answered it on the third ring.

"Hello?"

"Good morning. Malcolm Cobb, please."

"This is he."

"Mr. Cobb, this is Mrs. Winters from the attendance office at Ravenscroft School."

Malcolm sat forward in his seat. "Yes, Mrs. Winters, hello. How can I help you?"

"We're just calling to verify your daughters' absences. We didn't get a call or message from you saying they wouldn't be at school today."

Malcolm felt himself tense. "I'm sorry but Cleo and Claudia should both be in class."

"No, sir. They didn't report to homeroom this morning and neither has been in any of their morning classes."

There was a pregnant pause as Malcolm's head was suddenly spinning. His eyes flickered back and forth as he tried to reason why the twins weren't headed to their math and science classes.

"Mr. Cobb? Are you still there?"

He sputtered. "Yes . . . I'm . . . I apologize." He took a deep breath as he collected his thoughts. "I wasn't aware of any reason the girls wouldn't be there, Mrs. Winters. It was my understanding that my mother, their grandmother, was dropping them both off this morning. Let me give her a call and I'll be sure to send a note with them tomorrow to clear their absence."

"Thank you, Mr. Cobb, and if for any reason you

need to speak with me, please don't hesitate to call either myself or the headmaster."

Malcolm nodded into the receiver. "Thank you," he said as he disconnected the call.

"What's wrong?" Romeo asked, concern shining in his eyes.

The two men locked gazes. Malcolm didn't respond as he dialed one daughter's number and then the other's. Neither girl answered. He typed a quick text message to both but minutes later was still waiting for a response.

He shook his head. "I'm not sure," he said as he pushed the *speed dial* button to reach his mother.

Mama Claudette answered cheerily. "Hey, Sonshine!"

"Are the twins with you?" he asked abruptly.

His mother bristled. "No. They're at school. Why?"

"The attendance office just called me and they didn't show up today."

"That's ridiculous. I dropped them both off myself."

"Did they go inside the building?"

"They . . ." She paused in reflection, trying to recall what the girls had done. "They walked toward the door. I saw them stop to talk to that Murphy girl from Claudia's dance class and then one of the teachers spoke to them. That's when I drove off. I didn't actually see them go inside."

"I need you to go to the mall for me and see if they're there, please. And call Cilla for me. Let her know what's going on. I'll give you both a call back in a while."

"Do you think they're playing hooky?"

"That's what I'm praying they're doing!" Malcolm quipped. "I'll call you back," he said, disconnecting the line.

He dialed a second number. "Hey, Maxine, it's me. Is Shanell there with you?"

His ex-wife's mother answered, anxiety rising in her tone. "Boy, you know better than that. Shanell can't stay with me. Not while she's using. I know someone bailed her out of jail but I haven't seen her. Why? What's wrong?"

"The girls are missing. They didn't show up at school today."

Maxine seemed to read his thoughts. "I'll put the word on the street that I'm looking for her. If the twins are with her it'll get back to me."

"Thanks, Maxine. Keep me posted."

Neither needed to say good-bye.

Malcolm stood in the center of the room, suddenly seeming deflated. His daughters were gone and truth be told he didn't have a clue where to start looking for them. This was out of character for both girls and he was suddenly scared, the emotion creasing his brow.

"How can I help?" Romeo questioned, moving to his side. He dropped a heavy hand against his friend's shoulder.

Malcolm took a deep breath. "Pray," he said. "Just pray."

Shanell was talking nonstop as the car they were riding in careened down Interstate 95 toward the state of Maryland. Her chatter was nonsensical, not one word making any sense to either of her daughters. The man driving seemed oblivious.

Cleo tightened the hold she had around her sister's shoulders, fear ringing in her gaze. Tears streamed down Claudia's face. Both girls cowered anxiously in the backseat of the SUV they were riding in. Neither had anticipated everything going wrong when they'd agreed to meet their mother.

Shanell had been waiting for them in the school's parking lot. The girls had gone in through the front door and straight out the back. Their mother had waved them over excitedly, hugging and kissing them both as they'd raced into her arms. And then her friend had pushed them all into the car, yelling that they needed to get moving. Before either realized what was happening the vehicle was cruising onto the highway into early-morning traffic.

The man in the driver's seat was large and intimidating. A scar fanned one side of his face, running the length from his brow to just beneath his chin. It was dark and ugly, giving him a ghoulish appearance. He grunted and gnashed his teeth, speaking very little and the few words he did say were usually admonishments for them to sit down and shut up.

"Mommy, I have to go to the bathroom," Cleo said softly.

Shanell tossed her a bright smile, her eyes heavily glazed. "Not much longer. We'll be in Baltimore real soon, then you can go. Just hold it until then."

"But I have to go really bad."

"Me too," Claudia chimed. "Can't we stop someplace?"

Shanell shot the driver a look. The stare he gave

her back was venomous. He didn't bother to answer. She turned back to her children, suddenly hissing between clenched teeth. "We can't stop. Okay? Now don't be any trouble. I need you to be good."

"Then we need for you to give us our phones back. We need to call Daddy. He needs to know where we are," Cleo said, an air of defiance in her tone.

Claudia sat forward in her seat. "He'll be worried about us."

Shanell's gaze narrowed. "You're father knows you're fine."

"He doesn't. He doesn't know where we are and we need to at least send him a message to let him know so he doesn't worry," Cleo persisted.

"No," Shanell said. "You're not calling anyone." She suddenly smiled brightly. "Let's sing. You girls always liked to sing. We're going to have fun. I don't know why you want to spoil this for me. So sing!" she shouted, breaking out into a bad rendition of some Katy Perry song.

The man next to her suddenly spoke. "Shut up! All of you. Shut the hell up before I shut you up."

The two girls sat back against the seat. Shanell continued to hum softly under her breath, seeming oblivious to what was really going on. The man cut his eye at her. He shot a quick look to the twins in the backseat but said nothing, then refocused his eyes on the road.

Cleo entwined her fingers between her sisters, the two clutching tightly together.

Claudia nodded her head. She whispered, her voice as low as it could be. "Do you remember what Mimi told us to do if we were ever in trouble?"

Cleo nodded back, neither one needing to say anything else.

Cilla was at the family's home when Malcolm pulled into the driveway. She and his mother stood holding tight to each other, their faces creased with worry. He shook his head as he stepped into her arms, hugging her warmly.

"We saw the Amber Alert. Do they know anything yet?" Mama Claudette asked, the woman shaking nervously.

He blew a slow sigh as they moved back into the home, past the police officer stationed at their front door. Inside, he dropped down onto a padded seat in the kitchen. "I called your friend Randolph. He's running point on this. We viewed the security tapes at the school and the girls are with Shanell and some man."

"Well, that's something, right?" Mama Claudette said. "Shanell loves the girls. She wouldn't let anything happen to them."

Malcolm shot his mother a look. "I don't know, Mom," he said, his shoulders slumping. "The drugs are controlling Shanell right now. She'll do anything for them."

"But she wouldn't hurt the girls!"

Malcolm held up a hand and he snapped. "I can't right now, Mom. Okay? I really can't do this with you right now."

Mama Claudette took a step back and nodded. She took a deep inhalation of air. "I'm going to my room. I need to lie down for a few minutes."

Moving back onto his feet, Malcolm wrapped his arms around his mother and hugged her close. Her tears dampened the front of his shirt. "I'm sorry," he said as he kissed her cheek. "I know you're worried. And I want them to be safe just like you do."

Mama Claudette nodded. She kissed her son's cheek then moved up the back stairwell to her room.

When she was out of sight, Malcolm and Cilla locked gazes, staring at each other momentarily. "What are you not telling us?" Cilla asked. She reached for his hand and pulled him back to the seat beside her. "Because I know that Randolph wouldn't be the point man on a missing person's case."

Malcolm hesitated, tears burning hot behind his lids. He shook his head, fighting to control a sudden rise of emotion. He lowered his gaze, his head still waving against his thick neck. He took another deep breath and held it until his lungs began to burn. He shifted his stare back toward her as he slowly blew out the stale air. "Agent Taylor recognized the man on the videotape. He has a long history of crimes against children and women. Shanell's boyfriend worked for him. He's not a very nice man."

Cilla stared at him, disbelief crossing her expression. The look he gave her back gave her pause, emotion wafting through her gut. "There's something else, Malcolm. What is it? I want to know."

His expression was pained as he met the look she was giving him. "An hour ago headshots of both girls turned up on some underground website.

That bastard plans to auction them to the highest bidder."

"Oh, my God!" Cilla pulled a tight fist to her lips. She suddenly felt sick, bile threatening to spew. She swallowed hard, taking swift breaths. "What does Randolph say? What are they going to do?"

"He says to let them handle it but I think I'm going to Baltimore. I can't just sit here. I need to do something."

"Do you know that they went back to Baltimore? They might still be here in Raleigh."

"Taylor says this man is operating a porn business that's based in Maryland. The feds have been trying to shut it down but haven't been able to link it to anything illegal. And because of Shanell's connection to the town he's almost certain they'll go back to Baltimore."

Cilla nodded. "I don't think you should go. I think you need to trust the police. You need to be here when they bring the girls back."

He nodded. "I feel so helpless. Anything could be happening to them and I'm not there to protect them." He dropped his head into her lap, wrapping his arms around her waist. He clenched the back of her sweatshirt with his fists.

Cilla wrapped her arms around his shoulders. She kissed his cheek. "Everything's going to be okay. Trust your girls. I don't think they're going to be that easy to take advantage of this time."

The man was on his cell phone talking to someone in a language neither girl recognized. Frustration pierced his tone. Their movements were beginning to slow as traffic began to build, something down the road slowing their path. The stops and starts were abrupt and more than once the man slammed his fist against the steering wheel, cursing loudly as he did.

Their mother had fallen into a deep sleep, snoring softly from the front passenger seat. She'd admonished them one last time to not make any noise and then she'd dropped into a drug-induced stupor.

Cleo pulled her index finger to her lips, her gaze whispering for Claudia to be as quiet as she could be. Easing her backpack from the floorboard Cleo slipped her hand inside, searching with her fingers until she found a tube of bright red lipstick she'd hidden inside an inner flap and an ink pen from the bottom of the bag. When the backpack dropped to the floor with a low thud, the man tossed a quick glance to the backseat, his gaze shifting from one to the other. Neither girl moved a muscle meeting the look he was giving them. Claudia kicked the bag with her foot. When she swiped her eyes with the back of her hand he went back to ignoring them, focused solely on his call.

Cleo shifted toward the back window, easing her body against the door. Keeping one eye on the man in front of her she began to write backward on the side window. Their Mimi's words echoed in her memory. *You have to write it in reverse or no one will be able to read it,* she'd said. Cleo had practiced diligently until she'd been able to do it without thinking about it. The words HELP PLS CALL 911 were quickly printed in bright red against the glass. Easing back, she handed the tube of lipstick to her sister who did the same thing on the other side.

Each girl shot the other a look, their expressions hopeful. Whispering a quick prayer, they knew they didn't have anything to lose. With any luck someone stopped in traffic beside them would venture to report what they'd seen. If enough people called, the police might take it seriously. And if the police came, there was nothing that man or their mother could do to stop them from screaming for help like they had never screamed before. Holding hands, the twins knew that all they could do until then was wait for the next opportunity to make another move.

Chapter Eighteen

Cleo eased upright in her seat. She glanced out the window to the cars traveling in the same direction. Just outside of Fredericksburg passage had come to a complete standstill, bumper-to-bumper traffic impeding everyone's travel plans. Sitting in wait, some drivers had begun to cut off their engines, even exiting their vehicles to try to see what was holding them hostage on the highway, the northbound lanes seemingly closed.

Beside them a woman sat next to her husband, pointing at the message across the window. Cleo saw the two of them talking, the woman gesturing excitedly with her hands. Her eyes widened anxiously as the lady pulled her cell phone to her ear. She tossed a look at Claudia who was staring where she stared. The man with the scar driving them suddenly slammed his fists against the steering wheel in frustration.

He turned to stare at them and that's when he saw the red writing against the glass. His rage was palpable as he began to scream, the profanity piercing loudly through the space. He slammed his fists repeatedly then shifted the ignition into park. He turned, grabbing for whichever twin he could get his hands on first. Both began kicking at him, throwing every ounce of energy into causing as much damage as they could muster.

"What . . . what's . . . what's going on?" Shanell muttered, the commotion pulling her from her slumber.

The man continued to curse, venom spewing past his lips.

"Run!" Cleo screamed, pushing open the car door.

Claudia winced, pain shooting through her arm from the man's grip as he grabbed hold of her. She used her free hand to jam the ink pen in his face, just missing his eye. He shrieked loudly. Cleo pulled at his arm, then bit him, hard, drawing blood, and he screamed again as he took a swing in her direction. Shanell blocked the blow, taking the brunt of it as she threw her body between him and the backseat, trying fervently to scratch out his eyes.

Cleo pulled her sister by the leg, helping her exit the car and then the two girls began to run through the stopped traffic, screaming for help at the top of their lungs. The man jumped from the car, staggering slightly before he began to run after then. As the girls darted between the parked cars, racing toward the road's shoulder, curious onlookers began to take pictures and video, multiple cell phones hanging out car windows.

Five vehicles down the driver of an oversize tractor-trailer sensed something was very wrong. He'd seen the two girls racing past, screaming for assistance, then spied the man giving chase in his side-view mirror. He called for help on his CB radio before jumping from his cab. He wasn't the only man to suddenly exit his vehicle, wanting to come to the girls' help.

In the distance, sirens could be heard coming from the other direction. On the side of the road, three women were huddled around the twins, each with her cell phone to her ear, calling 911 for help. The man chasing after them suddenly came to an abrupt stop. He looked out over the crowd that was gathering between him and the twins. Overhead the Channel Eight news chopper had begun to circle. Realizing this was a fight he couldn't win, the man with the scar did an about-face, racing in the opposite direction.

Malcolm snatched his phone, answering it on the first ring. "Hello?"

Both Cilla and his mother stood anxiously at his elbow, listening as he spoke to someone on the other end.

"Yes . . . okay . . . yes . . . I will . . . thank you . . . yes . . . we will."

When he disconnected the line he threw his arms up excitedly, beginning to shake as relief flooded his body. "They found the girls!"

"Thank you, Jesus!" Mama Claudette cheered, laughing and crying simultaneously.

"Where are they?" Cilla questioned, concern still shimmering in her eyes.

"Fredericksburg. Agent Taylor is picking them up now. They're being flown into Raleigh-Durham

International. They should be landing in the next hour."

"Thank you, thank you, thank you!" Mama Claudette continued to chant.

Malcolm looped an arm around her, hugging her tightly. He kissed her forehead, his own tears dampening her brow. Cilla stood watching them, her hands clasped tightly together in front of her chest. Her own tears trickled down her cheek. Reaching out, Malcolm drew her into the embrace, hugging both women with the last ounce of energy he had left.

"Let's go get our girls," he said, clearing his throat.

The ride to the airport was rife with joy. Malcolm shared what little the federal agent had been able to share. He knew the girls were safe. He knew they had never made it to Baltimore. He knew that their mother and the man who'd taken them were both in police custody. And he knew that they would soon be home, safe and sound. He didn't care about the rest, wanting only to hold them both in his arms and never again let them go.

As if reading his mind Cilla reached out her hand, dropping it against his forearm. She smiled, giving him a slight nod of her head. "They're going to be just fine," she said. "But you can't smother them. Even though your first instinct is you wanting to lock them away to protect them, you can't do that. You just need to love them and keep teaching them how to protect themselves."

Malcolm blew a deep sigh. He cut his eye at her. "I'll think about it," he said as he pulled his car off the Lumley Road exit and turned onto Airport Road. "I promise. Next month, maybe even next year I'll give it some serious consideration."

In the backseat, Mama Claudette laughed, the warmth of it feeling good to them all.

The local news had carried the story of the twins' rescue. The family had gathered around the television with the girls filling in all the details the media had missed.

"We did like you told us, Mimi," Claudia said. "I stabbed him in the face with a pen. I tried to get him in the eye but I missed. It hurt though. You should have heard him scream."

"I bit him, too, and we didn't panic. We stayed calm and waited for the perfect moment to make a run for it," Cleo added. "And Mommy helped us. She jumped on him and we were able to get out of the car and run."

"And we stayed where people could see us so there were plenty of witnesses."

"Everyone came to help!" Cleo interjected. "A bunch of truckers gave that man a beat down!"

Malcolm looked from his daughters to Cilla and back. "Cilla told you to do all that?"

"Mimi's taught us all kinds of things," Cleo said, leaning her head against Cilla's shoulder.

Cilla gave him an uneasy smile. "It's never too early for a young woman to learn how to protect herself. Every girl should know some self-defense."

Malcolm nodded his head slowly.

Mama Claudette turned off the television, resting

the remote on the coffee table. "You girls have had a full day. It's time for bed," she said.

"Do we have to?" Cleo whined, looking toward her father.

"Can't we have a slumber party?" Claudia questioned.

He shook his head. "No. You two have school tomorrow."

"School?" both exclaimed. "We have to go to school?"

"Yes," Malcolm said. "You're going to school and then you're coming right home. You're on punishment until further notice for what you did."

Both girls groaned but neither protested. Claudia rolled her eyes as she moved toward the door. Cleo followed on her heels. Both girls paused in the entranceway, turning back toward their father.

"What's going to happen to Mommy?" Cleo questioned.

Malcolm took a deep breath. "What your mom did was wrong. She's going to have to go to court and the judge is going to punish her."

Cleo nodded. "Can we tell the judge that she helped us?"

Claudia's head bobbed in sync with her sister's. "Mommy didn't want us to get hurt. She really didn't, Daddy."

Malcolm looked from one to the other. "We'll see," he said finally. "Head up to bed. We'll all be up in a minute to tuck you in."

When the girls were out of earshot he turned his attention toward Cilla. "I see you and I have a lot to talk about," he said. "Self-defense? Really?"

She shrugged, a smile pulling at her mouth. "The more they know the better off they'll be. No man has a right to put his hands on them without their permission and if one does, they should know how to safely defend themselves."

Malcolm chuckled softly as he reached to kiss her lips. "Why do I get the feeling that tonight's story time is going to be a whole other adventure?"

He reached out his hand to pull her onto her feet and into his arms.

Cilla kissed him warmly. "Because love always is."

The girls were on the telephone with their grandmother Maxine when Malcolm and Cilla finally made it up the stairs. Mama Claudette stood in the doorway, her arms crossed over her chest as she watched them. She smiled as the couple moved to her side, both stopping to eye the twins. Everything felt right again.

Malcolm moved into the room, gesturing for the phone. "Hey, Miss Maxine," he said into the device.

He could hear the smile in her voice. "They're really okay?" she asked.

He nodded into the receiver. "They're both just fine."

She let out an audible sigh of relief. "Cleo said they arrested Shanell and the man she was with."

"They did."

"I imagine my daughter's not going to get out of this quite so easily this time."

Malcolm paused, sensing that everyone in the room was staring at him. "It'll work out," he finally responded. "I imagine that if we all pray hard enough that everything will work out the way it's supposed to."

"God is good," the woman whispered loudly.

"All the time."

There was a moment of pause as the two collected their thoughts. After a moment Miss Maxine changed the subject.

"I told the girls that I'm coming to see them this weekend. They had me scared so I need to come love on 'em for a few days. I hope that's okay."

"It's perfect," he answered. "We can't wait to see you."

He passed the phone back to Claudia. "Tell your grandmother good night, then give the phone to your sister so she can do the same," he said.

Obedient, both girls blew kisses into the receiver then hung up the phone.

"Once upon a time there were two pretty princesses, who had two fairy godmothers," Cleo started.

"One fairy godmother was poisoned by an evil witch, the dark spell making her sad and angry," Claudia said.

The two girls both swung their gazes in their father's direction.

Malcolm took a deep breath. "But the other fairy godmother was there to show them how much the pretty princesses were loved."

"And they were loved," Mama Claudette added, "more than anything else in the kingdom."

"And they all lived happily ever after," Cilla concluded.

The girls laughed.

"That wasn't very creative, Mimi," Cleo chimed.

"It was really bad," Claudia added.
"It wasn't that bad," Cilla laughed.
"It was," Malcolm teased. "Really bad."
Cilla looked to Mama Claudette for support.
The older woman smiled. "I liked it but then I'm always a sucker for a happy ending."

Chapter Nineteen

"How did I get engaged before you and you're getting married before me?" Bianca questioned. She sat sipping on a glass of champagne as her best friend tried on wedding gowns.

The two women were alone in the salon of Traditions by Anna, the North Hills bridal shop by appointment only. The consultant assisting them was smiling brightly.

Cilla shrugged as she stood in a classic off the shoulder design, eyeing her reflection in the mirror. "You're too flighty. It'll be another decade before you marry Ethan."

"No, it won't. I'm committed to marrying Ethan over the Christmas holiday. It'll be the anniversary of our meeting and falling in love. It'll be perfect. Besides, he's older than I am, remember? He might not have a decade."

"Bianca!"

"What? I've said the same thing to him. We can't afford to sugarcoat things. He's old!"

"He's not old."

Bianca looked at the saleswoman. "He's got some age on him. He looks good for his age but he's up there."

The woman smiled.

Cilla shook her head. "He's the best thing to happen to my friend. And she loves everything about that man. Even his dirty drawers!"

Bianca grinned. "I do love his dirt. I won't lie. Still doesn't explain how you're getting married first."

"Can you believe that next year this time we'll both be married?" There was no missing the sentiment in her tone.

Cilla's friend smiled. "Are you sure Malcolm's the one? You don't have any doubts?"

"It's the only thing I'm certain of. I love him more than I could ever begin to tell you. And I love our family."

Bianca laughed. "You get two teenage stepdaughters and I get a stepson almost as old as I am. How's that for some junk!"

Cilla shook her index finger at her friend. "Correction. I get two daughters. We aren't having any steps or halves in our family. I refuse to even start that. I love both his girls like they're my own and that's how I plan to treat them."

"I'd claim Ethan's son too but no one would believe I could have a son that old."

"Do it anyway. Give them something to talk about."

"I could do that, couldn't I. Lie about my age. Folks would be talking about how incredible I look. How fabulously young! I like that. I could work that."

Cilla and the consultant both laughed.

"Did I ever tell you that I love you, Priscilla Jameson? And that I'm glad you're my best friend and no one else's?"

"No. I don't think you ever have."

Bianca nodded. "There's a reason for that. I might tell you about it someday. When we're old and gray and we have little snot-nosed people calling us Grandma."

Cilla smiled. "I love you, too!"

Bianca changed the subject. "I'm not feeling that gown."

Her friend shook her head. "Neither am I. I look like a cake topper. All I'm missing is the bouffant hairdo."

Bianca laughed. "I'll take that as a no. That is not your dress!"

Minutes later Cilla stepped out in an Anne Barge design. The gown had a bateau neckline with a heavily beaded bodice that flowed into a skirt of silk organza. It fit her curvaceous figure to a tee. The cream colored fabric was ultra-flattering to her brown complexion, everything about the dress complementary. It was the most beautiful thing she'd ever seen and she was extraordinarily beautiful wearing it.

Bianca slapped her hand over her mouth fighting back hot tears that suddenly threatened to spill past her thick lashes. "Oh, my!" she gushed. "You look incredible!"

Cilla grinned. "I really love this one," she said. She spun left and then right, admiring her reflection in the mirror.

The consultant agreed. "It's stunning on you.

And it's one of the only designs that we have that you can get off the rack. It'll take very few alterations and we can easily have it ready by your wedding date."

Cilla turned to stare back into the mirror. Bianca moved to her side. The two friends clasped hands, swinging their arms between them.

"I think this is the one," Cilla said.

Bianca laughed. "So do I. And it's a good thing too because I might have to borrow it from you in a few weeks!"

The Starbucks coffee shop was the ideal venue for Malcolm and Cilla's wedding. The girls had suggested the casual location, insisting that the site of their first meeting would be the perfect place to seal their future together. The couple could not have agreed more. The space was inviting and familiar and the coffee shop's manager had been more than happy to oblige them.

The early evening ceremony had included their closest family and friends and a few strangers who'd wandered in for one of the business's renowned Frappuccino drinks. Malcolm had been a dashing groom in a black-on-black suit. Romeo had been his only groomsman, standing beside him in support. Side by side the two friends had looked like a *GQ* cover come to life.

Cilla had entered from the outside and Malcolm had been reminded of that first time she'd walked through the door and he'd laid eyes on her. As she'd stepped through the entrance she was even more stunning, the most beautiful bride that he could have ever imagined. Envisioning the gown Cilla had described didn't come close to the real thing. The beaded design shimmered beneath the lights, casting a warm glow over her face. Her curls were pulled atop her head in a loose chignon and a simple strand of pearls adorned her neck.

They took their vows with Cleo and Claudia standing between them, both beaming with joy. The minister said a prayer over their family as Cilla committed herself not only to Malcolm but to his daughters, as well. Everything about the moment was sheer perfection and when they were pronounced man and wife, both knew that they were playing for keeps, nothing and no one able to come between them.

After the ceremony, they danced the night away at The Playground, no other place more fitting for the occasion. Laughter was abundant and, side by side, Malcolm and Cilla couldn't imagine themselves any happier.

Everyone in the room stared in awe as they glided on the dance floor together. Malcolm had one hand wrapped around Cilla's waist, the other holding tight to her hand as it rested against his shoulder. Her eyes were closed as she leaned her head against his chest, the intense depths of their connection undeniable.

Romeo pulled Taryn closer against him, leaning to kiss the top of her head as she wrapped her arms around him. Cleo and Claudia sat beside their grandmothers, the matriarchs both lost in memory, thinking about the men they'd loved who had loved them back. Odetta stood off to the side, swiping at a tear that had fallen from her eyes. Her wide grin was a resplendent display of snow-white teeth. And the piano player danced with them, his hands racing across the black and white keys, the song a seductive melding of whole and half notes.

An hour later the couple stood with the twins as a photographer snapped photo after photo. When she saw an opportunity Bianca gestured for her friend's attention. Cilla kissed Malcolm's cheek as she excused herself, moving to the other woman's side. Bianca wrapped her arms around her friend and hugged her warmly.

"I'm so happy for you!" she exclaimed, tears misting her eyes. "And I'm so glad you didn't elope."

Cilla smiled. "So we do this for you next month, right?"

Bianca grinned. She tilted her head toward her fiancé, Ethan Christmas, staring at her from the other side of the room. "He says I'm the most beautiful maid of honor he's ever seen!"

"He's a good liar," Cilla said. "You're going to want to keep him."

The two women laughed.

The twins suddenly rushed to their sides.

"Aunt Bianca, are you going to dance with us?" Claudia questioned, pulling on the woman's arm.

"Please?" Cleo chimed.

Bianca tossed Cilla a look. *Aunt?* she mouthed, her eyes wide.

Cilla laughed heartily. "Yes, your *Aunt Bianca* would love to dance with you!"

As the trio skipped their way to the dance floor Malcolm eased behind her, gliding his arms around her waist. He pulled her close, nuzzling his face against her neck.

"I love you, Mrs. Cobb," he said as he spun her around in his arms.

Cilla smiled. "Mrs. Cobb. I really like the way that sounds."

The man grinned. "Not nearly as much as I do, I'm sure." He kissed her lips. "It has to be the sweetest thing I've ever heard."

She wrapped her arms around his neck and hugged him tightly. "I love you, too," she whispered against his mouth, the words blowing warm breath past his lips.

The sun was just beginning to rise on a new day. Malcolm opened his eyes as the first glint of the morning rays peeked through the window blinds. For just a quick second confusion washed over his face, his surroundings unfamiliar, and then he remembered where he was. He and Cilla had spent the night at the Renaissance Raleigh North Hills Hotel. It was the prelude to their honeymoon, time away before the whole family set sail on a cruise to the islands of Bermuda.

He smiled, nuzzling his body closer to hers. He rolled himself above her, supporting his weight against his arms. Cilla was still sound asleep and he lifted his torso up to stare down at her. He studied her face, amazed at how her long, dark lashes fluttered gently. He imagined she was dreaming and he wondered what decadent thoughts were tripping through her sleep. Hours earlier he'd gotten himself lost in her dark, lusty gaze and he knew that once she opened her eyes again, he'd fall headfirst back into the depths of her stare.

Malcolm raised his hand to her face, gently caressing the line of her profile. He cradled her cheek in the palm of his hand, allowing his thumb to lightly graze her flesh. She exhaled softly, muttering ever so slightly. He leaned forward, pressing his lips to her forehead in the gentlest kiss. He inhaled deeply, her sweet scent teasing his nose. It was intoxicating and he felt drunk with desire as he inhaled her again and again. He trailed his lips to her cheek and along her jawline, leaving a path of damp kisses against soft skin.

Malcolm kissed his way past her earlobe and down her neck, his lips parting and his tongue peeked forward to taste her skin. He swirled his tongue in circles and she trembled, sleep beginning to slowly leave her behind. She tilted her head as he hit that sweet spot beneath her chin, applying just the hint of pressure to her flesh. Cilla suddenly purred, the low murmur moving him to harden beneath the bedsheets.

His hands and mouth danced atop her skin until she began to thrust her hips up to meet his. She wanted him and he loved that he could elicit such a response from her. Her eyes fluttered open and then closed, then open again. He smiled down at her as she focused her gaze up at him. Malcolm could feel himself falling deeper in love with her as his reflection swirled in the depths of her dark stare.

She smiled, wishing him a good morning without uttering a word. Her hands snaked around his broad back and she pulled him to her, wanting to feel the weight of him against her. He pressed his mouth to hers and sighed as he hugged her closer.

His hands danced across her flesh, performing a ritual of their own design. His fingers kneaded one breast and then the other, the tips heated and teasing. His touch was indulgent, fulfilling every one of Cilla's dreams.

She parted her legs, wrapping them tightly around him. His body slid into hers easily, the connection as sweet as their very first kiss. He felt every muscle in his body tense and convulse with pleasure, unable to contain the excitement that raged through him. The moment was magical and Malcolm could see himself starting each new day like they were starting this new day.

He loved her. He loved her with every sinew and fiber of his being. He loved her like it was the first time he had ever loved anyone, holding on as if he never intended to ever let her go. His possessive touch marked her, claiming every inch of her for himself and she went willingly, following as he led her to sensual heights like she'd never known before.

Pleasure swept like a tidal wave between them. Malcolm craved more and more of her as he stroked her over and over again. And then he orgasmed, Cilla falling with him off the edge of the cliff at the same time. She clung to him, every dip and curve of her body meeting his evenly. Sweat washed over them both, moisture seeping from every pore. The moment was explosive beyond measure, him knowing that he was making love to his wife made all the difference in the world.

* * *

Cilla sat alone, lost deep in thought. It was officially fall, the changing weather beginning to take hold. The last of the Indian summer they'd been experiencing seemed to have come and gone. Earlier that morning she'd had to search her moving boxes for sweaters, maneuvering through the mess that sat in the home's spare bedroom. Both Malcolm and his mother had been bending over backward to help her assimilate her things in with theirs and Cilla imagined the task was not nearly as easy as they seemed to make it.

It had only been a few weeks since they'd come back from their family honeymoon, the girls still talking about their Bermuda getaway. Sharing a cabin with their grandmother, both had been ecstatic to roam the ship freely, spending much of their time in the vessel's teen center. During the day they'd been able to swim, rock climb, and play basketball with other like-minded young people. At night there had been the teen nightclub where both had danced until they were exhausted. Exploring the island had been one adventure after another and by their last day docked in the port at Hamilton, both had declared the island their favorite place in the whole wide world.

Cilla and Malcolm had agreed. The blue skies, pink sand beaches, and warm ocean waters had been a dream come true. From start to finish the experience had been nirvana, both feeling like they'd been dropped into their own personal Garden of Eden. Even those moments when the twins had interrupted their private time together had been glorious, both grateful that their little family was well and happy.

Now they were back to reality, negotiating school and work, schedules, homework, and a list of to do's a mile long. And Cilla was trying to balance moving from her townhome into her new home, still up in the air about whether or not she was going to rent or sell her old space. She blew a heavy sigh, taking a quick glance to the watch on her wrist.

Her cell phone ringing was unexpected. The girls were in school. She had already spoken to Malcolm and Bianca, and Mama Claudette was taking an impromptu nap in her room. She recognized the Baltimore area code but not the number.

"Hello?"

"Cilla? Hello, it's Maxine Perry."

"Miss Maxine, how are you?" Surprise registered in Cilla's tone.

"I'm good. How about yourself? How's married life treating you?"

Cilla laughed. "It's treating me well. I couldn't imagine being happier."

"I'm glad to hear that. And my granddaughters? How are they doing?"

"Always a challenge! Cleo just earned her orange belt in karate and Claudia will be dancing the lead in this year's *Nutcracker* performance. So they're keeping us running. But grades are good, both are full of energy and they like to keep their father on his toes."

"I'm so proud of them and you have been such a blessing to them both. You've also made Malcolm extremely happy. He deserved that more than you know."

"Well, I appreciate you saying so."

"I guess you're wondering why I'm calling," Miss Maxine said, dismissing with the small talk.

Cilla didn't bother to reply, instead waiting for the woman to continue.

"My daughter was transferred to the federal prison last week. She asked me to call you to ask if you would come see her and I promised her I would."

The woman's request came as a complete surprise. Cilla found herself suddenly contemplating her options. "I . . . I don't . . . why?"

"I asked the same question and she really didn't say. But I don't think her intentions are malicious. If I had any concerns I wouldn't have called and asked. I wouldn't have done that to you and Malcolm."

Cilla paused, thinking about the request. Her mind was racing as she pondered the possibilities. She nodded into the receiver. "I can do that," she said finally. "I can hear her out."

Miss Maxine blew a grateful sigh. "I'll have her attorney call you with the details. It was good to talk to you, Cilla."

"You, too, Miss Maxine."

"And, thank you," the older woman said before disconnecting the call. "Thank you for everything. You'll never know how much you mean to me."

"Why are you doing this?" Malcolm asked as Cilla tossed clothes into a suitcase, preparing for the two-day trip to the federal prison in Cumberland, Maryland, where Shanell had been incarcerated. "What are you trying to accomplish?"

Cilla dropped down onto the bed beside him. "I don't know. I just know that she asked and her mother wanted it too. I don't think it can hurt."

"I don't appreciate Maxine doing that and I plan to tell her so. You don't need to deal with Shanell's craziness. None of us do. I'm doing whatever I need to do to insure she never gets near the girls ever again. I don't think you should go."

"You're still angry. And I understand it but that doesn't make it right, Malcolm."

He rolled his eyes toward the ceiling. "You're too nice. I can't afford to be nice."

"It's not about being nice. It's about doing whatever needs to be done in the best interest of the girls. They haven't stopped loving their mother and they aren't still mad at her. They know she's sick and they want to see her well, whether you like it or not."

"Well, I don't like it and I'm asking you not to go."

She met his stare, holding the look he was giving her. "Please, don't do that. Don't give me an ultimatum."

"I'm not. I'm point blank asking you not to go see my ex-wife."

"Fine, and I hear you, but I am going to go see Cleo and Claudia's mother."

Shaking his head, Malcolm moved onto his feet. Not saying another word he exited the room, his footsteps fading off into the distance as he moved through the hallway and down the stairs. Cilla blew a low sigh. She was learning that Malcolm could be exceptionally sensitive about some things and with everything that had happened he was particularly sensitive when it came to Shanell.

He would pout for days, barely having two words to say to her and then the apology would come and the discussion they should have had from jump. Cilla could tell that this time he'd be angry until well after she returned, when he was certain that Shanell's actions couldn't blow anything else up in their lives.

She continued to toss her belongings into a carry-on bag, uncertain whether to pack for warm weather or cold. She and the girls had already had a conversation about her trip, Cleo and Claudia excited to have her pass on letters and drawings to their mother. Both had much to say and she appreciated the level of maturity they were showing. She only wished Malcolm would take some pointers from his offspring.

By the time Cilla found her way back downstairs, Malcolm was gone, he and the girls going for ice cream. Frustration creased her brow, unable to fathom what she needed to do or say to move him past his stubbornness. She caught a quick glimpse of Mama Claudette out in the backyard and she exited the door, seeking out the old woman for advice.

The sun was beginning its descent in the early evening sky. Mama Claudette was enjoying the last remnants of sunlight as she worked the gardens in the backyard. Cilla took a deep breath as she admired the matriarch's handiwork. She'd carved gardens out of the raw land, laying lines of growing color like a painter laying lines of paint against a blank canvas. Ivy crept up and over foundations of rock, trumpeting loudly against the base of fallen trees. She'd blown life in shades of green against a backdrop of dry dirt and blue sky and it was a blessing beneath Cilla's feet as she walked in the woman's direction.

On her knees Mama Claudette was pulling weeds from around the flower beds. With the changing weather she was beginning to prepare her plants for the cold weather that was sure to come.

"Mama Claudette, your gardens are so beautiful!"

"Thank you, baby," she responded as she stood upright, a hand falling against her plump hip. "Is everything okay?"

Cilla shook her head. "Malcolm's upset with me. He doesn't want me to go to Maryland to talk to Shanell."

Her mother-in-law nodded her head. "So what are you going to do?"

"I have to go. I think I need to hear her out. For Cleo and Claudia's sake if for no other reason."

"Then you should go. Malcolm will get over it."

"But I hate it when there's tension between us. He closes himself off and shuts me out. It's not a good feeling."

"No, it's not, but you know how to handle Malcolm. He gets frustrated when he can't control a situation but everything isn't for him to handle. One day he'll figure that out."

Cilla blew a gust of warm breath past her lips. Her gaze skated across the landscape as she tried to collect her thoughts, wanting to figure out what to do.

Mama Claudette chuckled softly. "Stop worrying. Everything is going to work out. Malcolm loves you and you love him. You going to speak with Shanell is not going to change that. Personally, I think it's a good thing. Malcolm is connected to Shanell as long as the girls are living and breathing whether he likes it or not. They don't have to like each other but there are going to be moments when they're going to have to get along."

Cilla nodded in agreement. She smiled brightly. "Do you think if I baked him a cake he'll be in a better mood?"

Mama Claudette smiled. "He might not be but I assure you it will make me and the girls very happy!"

Chapter Twenty

The medium security correctional institution in Cumberland, Maryland, was intimidating and only because Cilla knew it was a federal prison that housed some thirteen hundred offenders. As she pulled her rental car into the parking lot she took a deep breath to ease her rising anxiety. Shanell's attorney had added her to the approved visitors list and Cilla had called days earlier to guarantee the visit would be permitted.

Arriving the night before she'd gone over the lengthy list of visiting rules and regulations insuring there would be no issues that would necessitate her being turned away. Securing her car she followed the signs that pointed her in the direction of the visiting room. After enduring two body searches and numerous reviews of her paperwork she was led to the visiting room to wait.

Around her, wives, mothers, fathers, and children sat excitedly, anxious for the little time they would be able to spend with their loved ones. Despite the energy in the room Cilla found it all a little depressing. She blew a deep sigh wishing she had her cell phone and could text Malcolm. She missed him and despite his being mad she knew he missed her too.

When the door opened next a guard led Shanell into the room. The woman walking in Cilla's direction in no way resembled the woman she'd seen in Baltimore. She wore the mandatory tan jumper, which actually looked like a couture design on her ultra-lean frame. Her hair was pulled back into a single ponytail down the length of her back. Her hands were pushed deep in the pocket and she looked almost childlike as she tried to hide her nervousness. As she sat down across the table, Cilla noted that her eyes were clear and bright. Both women smiled, trying to ease the tension between them.

"Thank you for coming," Shanell said, initiating the conversation.

Cilla smiled. "I wasn't sure why you asked me."

She shrugged. "I've been practicing what I wanted to say for weeks. Now that you're here, my mind's gone completely blank."

Cilla smiled again. "The girls both wrote you letters and sent you their school photos. They confiscated them when I arrived. The guard said you'd get them once they were cleared."

Shanell nodded. "Thank you." Tears suddenly burned hot against her eyelids. "The girls are why I asked you to come see me. I was hoping you'd tell me about my daughters. My mother says that you've become very close to them."

Cilla nodded. "They're amazing young women. You should be very proud. They're resilient, independent, intelligent, spirited, and they both have big, big dreams. Claudia wants to be a doctor and she has such a compassionate spirit that I imagine she'll have an amazing bedside manner. Cleo's torn between being a pilot or a marine biologist. I actually think she'll eventually have a career in law. That one likes to argue."

"I never meant to hurt them. I can't believe I did what I did. I can't forgive myself for putting Cleo in such a horrible situation. I'm her mother and I failed her." Tears streamed down the woman's face, contrition heavy against her narrow shoulders.

Cilla wasn't sure what to say so she didn't say anything at all. She swiped at her eyes, fighting to keep her own tears from falling.

"I wrote them but I don't think Malcolm is going to let them read my letters."

"He's going to need some time. The girls are everything to him and he can't get past the fact that they weren't everything to you."

Shanell flinched, the honest assessment gut-wrenching to hear. She nodded her head.

There was an awkward moment of silence that wafted between them. Both shifted their gazes to eye the others in the room. Cilla found herself watching an elderly inmate sitting with a young woman who appeared to be her daughter. There was an uncomfortable air between them. Cilla suddenly imagined that their visits had become rote, the woman fulfilling her mother's expectations even though it wasn't what she really wanted to do. She suddenly wanted to cry for them both. Instead, she turned her attention back to Shanell who'd resumed the conversation.

"I've gotten past the withdrawals and now I'm

doing a twelve-step program. It's a daily struggle. But I'm going to be here for a while and I hope that when I'm able to see my girls again that they'll know I've been working really hard to be a better woman. I hope one day they'll be able to forgive me."

"Your daughters love you. They've already forgiven you. They just really want to see you healthy and they want a relationship with you. You're their mother!"

"So are you."

The two women locked gazes for a brief moment before Shanell continued. "I hated you when I heard Malcolm had married you. And I really hated you when I heard how close you were to my daughters. But I realize I was just jealous that you're able to do for them what I couldn't do."

"You know Malcolm and you know he would never have let any woman close to the girls who wasn't capable of loving them like they were her own."

"And that's the other reason I really wanted to talk to you. Malcolm trusts you with our daughters. And even if I didn't show it, I have always trusted Malcolm. He's an amazing man. I really screwed up there."

Cilla smiled, her head bobbing. "Yeah, you did. I hate to say that but your loss was definitely my gain."

Shanell laughed and the lilt of it brightened her face. "I hope that you and I can be friends one day. I don't know what's going to happen in the future but I do know that you're going to be able to have a relationship with my girls that I will never have. You'll be there for their first dates. Prom. Graduations. First day of college. I'm going to miss all that and I only have myself to blame. I would really like to be friends with the woman who does get to share all that with them."

"I would like that too, Shanell. I really would."

Shanell took a deep breath. "When they were little, Claudia liked to play the game duck, duck, goose. And when she got goose, instead of running, she'd spread her arms and would say she was flying and she couldn't be caught if she was in the air.

"And Cleo was obsessed with the Ying Yang Twins because she thought they were really twins like her and Claudia and she would go around whispering everything, doing her own version of 'The Whisper Song.' It was crazy but it made me laugh. They might not remember but we had moments that were very special. One day I hope they remember."

She stood up and gestured for a guard. "Thank you for coming."

Cilla stood with her, reaching to give her a warm hug. "Take care of yourself, Shanell!"

Shanell nodded, her tears falling one last time. With a slight wave of her hand she exited the room and disappeared from sight.

Back in her car Cilla sobbed. She cried for Cleo and Claudia and their mother and all the love they had for each other. Her tears were hot, burning down her cheeks, and all she wanted in that moment was to hurry home and be back in Malcolm's arms.

* * *

Malcolm was sitting alone in the club when his cell phone vibrated atop the bar. It had been going off for the last few hours and without looking he knew it was Cilla trying to call. They'd been playing phone tag for longer than either would have liked and even as he raced to answer it, knocking over two chairs in the process, he just knew that it would stop ringing before he could get to it.

He blew a heavy sigh as he stared at the blank screen. He redialed her number, and the call went right to Cilla's voice mail. He cursed, hitting the redial a second time. When she didn't answer he tossed the phone back to the bar top and moved to pick up the chairs.

Music was still playing in the background. Malcolm hadn't seen any need to turn off the sound system. He wasn't ready yet for the quiet. He had spent most of the day trying not to think about Cilla's trip to the penitentiary to see his ex-wife but he couldn't stop wondering what the two had needed to talk about. He didn't trust Shanell and her motives gave him reason to pause.

There was a knock on the outer door, the heavy rapping drawing Malcolm's attention. For a brief moment he thought about ignoring it but something about the urgency of it pulled him in its direction. He used his key to unlock the front entrance. He pushed it open slightly, preparing to tell whoever it was that they were closed for the night. His eyes widened as Cilla stood on the other side. She smiled, giving him a slight wave of her hand.

"Hey, you!"

"Hey, yourself."

Malcolm opened the door wide enough for her to step inside, locking it securely behind her. She wore faded jeans that hugged her firm legs and a white silk blouse with the top two buttons undone. He couldn't help but notice the way the dim lights overhead played against her skin, warming her complexion a brilliant shade of gold. A heated tremor crept through him, making him shiver.

Cilla stepped into his arms and hugged him tightly. "Were you busy?"

"I was trying to call you back. It kept going to voice mail."

"My battery just died," she said, gesturing with the device.

He took a deep breath. "How was your trip?"

She nodded. "It was good. I really think you'll be pleased."

He shrugged. "I trust your judgment. And I should have supported you. I'm sorry."

She pressed a hand to his cheek. "We can talk later. Right now, I just want you to hold me. I missed you."

Malcolm gently grabbed her hand and pulled her into the inner sanctuary. In the background the Danish singer Ayoe Angelica was singing her song "Get a Hold." The beat was thick and sultry, the seductive vibrato reminding them both of a really good time.

Malcolm turned and pulled her close. He had missed her more and there were no words to express just how much. He didn't need to speak, his body saying everything that needed to be said.

He eased his body against hers and eased both of them into the music. He wanted to touch her skin, to feel her graceful body pressed against his own. He pressed his check to her cheek, breathing in her sweet scent. He felt her body grow warm and languid at the prospect of what would eventually come. They did a slow drag across the dance floor, their movements reminiscent of the dances that made a blue-light basement party memorable. They danced until they were all danced out.

Leaving her car, they rode home together. Cilla leaned her head against his shoulder, holding tight to his arm as he maneuvered his car through downtown Raleigh. Lights flickered in the dark sky, everything more intense as both their senses were heightened.

Malcolm whispered her name in the late-night air.

"Yes?" She lifted her eyes to his, catching a glimmer of her reflection in his stare.

"Have I told you how beautiful you are?"

"You have."

"Have I told you how much I love you?"

She nodded. "You tell me every day."

He turned his focus back to the road.

Cilla smiled. "Why do you ask?"

"Just making sure I'm taking care of business."

"You're doing a great job," she said softly.

"You'd tell me if I wasn't, right?"

She laughed. "I would."

Malcolm reached for her hand and held it as he pulled the car into the driveway. Exiting the vehicle he moved from the driver's side to the passenger door and opened it. He extended his hand to help her out.

They walked arm in arm into the home, laughing

easily as she caught up on all she'd' missed. She'd tell him all about Shanell tomorrow. But tonight was about them. The home was dark save for one light in the family room. Everything was quiet, the mood easy and relaxed.

Cilla grabbed his hand and pulled him close, walking him backward until his back hit the refrigerator door. She pressed her body against his, still moving to the beat of the music that resounded in her head. Lifting her mouth to his she kissed him hungrily, having missed his touch more than she could ever have imagined. She shivered as he slipped his hands beneath her shirt, his palms heated against her flesh. Each craved the other's touch, the moment moving them both to want more.

The lights in the room suddenly flickered on, illuminating the space brightly. Standing in the entranceway Cleo and Claudia were giggling emphatically, the palms slapped over their mouths.

Malcolm and Cilla blushed profusely, feeling like they'd been caught with their hands deep in the cookie jar.

"Uh, why are you two still awake?" Malcolm snapped.

Cleo laughed. "We were waiting for Mimi to get home," she said as both girls rushed to Cilla's side, wrapping their arms tightly around her.

She laughed with them, kissing one and then the other. "You two should be in bed. You have school tomorrow."

Claudia nodded. "We just wanted you to know that we love you, Mimi!"

Cilla smiled. "I love you both too."

"And you missed story time."

"I did, didn't I!"

The girls nodded.

"Let's move it!" Malcolm exclaimed.

Cilla shot him a look, amusement painting her expression. "We have to do story time, Malcolm!"

He rolled his eyes, his expression incredulous. "You're kidding, right?"

She shook her head.

Mama Claudette's voice suddenly rang from the upholstered wingback chair in the corner. "Once upon a time there was a king and queen who thought they were sneaky."

Cilla and the girls laughed.

Malcolm's eyes widened. "Okay. Y'all think you're funny!"

"Say your line, Daddy!" Claudia admonished, her smile full and wide.

He shook his head. "The king and queen had two daughters who had devilish ways that always got them in trouble."

"But the daughters had a fairy grandmother who protected them and kept them safe from harm," Cleo said.

"One day the queen came back from a long trip bearing gifts of gold and diamonds for the two daughters!" Claudia added.

They all turned to look at Cilla. She looked from one to the other and grinned. "But the best gift the queen gave them was a golden goose with wings that flew sky high and a whisper song that they could sing every day."

There was a loud pause as they all stared at her. Malcolm nodded, understanding washing over his spirit. He leaned to kiss her mouth.

Cleo suddenly burst out laughing. "Mommy was never any good at story time either!" she said.

Claudia laughed with her sister. "Once again, Mimi. We're going to need a little more creativity from you. More creativity, people!"

"That's it. Bedtime! Hit the sack, ladies," Cilla said as she tossed up her hands. "There's nothing wrong with my creativity!"

Cilla grinned as the girls hugged their father, and then her, before racing up the stairs to their beds.

Mama Claudette cleared her throat. "Well, I guess I'll let you two get back to what you were doing before you were so rudely interrupted."

Meeting Mama Claudette's gaze, Cilla felt her cheeks become warm, a blush of color flooding her face. She tossed Malcolm a quick look, smiling as she noticed the glint of red that had risen in his face as well.

The older woman gave them both a nod and a wink of her eye as she rose to follow behind the girls. Wishing her son and daughter-in-law a good night, she kissed them both, then eased her way out of the room, shutting off the lights behind her.

Malcolm laughed heartily as he turned his attention back to her. He stared down at her before leaning to recapture her mouth with his own. Breaking the connection he hugged her tightly. "Welcome home, baby! Welcome home!"

Don't miss Deborah Fletcher Mello's

Playing With Fire

On sale now!

Chapter One

The line into the Playground Jazz and Blues Club extended past the bolted doors and barred windows of Lem Young's Chinese Cleaners and Harper's Florist, which neighbored the old brick building. Except for the patient souls waiting to get inside, the street was bare. A crisp breeze blew teasingly under tight-fitting skirts, while firm bodies, suited to the nines, paced anxiously, examining the evening's offerings.

Once inside, having paid the ten-dollar cover charge, the privileged few permitted admittance walked a dimly lit corridor, past a mirrored wall reflecting a kaleidoscope of characters. Romeo Marshall, the club's owner, stood in the entranceway, greeting each of them personally, many by name, as he pointed them to the few remaining tables and the stools at the bar.

Within the inner sanctum of the club, a pale blue light cast an eerie glow over laughing, crying, flirting faces. On the dance floor, couples clutched each other tightly. Shuffling in small circles, their bodies melted one into the other. The heavy aroma of strong perfumes and stale tobacco filled the air, and vision was dulled by swirls of thick smoke that clouded the room. It was Saturday night and the room was filling to capacity as scented, powdered bodies swayed eagerly inside. The audience pushed toward the stage, rollicking to the music, bodies bumping shoulders to shoulders, hips to hips, barely enough room remaining for a swallow of air to pass between them all.

Heads bobbed in time to the music. Bodies swayed to the beat. The music was hot, the room was hot, and the heat was rising with each new body that entered the room. The sounds were low and husky, the guttural strains pressing at skin moist with perspiration. The vibration of the music could be felt deep down inside, creeping from the pit of liquor-filled stomachs, up into haze-filled minds, spreading its infectious spirit copiously throughout relaxed muscles, down into tingling limbs.

Along the rear wall, bodies were pressed tightly against the salmon-colored stucco. At many an occupied seat, creeping hands could be caught pressing along trembling thighs, groping anxiously at knees pressed tightly together. You could smell the passion, a heavy, musky aroma of wanton lust, its dampness glistening like stardust against sun-blessed skin drenched in salted sweat.

Romeo guided his staff with lingering looks, slight nods, and every so often a slight gesture of his hand. His body spoke for him, his eyes mouthing his words. He stood imposingly, his six feet, six and one-half-inch stature long and lean. Taut muscle massed his solid frame, his smooth, sable complexion complementing the vibrancy of his blue black eyes. He had a penetrating stare, piercing through the chaos of the crowded room. His eyes missed nothing, catlike in his observations, and observe he did. The Crayola cast that paraded about from night to night fascinated him.

The Playground was his personal concourse, nurturing the childlike qualities hidden within his soul. Moving passively from table to table, he'd instigate the games and establish the rules. His massive hands would tease, the long chocolate fingers stroking a bare back or resting lightly atop a crossed knee. Laughter danced on his thick lips, curling past snow white teeth lined perfectly in a row. His laugh was deep and rich, echoing in the hollows of his dimpled cheeks.

Born Lawrence Alexander Marshall, he'd been called Romeo since he'd been four years old. His mother's best friend had blessed him with the nickname, proclaiming the moniker his as he'd batted his long, ebony eyelashes at the old women in the Laundromat for a small piece of candy or an extra sugar cookie.

"He's going to be a Romeo," she'd remarked, pinching his dimpled cheeks and planting kisses on his curly head. "Going to romance all them pretty girls, he will."

For him, it had always been a game. A game he could play better than most, and now he only played whenever it suited him. Music had always fascinated him, but he had no particular talents in that direction and his mother had insisted he focus his attentions elsewhere. He had excelled athletically, baseball and track being his fortes. An athletic scholarship, betrayed by a knee injury his sophomore year, had opened the doors for a degree in engineering. After graduation and two years of starched white collars and navy blue suits, he'd realized the corporate boardroom was definitely not his calling.

Taking a yearlong hiatus, he'd traveled across the United States, settling for brief periods in the bars of New Orleans, New York, St. Louis, and Chicago. He'd spent his nights studying people who wandered as aimlessly as he did, searching for something that belonged only to him. Then one day, shortly after returning home to North Carolina, he'd found the Playground. It had been a deserted shell, inhabited by a dark infestation tainted with dirt and grime. Together with his fraternity brother Malcolm Cobb, they'd nursed it to health with the help of their savings, a small bank loan, much backbreaking labor, and their own salted sweat. Everything else had fallen into step with the music.

No night at the Playground was ever the same. The mood of the evening moved with the flow of the crowd, influenced by the voracity of the music. The tones would be sweet and rich one night, wicked and sultry the next. Romeo liked it that way. He'd spend his days ordering booze, balancing ledgers, paying bills, and counting cash. The daily routine was the same, never changing, but his nights were always varied. He'd successfully recreated a gin joint comparable to any of the hottest clubs that had rocked well before his time. Relishing the satisfaction of his accomplishments, he welcomed the onset of evening and all of its uncertainty.

The Playground was now the place to be and Romeo and Malcolm the men to know. The success of the Playground had propelled both right into the spotlight. Although Romeo was still driven by the desire to do and be more, he could bask silently in the warmth of already having attained a level of contentment and accomplishment others would never know. He found great satisfaction in that fact.

Warm air suddenly blew eerily against Romeo's neck as long arms snaked seductively around his chest. Soft lips, painted a vibrant red, brushed gently along his neck, teeth nipping lightly at his flesh. As pink polished nails were clasped firmly across his midriff, a familiar voice whispered hot against his ear.

"You still feel too good, lover."

Romeo laughed, turning to encircle his sturdy arms around a lithe body draped in a fluid, black silk pantsuit. Brushing his lips against the woman's, Romeo savored the taste of wintergreen and mint. Allowing his hands to glide down her lean back, he rested his palms lightly at the rise of her buttocks.

"Not as good as you do, Roberta. How are you, darling?"

"Better. Now."

Romeo laughed again. "So where have you been hiding yourself, lady?" he asked, the scent of her perfume suddenly too familiar.

Roberta shrugged, pressing herself closer to Romeo. "I wasn't hiding, honey. I just found a man who would *marry* me. I got tired of waiting for your good-looking behind."

Romeo squeezed her gently. "So, you're happy?"

"Would have been happier if you'd married me, but I'm not complaining." Roberta goosed him gently, resting her hand warmly on his backside.

"Woman, you know I am not a marrying man," Romeo exclaimed. "I would have never made you happy."

The woman chuckled. "True, but you sure knew how to make me feel good," she said, kissing him again.

Romeo laughed with her, shaking his head from side to side. "So, where's this new husband of yours?" he asked.

"Home with the baby. It's ladies' night tonight."

"A baby too!" Romeo exclaimed. "Damn, girl, you work fast!"

Roberta laughed again, a warm rise of noise that filled what little space there was between them. "So how about you? Who's got your heart?"

Romeo grinned. "You know that's a game I don't play, girl. I'm too busy trying to keep myself afloat to be in a serious relationship."

Roberta nodded. "But business is good, right? I mean, the place is bumping! And everyone's talking about it."

Romeo gestured toward the crowd, releasing his hold on the woman. "I can't complain. This place definitely keeps me on my toes."

"I'm really happy for you, Romeo. You really deserve all your success," Roberta said with a nod, her shoulder-length bob swaying from side to side.

He smiled, the lift to his mouth warm and seductive. "Thank you. I really appreciate that."

Roberta smiled back. "Well, I need to get back to

my friends. I know they're peeing in their pants with envy," she said, pointing to a table of women staring intently in their direction.

Romeo nodded, pulling her back tightly against him. "Mmmm," he hummed. "Too bad you have a husband now."

"Liar," Roberta said with a slight giggle as she punched him playfully in the chest. "Stop by the table and say hello," she said. "I'd love to introduce you to my girls."

"I'll do that. And you take care of yourself," Romeo said, placing his lips lightly atop hers, savoring the quivering lips one last time. He moved to kiss her gently against the cheek, whispering in her ear. "Got to give your girls something to talk about," he said with a soft chuckle.

"Damn," Roberta said, shaking in her six-inch heels. Squeezing his hands between her own, she paused briefly as a chill swept down her spine. "We could have been so good together, Romeo. Too bad you messed up."

Romeo smiled broadly as he watched Roberta walk away, the familiar scent of her perfume fading with her departure, then lifted his hand to wave at the other women who still sat staring at him.

"You need to stop!" Odetta Brown, the head waitress, said with a deep laugh as she brushed past him.

"What?" Romeo asked. "I'm not doing a thing."

"Uh-huh," Odetta said, shaking her head. "Just keep it up and see if you don't get yourself in trouble."

Romeo laughed with her. "I just can't help myself,

Odetta. Some of my clients require a bit more attention from me than others."

As Roberta sat back down her best friends began talking over themselves, each one eager to comment on what they'd just witnessed.

"I cannot believe you kissed that man!" Taryn Williams exclaimed, her tone scolding. "Did you forget you had a husband?" She narrowed her gaze on her associate.

Roberta giggled. "What I remembered was that my husband's not here right now and how that man could make me feel back in the day," she replied. She took a big gulp of her vodka tonic, fanning herself rapidly as she swallowed. A wide grin spread across her face.

Taryn shook her head. She tossed Romeo Marshall a quick look, the man knee deep in conversation with another woman at another table. She rolled her eyes skyward. Everything about his demeanor told her he was no good for any woman looking for a relationship worth more than an ounce of salt.

"Please, tell me you did not date that man for long," she said, giving the other woman a questioning look.

Their friend Marsha chimed in. "They didn't date. All they did was—" she started.

Roberta interrupted. "What we did was enjoy a mutually satisfying adult relationship. Don't hate," she said.

Marsha laughed. "Like I started to say. What they

did never took them out of bed. I doubt she even got a meal out of the deal."

"Oh, I ate," Roberta said with a laugh. "I ate very well, thank you very much! And he did too. In fact—"

Taryn held up her hand, stalling the crude comment she knew was coming from her friend's mouth. "Please, spare us the nasty details."

Laughter rang around the table.

"Actually," Roberta said after downing the last of the beverage in her glass, "Romeo is a really great guy and one day he's going to make the right woman an incredible husband. I just wasn't the right woman and we both knew it. But we knew how to have really great sex!"

Marsha shook her head. "I sure wouldn't mind riding him," she said with a woeful sigh. "Just one time."

Roberta laughed, her head waving from side to side. "He's not your type," she said matter-of-factly. "I was thinking he'd actually be a great catch for you, Taryn." She tossed her friend a raised eyebrow.

"Girl, please! That man's a dog. Pure hound," Taryn answered as she rolled her eyes skyward. She tossed Romeo another quick look. "No, he's too much of a player for me," Taryn added.

Roberta shrugged. "Girl, he is not that bad! I wouldn't count him out if I were you. He's one of the good guys and there aren't too many of them left. Trust me when I tell you!"

Taryn's gaze moved back across the room, eyeing Romeo curiously. As if he sensed her staring, his gaze suddenly turned in her direction, meeting the look she was giving him. Their eyes locked and held and then he smiled, a sly, seductive bend to his mouth that illuminated his dark face. She felt her breath catch in her chest as she tore her gaze from his, suddenly dropping her eyes to the table and the empty wineglass she twisted nervously in her hands. She took a deep breath and then a second.

Roberta bumped her shoulder. "If I were you I definitely wouldn't count that man out just yet."